THE NEW RULES FOR

Blondes

Highlights from a Fair-Haired Life

THE NEW RULES FOR

Blondes

Highlights from a Fair-Haired Life

SELENA COPPOCK

itbooks

AN IMPRINT OF HARPERCOLLINS PUBLISHERS

*it***books**

THE NEW RULES FOR BLONDES. Copyright © 2013 by Selena Coppock. All rights reserved. Printed in the United States of America. No part of this book may be used or reproduced in any manner whatsoever without written permission except in the case of brief quotations embodied in critical articles and reviews. For information address HarperCollins Publishers, 10 East 53rd Street, New York, NY 10022.

HarperCollins books may be purchased for educational, business, or sales promotional use. For information please e-mail the Special Markets Department at SPsales@harpercollins.com.

FIRST EDITION

Designed by Paula Russell Szafranski

Library of Congress Cataloging-in-Publication Data has been applied for.

ISBN 978-0-06-213181-2

13 14 15 16 17 OV/RRD 10 9 8 7 6 5 4 3 2 1

For my parents: Susan and Mike.

Your combined DNA gave me a phenomenal head of hair

and your strong values, unconditional love, and unending

support gave me a great head on my shoulders.

Thank you and I love you, Mud and Pud.

Contents

Contents

Introduction

How old were you when your heard your first blonde joke? Usually indoctrination happens in childhood, when tow-headed tykes are taught that their hair color makes them stupid and hundreds of jokes exist to support that premise. *How do you know that a blonde was just using the computer? Because the screen is covered in whiteout. Why did the blonde tiptoe past the medicine cabinet? So she wouldn't wake up the sleeping pills. Why did the blonde return the scarf? She said it was too tight.* How many of these classic blonde jokes have you heard before? How many other blonde jokes?

Light-haired ladies have faced patronizing prejudgment since time immemorial. Historically, society has embraced old rules of blondeness that characterize all blonde-haired ladies as either clueless, naïve simpletons or gold-digging, unrepentant sexpots. If you're a blonde, you must be one or the other. Either you're Sandra Dee or you're Marilyn Monroe. The old rules of blondeness reinforced this limiting, narrow dichotomy of the

Madonna/whore identity, and for that reason, the old rules are obsolete. We are living in an age of intelligent, self-sufficient, gutsy blondes such as Hillary Clinton and Lady Gaga, and the blondes of today need not be defined and inhibited by the tired blonde stereotypes of yesteryear.

To my fellow blondes, I decree that it's time for new rules. It's time to laugh in the face of those retrograde, inaccurate stereotypes (or at least giggle while we toss our amazing hair). If there's one thing that blondes are not, it's shrinking violets (though we often use violet shampoo). Leave that act to other hair colors—blondes won't do it. Just as fresh highlights mix both whitish and yellowish tones, every blonde possesses a fascinating mix of experiences, personality traits, and opinions. She's not just an ignorant prude or a hypersexual knockout. She can't be reduced to a black-and-white stereotype of a Sandra Dee or a Marilyn Monroe. She's multifaceted, unpredictable, and wholly unique.

As a natural-born blonde who now has to see a colorist to maintain that hue, I'll admit my blonde color is a bit of an obsession. At the end of high school when I was given the senior superlative of "Best Hair" in my graduating class, I knew that the hair on my head was something special. In the years since then, I have been stopped on the street and asked about my voluminous locks by complete strangers. I have listened to pals' stories of follicle frustration and guided those friends to the land of deep conditioning and root boost spray. I have crusaded for healthy golden tresses and given my colorist many referrals. In short, hair is of utmost importance in my life, and good hair is an integral part of my identity.

Are you in the same boat? Are you unable to watch the groundbreaking miniseries *Roots* without thinking about the last time that you saw your colorist? Are you unsure of how to answer that ultrainvasive question "Do you dye your hair?" When blonde celebrities dye their hair red or brown, do you take it as a personal affront? Are you tired of people assuming that you can't read a map because your hair is platinum and fantastic? Then you need *The New Rules for Blondes*.

Let's explore all facets of blondeness: the history, evolution, stereotypes, references in popular culture, and more. In this journey of self-discovery and blondeness, we'll explore the ups (the staying power of iconic blondes, blonde anthems, platinum friendship, catching eyes wherever you go) and the downs (botched color, tears, catching eyes wherever you go) and establish new rules for the twenty-first century. I will address those tired stereotypes head-on, impart crucial hair care and hair color tips, explore representations of blondeness in popular culture, and share my personal triumphs and trials from blonde life. In this *künstlerroman* of the blonde artist, I will even encourage you to experience life as a nonblonde (hear me out!) as a blonde *rumspringa* of sorts. See what it's like out there in the dark-haired world, and you'll come back to the community with a renewed appreciation for blondeness. With all of that, you, dear reader, are embarking on a crash course for the modern blonde. Let's be bold blondes! This will be a journey to your roots (be they brown, black, blonde, or nonexistent) and back again, but I promise that all of it will be fun. After all, that's what blondes have more of.

PART ONE

Blonde Pride

CHAPTER 1

RULE: *Know Thyself*

An old friend once told me, "There are two types of people in this world: people who get the joke and people who don't get the joke." Once I stopped laughing at his comment (to thwart any doubt as to whether I'm part of the elite team who gets the joke—oh, I get the joke, I sure as hell get the joke), I thought about his odd way of dividing *all* people into two neat categories. I must admit, though, that I see the blonde world in a similarly dichotomous fashion. There are two types of blondes in this world: Ashy Blondes and Brassy Blondes. I didn't make up these categories, either—there's science behind this. Two types of pigment give hair its color: pheomelanin (which colors the hair orange and yellow) and eumelanin (which determines the darkness of hair color). Blonde hair can have almost any proportion of pheomelanin and eumelanin, but in small quantities. More pheomelanin creates a more golden, brassy blonde color, and more eumelanin creates an ashier blonde. It's the split of the century: ashy or brassy.

To the uninitiated, these categories might sound confusing and nebulous, so let me break it down for you. Contrary to what you might be thinking, ashy blondes aren't ashy in that they need to apply lotion (the more common use of "ashy" as a descriptor). This category has nothing to do with Howard Stern's sidekick Ashy Larry (now *that* guy should get some lotion). Ashy blondes are sometimes known as Hitchcock blondes after the gorgeous Grace Kelly, who was seen in several of Alfred Hitchcock's films (*Dial M for Murder, Rear Window,* and *To Catch a Thief*). They have platinum, almost grayish-blonde hair. Their hair hue isn't yellowish at all—it's closer to platinum—and ashy blondes must use a lot of purple shampoo to keep the color from getting brassy. (More on brassy later.) This shade is favored in salons on the Upper East Side of Manhattan and with the older blonde set. It's not a bold, bright blonde—rather, it's an understated, regal, country club blonde. It's popular among WASPs (not the insect). Ashy blondes are often seen wearing preppy clothing or pashmina shawls with pearls. This shade is often paired with a bit of an attitude, or at least a wicked poker face. Think Tinsley Mortimer, Princess Diana, Paris Hilton, LeAnn Rimes, Reese Witherspoon, Dakota Fanning, Gwyneth Paltrow.

On the other extreme of the blonde continuum is the brassy blonde. This is the more stereotypically "blonde" blonde. Her hair is bright, bold, and almost yellowish. The wearer of brassy blonde might wear it with pride, or might be the unfortunate victim of a bad colorist who was shooting for ashy but ended up at brassy because her original hair color featured red or brown undertones (more on that in Chapter 7). Hair coloring is an intricate dance, and you can't always get *there* from *here*. The brassy blonde who treads into that realm deliberately is usually outspoken, fun, and opinionated. She's not as preppy as the ashy blonde—the brassy blonde is more funky, spunky, and playful. Think Pamela Anderson, Kelly Ripa, Britney Spears, Jessica Simpson, and Chelsea Handler.

Let's break it down, Jeff Foxworthy style:

YOU MIGHT BE AN ASHY BLONDE IF . . .	YOU MIGHT BE A BRASSY BLONDE IF . . .
your friends would describe you as demure, subdued, and subtle.	your friends would describe you as tons of fun, pretty wild, and spontaneous.
you refer to a platter of vegetables and dip as "crudités."	you refer to a platter of vegetables and dip as a "veggie platter" or simply "a step closer to my dream of drinking ranch dressing."
your nickname is Ice Queen.	your nickname is Sunshine.
you've been known to wear a silk scarf with a plain T-shirt to "jazz it up."	you've been known to mercilessly mock people who use phrases like "jazz it up."
you live by the mantra "Before you leave the house, take off one piece of jewelry to avoid overaccessorizing."	you live by the mantra "When it comes to accessories, less isn't more—*more* is more!"
upon first impression, people have told you, "You act a lot like Amanda Woodward from the original *Melrose Place*."	upon first impression, people have told you, "You act a lot like Kelly Bundy from *Married with Children*."

YOU MIGHT BE AN ASHY BLONDE IF . . .	YOU MIGHT BE A BRASSY BLONDE IF . . .
when you're shopping and a pair of pants is only available in a size a bit too large for you or a bit too small for you, you go with too large so that you don't look tawdry.	when you're shopping and a pair of pants is only available in a size a bit too large for you or a bit too small for you, you go with too small so that you don't look dumpy.
you wear pearls without irony (and often with cardigans).	you once wore pearls to a 1980s-themed party.
you date around but have one cardinal rule: no tattoos and no piercings.	you date around but have one cardinal rule: If the person has no tattoos and no piercings, you say no thank you.
you have a pretty standard routine with your colorist, and that's generally light ashy/platinum in the summertime and some lowlights in the wintertime.	your colorist never knows what you'll be in the mood for. Reddish lowlights in wintertime? Bold streaks of blonde in summer? It all sounds good to you.
you appreciate a nice glass of Malbec.	you appreciate a beer + shot deal.
you shop at the Loft.	you're only familiar with lofts as party venues.
you often find yourself saying, "Everything in moderation."	you often find yourself saying, "I'll try anything once!"

when you see a guy make the hand gesture known as "Hook 'em Horns" or the international sign of rock and roll, you probably think, *Does that guy worship the devil?*	when you see a guy make the hand gesture known as "Hook 'em Horns" or the international sign of rock and roll, you probably think, *Rock and roll, buddy!*
Us Weekly and *People* magazine are your guilty pleasures, but you wouldn't be caught dead reading them in public.	you're comfortable reading *Us Weekly* and *People* magazine in public. Who cares?
you're hard to read, so friends sometimes say, "Tell me what you really think."	Friends sometimes sarcastically say to you, "Tell me what you *really* think."

Now that I have regaled you with broad generalizations about blondes, let me get a bit more nuanced in my summation of light-haired ladies. Most blondes aren't actually 100 percent ashy or 100 percent brassy—most of us are a mix. Painting in broad strokes is fun but rarely representative of how people actually are. Most blondes are a bit brassy and a bit ashy simultaneously, and that combination makes for a good shade with depth and dimension. There's a little bit of ashiness and a little bit of brassiness in each of us, and we can call on either of these sides when the situation is appropriate. Going out to the opera with your new crush's parents? Perhaps it's time to put on a Grace Kelly–style steely reserve and pull the ashy card. Going to a rodeo with your cousins from Arkansas? Break out the good-times, Kelly Ripa enthusiasm, and embrace your inner brassy gal.

Whichever shade of blonde you choose (or with which you

are naturally blessed), you are probably painfully aware of the preconceived notions heaped upon the golden-headed populace. The human instinct to judge a book by its cover is inevitable, despite what people say to the contrary. Every skin color, hair color, and aesthetic comes with a set of baggage that can help others form judgments. But no hair color is the dumping ground for as many stereotypes, preconceived notions, jokes, and negative assumptions as blonde.

There's a reason that city cabs are painted bright yellow: It catches the eye. A head of yellow-blonde hair acts like a lighthouse, drawing attention, reflecting light, and stopping sailors from crashing into the beach (well, two out of three ain't bad). The color yellow (and blonde) stimulates mental processes, activates memory, and encourages communication. School buses are yellow because that color jumps out, visually, so drivers will be careful around the children getting on and off and crossing the street.

Combine this tendency to stick out with the stereotypes heaped upon blondes, and now a yellow-haired lady might feel like she is a moving target. Based on hair color alone, strangers make myriad assumptions about her, the first of which is that she's stupid. The earliest suggestions of blonde as a negative thing date back to medieval Europe, when members of the upper class tended to be paler and darker-haired than the peasantry. Lower classes toiled away outdoors, acquiring sunburns or tans and (probably) natural highlights (which women now pay top dollar to mimic). Since peasants were uneducated laborers and considered less intelligent than the upper classes, a link between light hair and presumed idiocy was born.

Some scholars trace the emergence of the dumb-blonde archetype to blonde French courtesan Rosalie Duthé, who lived during the eighteenth century. You've got to be a pretty huge moron to inspire a negative hair color reputation that will persist for centuries. She inspired the satirical play *Les Curiosités de la Foire* (1775), which highlighted her habit of taking long pauses before speaking, thus appearing not only stupid but also quite literally dumb (as in mute). After that, the dumb-blonde characterization cropped up again in vaudeville theater of the 1870s and 1880s, when a troupe of women known as the Dizzy Blondes toured the United States. It is believed that the "dizzy blonde" of this era was the precursor to the "dumb blonde" that would emerge only a few decades later and continue to this day.

The next stereotype heaped upon my blonde sisterhood is that she's conniving and gold-digging. Seems to run completely counter to the dumb-blonde characterization, huh? This negative reputation may have emerged from the 1925 novel *Gentlemen Prefer Blondes: The Illuminating Diary of a Professional Lady* by Anita Loos. Yes, it was a book before it was a movie before it was a Madonna video. In this book, the protagonist, Lorelei Lee, is a blonde Southerner—beautiful, gold-digging, and materialistic—who plays dumb brilliantly to get whatever she wants. When this novel was made into a film in 1953, iconic blonde Marilyn Monroe played the role of Lorelei and sang about how "Diamonds Are a Girl's Best Friend." Two years after the publication of *Gentlemen Prefer Blondes*, author Anita Loos published *But Gentlemen Marry Brunettes*, aligning with the stereotype that blondes are frivolous and fun but not suitable for the serious contract of marriage. Brunettes (or any non-blondes, really) are a better fit for that.

Only a few years after the critical and commercial success of Loos's *Gentlemen Prefer Blondes*, another iconic blonde was born: Barbie. Barbie was invented by Ruth Handler (who named the doll after her daughter, Barbara) and later purchased, produced, and marketed by Mattel. While the original doll came in two shades, blonde and brunette, we all know which look adhered to the public consciousness. You can't necessarily think that a doll is especially smart or stupid, but you can judge a doll by its body (umm . . . gross) and the Barbie doll was controversial because of Barbie's tiny waist and distinct breasts. Barbie was a departure from her doll contemporaries in that she was the first doll for children that wasn't a baby—she was an adult. Barbie's pronounced breasts, tiny waistline, and feet stuck in high-heel position seemed to indicate one thing: Barbie was just another party girl.

Some people think that the average blonde is not only stupid but also a hypersexual vixen. The alliterative characterization of a blonde as a "blonde bimbo" dates back to the Roman Empire, when blonde hair was associated with prostitutes. Because of that association, fair-haired women in the early period of Ancient Rome used to dye their hair dark. A denial of blondeness was the trend until Greek culture (where the opposite practice—bleaching hair blonde—was popular) reached Rome. Unfortunately, blonde hair dye in that era was quite barbaric and would burn and irritate the scalp and hair. Hair color concoctions made from rock alum, quicklime, wood ash, saffron, and yellow mud were the most popular routes to blondeness, and these pastes resulted in scalp irritation and mixed results.

Religion jumped into the fray during the late fourteenth century, when Eve was usually depicted as a blonde and the Virgin Mary as a brunette. In John Milton's *Paradise Lost* both Adam and Eve are described as having "golden tresses," and I'm glad Adam isn't immune from some blame here because dude got in on that apple-eating action, too. But of course the Virgin Mary is almost always shown as a brunette. Being blonde ain't easy, I tell ya.

Whether you are ashy or brassy, you'll face the aforementioned stereotypes and assumptions. There's strength in merely knowing who you are and where you fit in, though. I was born of an ashy-blonde mother and a brown-haired father, and yet I'm a brassy blonde. Weird science, I know! This result is not a scientific impossibility, just as two pigmented parents can indeed produce an albino child. I wear my bright, brassy yellow hair with pride, despite the haters. I'm spunky, opinionated, and somewhat loud—the textbook brassy blonde. You should wear your color, whatever it may be, with pride and without apologies. If you get backhanded, patronizing "compliments" from coworkers or acquaintances, let them roll off your back, because your chosen color works for you and makes you happy. Trust me, I've gotten many a backhanded compliment in my day.

Years back, a coworker (with a horribly patronizing attitude, a wry smile that silently communicated constant disdain for others, and a head of mousy brown hair) tried to make me feel bad about my eye-catching, voluminous hair. We were standing by the copier in the oppressive law firm where we were both working as paralegals. In truth, most of my day was spent avoiding work and perfecting the "silent weep" in the bathroom stall. It was a sad time in my life—I was fresh out of college, perpetually broke, living in an unfamiliar city, and super lonely. I was too poor to afford a colorist, so I painted in my own blonde highlights at home. Very badly. But I was still blonde, and that gave me a sliver of happiness. Miserable Coworker and I were chatting about the TV show *The Sopranos* and making small talk when I made a joke:

"I'd love to be a Mafia wife—it would be so easy! Just bring home the money, husband, and don't tell me where it came from," I joked, attempting to break the ice with a coworker who seemed only capable of spewing harsh judgment and mean-spirited sarcasm.

"You could definitely be a Mafia wife. You look the part. I mean, look at your hair." She gave me a smarmy look that clearly communicated her real meaning.

"Ya know—I think that you meant that comment as an insult, but I take it as a compliment, because I like the way Mafia wives do their hair. They have nice color and a lot of volume, so thanks." And I marched out of the copy room. Mousy Brunette Coworker and I kept our distance after that. You know that saying, if you mess with the bull, you'll get the horns? Well, I'm a Taurus (bull) and I have my own version of that saying: "Mess with my hair and you'll get . . . well, you'll get nothing. My hair will not be messed with. I love it and I don't give a rat's ass what you think. You might think it's tacky or too bright, but I love it." I need to work on tightening up that saying. It doesn't quite roll off the tongue.

Blondes—whether ashy, brassy, combination ashy and brassy, well coiffed, badly coiffed—take a lot of abuse. Many people see our hair color and simply assume that we're stupid, conniving, materialistic sluts. You know who you are, though. Whether you're mostly ashy and only a little bit brassy, or 100 percent brassy, or ashy for life, you should hold your head high. After all, in the grand scheme of things, a little bit of negative prejudice is a small price to pay for having amazing hair.

CHAPTER 2

RULE: *Don't Be Afraid to Run in Heels*

For two years running (heh), bubbly blonde Kelly Ripa gathered a posse of women to quite literally run in heels in Central Park in New York City. Ripa teamed up with the Foundation for the National Institutes of Health to run a 150-yard sprint in stilettos to raise money for the Heart Truth campaign. It's good that this is a short race because sprinting in stilettos is actually terrible for you since it puts a ton of pressure on the balls of your feet. But sometimes it simply cannot be avoided and you must do it for your sanity and your safety. A few years ago, I ran in my heels down Newbury Street in Boston, in pursuit of a mugger who had stolen my cute satin purse. He probably had scoped me out thinking, *She seems a bit tipsy . . . her purse is dangling from her wrist . . . and she has a great head of blonde hair—easy target.* But the assailant messed with the wrong lady. Because I'm certainly not afraid to run in heels, especially if I'm hustling in pursuit of a cute, retro-style purse.

It was the night before Thanksgiving—that dreaded night

when Americans migrate back to their childhood homes, not unlike Mary and Joseph returning to Nazareth to be counted. Only Americans aren't going anywhere to be counted; rather, they are heading back to their hometown bars en masse to bump into old middle school and high school "friends" and assure everyone that *life is good*! Everything's coming up *roses* for me. On Thanksgiving Eve 2006, my best friend and fellow peroxide addict, Suzanne, and I were doing just that in downtown Boston.

Suzanne and I were all dolled up—heels, tight jeans, big earrings, dope hair (my dope hair being the only constant, other than death and taxes, in this topsy-turvy world). When we inevitably bumped into the old Weston High School crew, I wanted to show them that Weston High School's Class of 1998 winner of "Best Hair" could still defend the title. We drove into downtown Boston from the suburbs, parked her black Jetta on posh Newbury Street, and had a lovely dinner at our favorite restaurant, Croma.

"All the other Weston High alums are at that bar that used to be called McCarthy's," Suzanne informed me.

"McCarthy's is gone? I move away to New York City, and within two months, the bar where we've been drinking with fake IDs for years is now gone?"

"There's still a bar in there—same exact setup—just now it's called Lir, I think. Anyway, that's where everybody is." Suzanne always had more connections than I did. We had both been popular in high school, but I was always a bit too loud and opinionated for some people, and by "some people" I mean "every male in my town." An encyclopedic knowledge of Guns N' Roses trivia and quotations from comedy movies will win you big points during college but won't even get you on the scoreboard in high school. In fact, those things will earn you a reputation as a bit of a weirdo in a town where most girls are Stepford Wives in training and boys are American Psycho wannabes.

"Well, I'm glad we're getting a little liquored up before we head over there. I can't deal with seeing most of those characters sober," I responded. In fact, I was secretly hoping that we'd somehow end up at the Thanksgiving Eve reunion of another high school—any other high school. In high school I'd been seen as a spazz, and even when I was sixteen years old, I just couldn't abide the sight of sixteen-year-olds driving brand-new luxury cars. Plus, the mix of flagrant entitlement and complete ignorance to the value of a dollar worked like an antiaphrodisiac on me, so I tended to fall for more blue-collar-type guys from our rival high school. Nothing puts a target on your back during the already arduous days of adolescence quite like dating guys who your entire hometown summarily hates based on geography alone. But I'm like Mary Chapin Carpenter, and everything I get, I get the hard way.* I could picture it now—Suzanne and I would walk into the bar just next door to our high school reunion at Lir but a world away. It would be another high school's T-giving Eve reunion, where we'd stumble upon a phalanx of guys I could date: tough guys who were dude's dudes—cops, firemen, carpenters. Guys who knew the value of a dollar and had worked hard their whole lives. Guys whose palms felt like sandpaper when they rubbed your neck during a good-bye kiss in the front seat of a pickup truck.† Guys who had season tickets to all Red Sox and Patriots games and whose cell phone ringtones were a mash-up of "Dirty Water" and "Tessie" (if such a

---

* I also take my chances and don't mind working without a net, just like MCC.
† Ford F-150s preferred, Chevy and Dodge trucks accepted.

mash-up is possible). Real, pure Masshole thugs. Bonus points if they had Boston accents and said stuff like "When I go to M Street Beach in Southie to get col-uh, I go straight from Caspah the Friendly Ghost to friggin' lobstah!"

But I knew that meeting such a star-crossed Romeo wasn't in the cards that night. It was inevitable: Suzanne and I would go to the Weston High School reunion and rub elbows with guys who we had known since we ruled the sandbox at North Avenue Nursery School. Guys who we had witnessed projectile vomiting during an ill-conceived sixth-grade whale-watching trip in Boston Harbor. Guys who had bobbed in the rough waters of puberty, braces, and breakouts while Suzanne and I treaded those same waves.

Despite the impending high school reunion festivities later that night, we had a delightful dinner consisting of gourmet pizza, a few dirty vodka martinis, and a bottle of wine. We probably should have been worried about the potential for a DUI at the end of the night, but instead we were nervous about our fashion choices. Would our outfits properly showcase just how fantastically well we were doing in adulthood? We hoped so.

After dinner, we walked along a surprisingly desolate Newbury Street to head up to Lir, where a flood of disingenuous "Great to see you"s and half hugs with back slaps awaited us. But we never made it to Lir that night.

That night, I was carrying a black satin purse, a 1970s-style sack hanging from two silver rings that I clutched in my hands. So the sack hung down from the rings, not unlike a nutsack from a dude's body. (It's not gratuitous dick talk when it's an illustrative explanation, right?) My fashion style is very 1970s—I was born in the wrong era. I'm perpetually inspired by the look and style of the late Farrah Fawcett in her heyday. I was wearing tight bell-bottom jeans, big earrings, a tight black shirt, and black high-heeled boots—an outfit also known as "the Uniform." On top of all this was my jazzy 1970s-style tan puffy vest with a horizontal stripe across the chest and fur around the hood. (That vest is so disco '70s, it should come with Quaaludes in the pockets.) Suzanne and I probably looked like a blonder version of *Charlie's Angels* in which one angel had been tragically killed in a roller-skating accident but the other two knockout, platinum-haired crime fighters soldiered on. Or perhaps we looked more like a walking target—two drunk blonde chicks, one of whom had a purse dangling from her dainty wrist. To this day I'm convinced that the stereotype of blondes as helpless pushovers laid the groundwork for the events that unfolded after we left dinner.

"So will all the usual suspects be in attendance?" I nervously asked Suzanne as we walked down Newbury Street. As she answered my inquiry, we saw a teenager riding an undersized dirt bike down the sidewalk directly toward us, so we moved into single-file formation to let him pass (because we weren't raised by wolves and we're polite). Just as he pedaled past me, he scooped my satchel purse from my hand and kept biking down Newbury Street.

"What?" It took a moment for me to register what had just happened. That kid had just ripped my (retro-style) Gap purse from my hands and was now pedaling for dear life down Newbury Street. The Gap purse that contained all of my designer makeup (OK, there was some CoverGirl in there, but the rest of my makeup was from M·A·C and Sephora, I swear), my money (six dollars cash!), all of my credit cards (mostly maxed out), and my ID (featuring my name and an old address from when I lived between two projects in South Boston and had blue-collar thugs at my fingertips—those were the *days*!). My ID! My ID! I'd be unable to get on the bus back to NYC without my ID! I was about to start a new job the Monday after Thanksgiving—I had to get back to New York!

Once I was done processing the fact that I had been robbed (it probably took one-tenth of a second, but it felt like forever), I turned on my heels and started chasing the punk-assed perpetrator. I was half in the bag, and I had something to prove: Blondes might catch your eye and stand out and seem like easy targets, but we are *not* to be fucked with.

"HELP! HELP!" I shrieked as I chased the cycling criminal over the uneven slabs of sidewalk, my high-heeled leather boots propelled forward by surprise, anger, and fear. I then remembered something that Oprah had told me (and a million other women, via the television): During an emergency, you shouldn't yell "Help," because people are inherently selfish (don't I know it!) and won't respond to cries for help, but they will respond to screams of "Fire," because they think that *they* could be harmed by a fire. Humanity, I tell ya. With this newfound knowledge, I changed my refrain.

"FIIIIRE! FIIIIRE! FIIIIRE!" I yelled, as if doing an awful impersonation of Jim Morrison belting out the Doors' most famous song. Suzanne gave chase just a few steps behind me as she dialed 9-1-1 on her cell phone. We ran for blocks down Newbury Street, passing an Indian couple who then joined in on our little crime parade, bless their hearts. We also cruised by a few jaded valet attendants, who must have seen this type of thing a million times, as they simply watched the chase scene zoom by without doing anything to assist. This pissed me off, and I was already shrieking for my life, so I let a few choices words fly for the cowardly valets: "Fuck you! Fuck you! I hate you!"

I finally caught up to the thief on his bike, and for at least one full block I was running directly along his right side and screaming. There was nothing left to do but swing my arm at him and hope that I made contact, so I did just that. My fingers were knotted up, and I heaved my fist and arm left, directly into his chest, prompting him to lose his balance on the bike. As if in slow motion, the bike began tilting dramatically to the left, then to the right, being pulled downward by the blessed force of gravity in the bizarre motions that precede a person eating pavement. He fell over on his left side as the bike shot out from between his legs and directly into my running lane on the sidewalk. Thank God I used to be a dancer and I took figure skating classes in childhood (mostly for the post-skate hot cocoa, but apparently I retained some skills) because I was able to jump over the bike as it slid across the sidewalk and stick the landing on the other side, like a little Romanian gymnastics wunderkind.[*]

But the moron mugger wasn't ready to throw in the towel— the chase continued on foot. I was ready for it, though—I could run up and down Newbury Street in heels while screaming swears *all night long.*[†] The ridiculousness of the situation was starting to affect my moves, and I decided to change my message to the perpetrator. I'd reason with him and make my purse seem like it's not worth all the trouble.

"I'm so broke! I work in publishing! I only have six dollars in there, asshole!" I screamed. After a few blocks of sprinting

---

[*] Could I get a hug from Bela Karolyi, please?
[†] I just wish I had had the Guns N' Roses *Appetite for Destruction* album blaring in my ears, as I usually do when I run. There's no better way to start a workout than with Axl Rose screaming a siren imitation into your eardrums.

while learning about the financial hardship of a publishing career, the thief gave up, either out of pity for this poor publishing drone or because his abandoned bike was more important than my forty-five-dollar Gap purse. He tossed my purse into a bush to his left, cut right and crossed the street, then bolted back down Newbury Street in the direction we had just come from. Shaken and shocked, no doubt, he grabbed his bike and pedaled away into the darkness.

"Holy fuck. Holy shit. What the . . . holy fuck—" I could barely form words. Retrieving my purse from the bushes, I unzipped it and found everything still present and accounted for—makeup, money, ID, credit cards—everything.

"Dude—he didn't even take anything. Everything is still here!" I marveled.

"Yeah, well, how would he have unzipped your bag while he biked and fended off your punches? He probably didn't have time to grab the wallet or anything," Suzanne said.

I couldn't believe it—everything was there. I kept fingering the contents of my purse. It had been in a stranger's hands for a few blocks, but here it was, back with me and no worse for wear. Would it become my bad-luck purse now? Was the hoop-sack formation just asking to be snatched away, or was my hair color just asking for trouble?

"Oh, cops are on their way," Suzanne informed me.

"Holy shit. That was insane." I said, exhaling a puff of warm air into the chilly night.

We thanked the Indian couple for their instinct to help, and they moved along, perhaps to their own Thanksgiving Eve high school event. Suzanne and I stood on a corner and ruminated about how the bizarre chase had unfolded.

Within a minute or two, an assortment of Crown Victoria

cars pulled up and assembled around us. Some were obvious cop cars, others were unmarked cop cars, all were Crown Vics—proving a point that I had argued with my dad the last time he was car shopping: Purchasing a Crown Vic for use in civilian life would be like purchasing a fire engine to drive around town. It's a utility car, and it's not for civilian use.*

The officers driving the Crown Vics parked every which way all over Newbury Street, the abutting side street, and the sidewalk. Within moments, Suzanne and I were surrounded by cops—some were in traditional uniforms, others were in street clothes, all were hot (to me). *They are public servants—show some respect (in the form of shameless flirtation),* I thought. Perhaps this night wouldn't end badly after all. I didn't stumble into a blue-collar high school reunion where I met some hardworking natives of Kickassachusetts—they stumbled into me.† You could practically smell the Dunkin' Donuts French Vanilla coffee on their breath, they were so Boston.

"Can you please describe exactly what happened, as best as you can rememba?" asked a young cop with a notepad. I carefully recounted the night's events, and Suzanne assisted: nice dinner, walking down Newbury Street, then the next thing I know I'm chasing some crazy teen on a bike and screaming swears, then I'm punching him, then I'm jumping to clear the bike, then we're on foot, then my bag is in the bushes and he's gone.

"Wait, the perpetrayta didn't get away with ya packetbook? You have ya packetbook now?" the cop inquired. It struck me

---

* So instead, my father bought a Buick Roadmaster—a mammoth station wagon we nicknamed "the Land Yacht" and that he covered in layers of Republican bumper stickers. Sigh.
† Much like the Malcolm X saying about Plymouth Rock.

that *this* is exactly how things get confused at crime scenes. What seems so obvious and clear to the witnesses can actually translate as quite confusing and illogical when explained. Of course I knew that I chased down the guy and gotten my bag back—Suzanne, the Indian couple, and some lazy valets had witnessed the whole thing! Said forty-five-dollar Gap purse was dangling from my wrist! But the police officers had no knowledge of this—they only saw two frightened and keyed-up, perfectly coiffed young ladies telling a very unlikely sounding story, in tandem. It also struck me that the cop referred to my purse as my "pocketbook," and I wondered what other Massachusetts-isms he had up his sleeve. *I bet that he refers to sprinkles as "jimmies" and calls Stop & Shop Supermarket "the Stoppie," and when he visits towns on the south shore of Massachusetts, he calls it "going down the shore,"* I thought.

His beautiful accent kept flowing: "So the perpetrayta did not get away with ya purse, but did he remove anything from it?"

"No—everything is in here," I responded.

"So, just to be showa I fully understaaand, ya purse was taken from you, but you chased down the assailant and managed to retrieve ya purse, then he fled west on Newbury Street toward Mass Ave?"

"Yes, exactly," I said.

"Huh." The cop seemed bewildered and delighted. "You must got some bruthas at home, right? You got a lotta hustle in ya."

"Ha—thanks. No brothers, actually. You just never know how you'll react to a situation like that. And I guess I'm tougher than I look," I conceded.

And you're tougher than you look, too, my friend (unless Dog the Bounty Hunter is reading this book, then no, you are exactly as tough as you look). There are many ways to "run in heels," and they don't all involve slamming your entire body weight into the ball of your foot while screaming obscenities. You can metaphorically "run in heels" by doing something strong and bold for you. By stopping the guy at Dunkin' Donuts who is deliberately ignorant of how the line works and saying, "Yeah, I'm next in line—the end of the line is back there. Thanks!" By driving decisively and defensively. By speaking with authority and confidence. The world will never have enough gutsy women—blonde or not. So follow in the footsteps of a savvy, gutsy, confident blonde Kelly Ripa and don't be afraid to run in heels.

CHAPTER 3

RULE: *Crank Up the Pro-Blonde Anthems*

All people have bad days now and then—even dope blondes. On days like those, it's good to crank up some pro-blonde anthems to help pull you out of your funk. Or feel free to wallow in it and only pull yourself out when you feel completely ready. If there's one thing I hate, it is forced, inauthentic cheeriness. So go ahead and marinate on whatever has got you down for as long as you need, then formulate a plan to move on and bounce back. I recommend cranking up some sweet tunes and either going for a run or dancing around. Here's an assortment of my favorite pro-platinum jams:

- Anything by Blondie. A hard-rocking band led by a gorgeous platinum-blonde ball-breaker (Debbie Harry) with an amazing voice and a mean smirk.

- "As a Blonde" by Selena Gomez. I feel a special kinship with Selena Gomez since we share the same first name. The similarities end there, though, as Selena Gomez is a dark-haired tiny singer whose longest relationship was with a guy who I could probably take down in a fistfight.

- "Feelin' Love" by Paula Cole. A hugely underrated song, this gemstone appeared on the soundtrack of the film *City of Angels* (1998). The line "You make me feel like I want to be a dumb blonde in a centerfold, the girl next door" reinforces a blonde stereotype, but I'll give it to her. This song's too hot to ignore.

- "Blonde Over Blue" by Billy Joel. Admittedly, this song isn't one of his best, but it's about blondes (specifically Joel's ex-wife Christie Brinkley) and it has a unique sound.

- "Bed of Roses" by Bon Jovi. In this beautiful ballad, JBJ sings, "Some blonde gave me nightmares, I think that she's still in my bed." Hell yeah, blonde shout-out and a song about blondes getting laid!

- "What's Up?" by 4 Non Blondes. You couldn't live through 1993 and 1994 without hearing this song a lot. "What's Up?" is a catchy, belt-it-out tune, and it catapulted the San Francisco–based quartet 4 Non Blondes to stardom. It might seem counterintuitive for me to embrace a band whose existence is predicated upon their nonblondeness, but I put them on here in the way that one might retweet an insult on Twitter. I embrace 4 Non Blondes as a move to reclaim power.

- "Suicide Blonde" by INXS. I love the music of INXS, from "Need You Tonight" and "New Sensation" all the way through "Elegantly Wasted." But "Suicide Blonde" is something special.

- Anything by Madonna. Nobody is more of a balls-out, brassy, no-bullshit blonde than the Detroit native with a

British accent, Madonna Louise Ciccone, a.k.a. Madonna. Her career has spanned decades, and she's a cornucopia of talent: dancer, singer, filmmaker, writer, director, mother, and more. Blondes should love her the most, though, for her Blond Ambition World Tour in 1990.

- "Platinum Blonde Life" by No Doubt. This track was on No Doubt's phenomenal 2001 album, *Rock Steady*, which also featured the hit single "Hella Good" and the majorly underrated ditty "Making Out." "Platinum Blonde Life" is a song about wanting the world to go away—not answering the door, just rolling over in bed.

- "Joey" by Concrete Blonde. It's like an intervention set to music, and never has the story of an alcoholic named Joey sounded so sexy. This song has nothing to do with being blonde—it just rules.

- "Tired of Being Blonde" by Carly Simon. This song addresses the assumptions inherent to blondeness. Carly Simon knows what it's like—she's a gorgeous blonde. The video features some classic 1980s footage of blondes and Simon in an assortment of colored wigs. When you're not feeling the pro-blonde anthems or you've heard a few too many blonde jokes, crank up "Tired of Being Blonde" for a change of pace.

CHAPTER 4

RULE: *Don't Date a Guy or Gal Who Is*
as Hair-Obsessed as You Are

When it comes to gorgeous locks in the context of a romantic relationship, the *Highlander* rule applies: There can be only one (person in a relationship who has phenomenal hair). If both people in a relationship are hair-obsessed, one person will eventually feel inferior about his or her hair and be unhappy. Two people whose identities hinge upon their personal possession of gorgeous locks coming together for a romantic union is a recipe for disaster. It's akin to two hugely insecure actors dating while on set. You might think that this arrangement would be ideal—they have the same experiences, concerns, career issues—but it's ultimately toxic. Competitiveness, insecurity, and paranoia can crop up when both parties place so much importance on the same exact quality. Catastrophes can occur: Fuses can be blown (if both partners are blow-drying simultaneously), curling irons can be worn out (if both partners possess long, luxurious locks), conditioner can run out (if both partners have thick hair with natural curls and thus require regular conditioning)—it can get *that* bad.

That is why, dear reader, *you* should have good hair, but your partner should not. You must wear the pants in the relationship by wearing the overhead dryer at the salon every four to six weeks. I'm not suggesting that you swallow your hair pride and date a guy who has a cascade of what resembles pubes cresting off his crown. Rather, I'm suggesting that you date a guy who doesn't care about his hair *that much*—there's a difference.

A guy who is hair-obsessed is a modern-day Narcissus. In case you skipped fourth grade, let's review the myth of Narcissus: Before it was a perfume or a song by Alanis Morissette or a club beneath the Citgo sign in Boston, Narcissus was a hunter in Greek mythology. He was extremely proud, egotistical, and disdainful of those who loved him. That last trait sounds more like a Groucho Marx phenomenon (the ol' "I don't care to belong to a club that accepts people like me as members") more than narcissism, but let's not split hairs.* A Greek goddess named Nemesis (with a name like that, how did the girl make any friends?) assessed Narcissus's character flaw and attracted him to a pool, where Narcissus laid eyes upon his reflection for the first time. Much like a young starlet newly introduced to celebrity and cocaine, Narcissus was immediately hooked. He didn't understand that he was simply staring at a reflection—an image—and he fell in love with the creature staring back at him. (Apparently mirrors weren't big during that era—think of it as the opposite of the 1970s.) Narcissus was unable to stop staring at this beautiful creature, so he never moved and simply died there on the water's edge. Presumably Narcissus starved to death because he couldn't be bothered to eat—his commonalities with young starlets just keep on coming! In present-day

---

* HEYO!

society, a guy who worships his own hair probably won't starve to death while staring at his reflection, but he might take off for the weekend and pack your blow-dryer and forget to tell you.* Or he might use the last of the mousse and forget to replenish.† Heed my warnings, dear reader: Never date a guy who is as hair-obsessed as you are.

There is a lone exception to this rule and, ironically, it's a man who hails from a state inextricably linked to the overuse of hair products: New Jersey native Jon Bon Jovi. Yes, JBJ is the exception to my rule, and from my extensive research I can confirm that he is the lone anomaly. Mr. Bon Jovi's hair is celebrated around the world, almost as much as his music. He's never had a hair failure, but his band has released such musical bombs as "Have a Nice Day," "Someday I'll Be Saturday Night," and "I Love This Town." Bon Jovi's music often explores themes of persistence and hard work ("Keep the Faith," "Wanted Dead or Alive," "Blaze of Glory"), and his consistently amazing hair has been putting in hard work since 1984, when Bon Jovi burst on the rock music scene (or, more accurately, since 1962, when Jon was born). It's evolved over the years, but JBJ's hair has always been voluminous, well styled, and on-trend. Has this crown of amazing hair gone to Jon's head, though?‡ Has it manifested in narcissism, toxic bad-boy behavior, and a trail of tears and blown fuses? It has not. Mr. Bon Jovi has been happily married to his hometown sweetheart, Dorothea Hurley, for more than twenty years, and they have four children together. Normally I think that marrying your hometown sweetheart is the most

---

* Word to the wise: Always have an emergency blow-dryer.
† Another word to the wise: Never let it come to that. Have an emergency stash of hair products everywhere you go.
‡ I'm like a hair joke writing machine!

podunk, unimaginative thing you can do, but not in this case. JBJ has a sweet head of hair and legions of fans around the world, and is completely committed to his equally well-coiffed (though brunette) wife. It's admirable behavior and completely unexpected from a guy with hair that good.

But let's not get too caught up in this sole exception. A rule is a rule because 99 percent of the time it applies, so let's not let JBJ's great hair and romantic commitment distract us from the rule at hand: Don't date a guy who is as hair-obsessed as you are. I became intimately familiar with this rule back in late 2009, when I developed a kind of joke crush on *American Idol* contestant, Broadway star (*Rock of Ages*, *The Wedding Singer*), and alleged ladies' man Constantine Maroulis. He is a man of Greek descent (by way of New Jersey) with long, curly brown hair; a bump in his chin that makes it resemble a tiny bum on his lower face; and a love of making the rock-and-roll hand gesture (often confused with the University of Texas's "hook 'em, Horns" and the sign of the devil). He's supposedly a lothario in the musical theater world. Yes, that's what drew me IN. This is consistent with my type—the rest of the world's deal breakers are my aphrodisiacs. My preferred "type" is a guy who is bit overweight and hairy, and drives a truck. Added bonus if he is estranged from his parents, has a Boston accent and tattoos, and possesses a wicked temper that he justifies based on his heritage (whether they were Irish or Italian or whatever, everyone thinks his ancestors were the most hotheaded).

Even though Constantine was much thinner than my normal type, I gave him a shot anyway. At least he was hairy enough, and that sweet head of brown curls called to me, as if to say, "We can talk about conditioning and overconditioning for hours." He appealed to me and drew me in like a pile of positively charged metal shavings to his hulking negative man magnet. So in August 2009, I dragged my fantastic fellow comedienne and gorgeous redheaded friend Heidi to the Broadway show *Rock of Ages* to enjoy delightful power ballads and stalk my D-list joke crush. *Rock of Ages* is a Broadway show that is a mash-up of music by Journey, Night Ranger, Styx, REO Speedwagon, Pat Benatar, Twisted Sister, Poison, Asia, Whitesnake, and more, all connected via a thin story line about following your dreams and getting the girl. In other words, it's the most important piece of theater to ever grace the Great White Way. As my luck would have it, that first night I saw *Rock of Ages* was a night when Constantine's understudy was performing, and my love/hate crush was not. I was pretty disappointed, but the show was awesome nonetheless and definitely "took me high enough," to quote Damn Yankees' masterpiece "High Enough." And back in the innocent days of summer 2009, I wasn't in *that* deep.

About six months later, I began following Constantine on Twitter (twitter.com/ConstantineM) and falling prey to what every celebrity Twitter follower experiences: the deluded sense that you *really* know this person via their 140-character proclamations. Constantine's tweets cracked me up because they were brimming with arrogance, masturbatory self-promotion, and deluded self-importance. Most of his tweets were full of faux humility and excitement but were really just bragging notes. Thanks to Twitter, I got to know both Connie Maroulis and his nutty fan base. His fans are a loyal bunch whose love for Constantine can only be matched by their love of misspelling "rock" as "rawk." I didn't think it was possible, but his fans seem to be more loyal and crazed than Clay Aiken's "Claymates." Constantine's fan base seems to consist mainly of mothers aged forty-plus hailing from New Jersey, which is, not coincidentally,

Constantine's home state. They have Twitter handles such as AshWantsToRock and HottieMama, and they tweet things like "Going to Rock of Ages for the 10th time tonight! Can't wait to RAWK!" One Constantine fan's Twitter profile might read: Stay at home Mom of 2 boys and a dog. Constantine's my #1 guy!"* The gals of Constantine's Twitter posse are not especially good-looking or chill with their affections for Constantine. I figured, *Easy competition*. And thus, I began sliding down the slippery slope of joke stalking a celebrity who you somehow simultaneously find attractive and repellant. (We all know how that old song goes, right? Right? Is there anybody out there who understands this bizarre phenomenon? Just me?)

I thought to myself, *His fans are such weirdos, it would be like shooting fish in a barrel if I showed up at one of his shows and tried to lure him in. It would be fun to lure in a legendary womanizer and then eat him alive, black widow style. That would teach him a lesson he'd never forget. Plus, if nothing else, it's a great story— just great material.*

And so my Constantine crush developed as a funny, ironic joke—I'd lure him in, make him fall hopelessly in love with me, then walk away with just a funny story of how I wooed a D-list celebrity, and isn't that (somehow) funny. It would be a spite relationship, really. The romantic version of how I used to collect New Kids on the Block trading cards as a kid or how I currently listen to Nickelback when I work out. It's just something that I love to hate—it nauseates me, yet I love it. Plus, romancing a D-list celebrity would make great cocktail banter.

I could see it now. I'd be at a comedian cocktail party

---

* I'd be pissed if I were one of her two "boys"—they're her sons, yet her "#1 guy" is some long-haired singer?

somewhere in Brooklyn—probably on a filthy rooftop in Bush-wick. I'd be dressed in a black sheath and red pumps, with my voluminous locks forming a halo of blonde perfection,[*] when the subject of heartless romantic manipulation would come up, as it so often does in polite company (right?).

"You guys have *got* to hear Selena's story about wooing a D-list celebrity and then walking away and ruining him," Heidi would insist to the assembled literary and comedic heavyweights. "Come on, Selena, tell them the story!" she would press me as I cranked a cocktail straw around my dirty vodka martini, like a tiny boat engine in a miniature pond made of delicious brackish booze.

"Oh, it's silly—nobody knows who Constantine Maroulis is—"

"Constantine Maroulis!? From *American Idol* and *Rock of Ages!*" my gay friend would exclaim, rattling off Mr. Maroulis's résumé for the edification of the party.

"Oh, it was silly," I'd respond, pretending to be bashful and unimpressed with my own achievement but secretly hoping they'd pry it out of me because *this* is exactly why I had done it. This exact moment of cocktail chitchat. This moment, on the dot right here, as Buddhist nun Pema Chödrön would say.[†] And thankfully, the assembled people would push me, so I'd share the funny story.

"Ha—so yeah, so I lured him in with my amazing hair and

---

[*] I realize that wearing a sheath dress and pumps on a Bushwick rooftop probably doesn't make sense, but this is my fantasy, and in fantasy world, your feet never hurt from standing in heels for too many hours. Go with it.

[†] Although I doubt her Buddhist teachings were ever meant to be applied to cocktail banter about spite fucking an *American Idol* reject.

we hooked up, then I never called him again. It was just a funny thing. Just for fun. What an idiot, right? Fuck him!" I'd laugh.

"You think that *he* is losing sleep over *you*?" my no-bullshit, uncouth dude friend would ask. "I mean, that's every dude's dream! Especially every celebrity's dream! You find a hot groupie and you hook up with her, then it's like, 'See you in hell,' ya know? I'm sure he has a million groupies lined up and doesn't even remember who you are." He had a point. And suddenly my hilarious story of negging a D-list celebrity didn't seem quite so jazzy anymore.

But this flash-forward moment of clarity wasn't going to stop me. I was going to meet Constantine Maroulis and see his dope hair firsthand, even if it meant traveling from New York City to the wilds of New Jersey.

I carefully read his tweets every day for months, and then in May 2010, I had another outbreak of Constantine Fever.[*] My supportive friend Heidi, who had accompanied me to the understudy *Rock of Ages* night (back in the summer of 2009), was willing to act as my wing woman once again. But this time we had to get serious. I did extensive research online (constantinemaroulis.com, twitter.com/ConstantineM) and learned that on his rare nights off, Connie performs in a live music concert called "A Night at the Rock Show" with a band. It's a concert during which he plays covers of other people's songs in a minimally rock-and-roll atmosphere. Almost like an Epcot experience of a rock-and-roll concert, where it's basically a simulated rock concert environment, but without the actual smoke, coke, drunk people, antics, and mayhem of a rock concert. "A Night

---

[*] Constantine Fever is almost like Cat Scratch Fever, only with less Ted Nugent and more hives.

at the Rock Show" would appeal to people who visit Las Vegas and see the Paris and Venetian hotels so that they'll never need to actually travel to France or Italy, God forbid. A sterile, simulated version of the real thing is preferable to them. These people probably love photocopies of photocopies. My interest in spending "A Night at the Rock Show" was twofold: (1) woo a D-list celebrity and (2) witness what people were like in there. I was genuinely curious. What's the scene like at a show of cover songs played by an *American Idol* reject? Who goes to "A Night at the Rock Show" earnestly and unironically? For me, going to that concert was like visiting Red Lobster or the Olive Garden—hark, who goes there? Who is actually inside this type of place?

So I rented a car, driving the streets of New York City for the first time in my life, and Heidi and I journeyed out to Teaneck, New Jersey, where "A Night at the Rock Show" was happening in a performance venue *slash Mexican restaurant*. Yes, a place where you can enjoy a subpar live show while you munch on soggy burritos. The D-list-ness of it all just kept getting better.

Heidi and I carefully planned my outfit—hot stuff, but not trying too hard and certainly *not* a Constantine Maroulis fan like everybody else at the show. We assembled an outfit that clearly communicated, "I'm just a hot blonde with a head of award-winning hair* who you'd probably want to pick up in a bar, but instead I'm here at your concert. But I'm not here because I'm a 'fan,' let's get that straight. Quite the contrary. I'm here because I'm hot and so are you, so you should fall for me so that I can then give you the Heisman."† This message was

---

* Weston High School, Class of 1998, "Best Hair."
† The Heisman is awarded to one college football player each year. It's a

communicated via tight jean capris, wedge-heel espadrilles with long laces that tied up my calves, a blue tank top, and big gold earrings.

Heidi and I made our way across the George Washington Bridge and over to a land that I'd previously only seen in the opening credits of *The Sopranos*: New Jersey. We found Mexi-Cali Live (the infamous Mexican restaurant/performance space) through the sweltering summertime heat and parked the rented midsize sedan across the street.

"Wait—this is it? That nondescript building we almost drove right by! That's it?" Heidi remarked incredulously. It didn't look like much from the outside, and I suppose that I didn't expect much.

"Yup, this is it. I mean, this is effectively a cover band concert on a Wednesday night in the suburbs. I guess this is what you get." I laughed.

We walked from the glaring late-day sunshine into the darkened venue, paid the twenty-dollar cover (I paid for both of us since I was, again, dragging Heidi along to be my wing woman), and received bracelets whose color indicated that we hadn't purchased tickets to sit down and eat Mexican food while we watched the show. Yes, that was an option. "A Night at the Rock Show" is like a glorified dinner theater, apparently. Going from

---

big deal among collegiate football players. The trophy is a statue of a football player cradling the ball with one arm and pushing away any oncoming players with his other hand out. Thus, being rejected can be called "getting the Heisman" because you are being pushed away. The trophy's existence and the fact that "sacking" is something that happens to the quarterback comprise the extent of my football knowledge. Oh, and that when a team decides to blitz, shit gets crazy. More on that in Chapter 14.

the bright sunshine outdoors into the near pitch-black, over-air-conditioned venue felt like that scene from *Varsity Blues* when they stumble out of a strip club and walk into glaring daylight. Only in reverse. There was a small stage toward the front of the venue (with an adjoining "green room" that would have been the size of a telephone booth, if those things still existed), a bar in the back, tables in between the bar and stage, and a small area for people to stand and dance. Or rather, as it was used for this concert, a small area for women to stand and sway while grinning creepily.

The place was packed with women who were either creepy-old to be there or creepy-young to be there. The "creepy-old to be there" contingent looked like the Twitter ladies who followed Constantine, and thus, they enthralled me. They had big hair, outdated fashion sense, and gargantuan, dumpy purses.

"I bet they're going to tweet about how hard this show 'rawked,'" I joked to Heidi. The assembled ladies scoped one another out, as if on a tacky reality TV dating show. Much like the fat, gay nudist in season one of *Survivor** and every girl who has ever been ostracized on *The Bachelor*, *I REALLY didn't come here to make friends*, I thought.

The lights of MexiCali Live dimmed, and the band members took their places on the tiny stage. The excitement was palpable as the band played the first few chords of "Rock On" (the David Essex song, not the Gary Glitter creepfest) and Constantine emerged from backstage. The multicolored theater lights caught the perfect, natural highlights of his long, brown mane as I thought, *Whoa—nice hair.* He was surprisingly thin and tall,

---

* Richard Hatch, who failed to pay taxes on his prize money and served jail time because of it.

dressed in a white V-neck, a vest, and a necklace. For the next ninety minutes, Constantine and his band played covers of every second-rate rock song you've ever heard, which makes me think that he probably couldn't license any songs from *Rock of Ages*.

"A Night at the Rock Show" was fun, albeit corny. At one point, Constantine took the microphone chord and wrapped it around his back, then shimmied almost like in those old "Zest-fully" clean commercials. Heidi and I looked at each other and began laughing as the surrounding crowd shushed us so they could capture his every movement on their iPhones.* Constantine sings well, no doubt, and I appreciate that he's found a profitable niche as the master of all rock music covers, but I still had a case of the dumb chills.† That is, until he pointed at me and we made eye contact.

Toward the end of the concert, Heidi and I had scooted our way to the front of the "crowd" of a few dozen ladies as Connie was crooning a power ballad. I flipped my hair, sipped my Corona, and stared up at the hairy Greek Romeo. Just then, we

---

* I hate people who videotape or photograph an experience in its entirety rather than actively living that experience as it happens. That behavior makes me insane. I saw people doing that inside the Sistine Chapel in Rome—obsessing over capturing imagines of the ceiling (illegally) with their crappy cameras. You can buy a postcard with a clear image of that gorgeous ceiling that will be better than you could ever capture and you can look at that postcard later on, but right now you're here beneath this amazing fresco. Just lean your head back and enjoy looking up at the real thing—this gorgeous ceiling that Michelangelo painted. Just stop and *be* here for a moment—enjoy this live experience. Why are you taping or photographing this? Preserving it for posterity? Ya know what's a lot more fun? Being actively engaged in what's happening right here and right now and having a great memory of this experience. Fucking morons.
† Dumb chills are goose bumps that you get when something is super corny or lame.

locked eyes, and he pointed at me and made an upward motion with his chin, Dylan McKay style, and made me feel like the only girl in the room.

"Holy shit, he just totally pointed at you!" Heidi squealed while trying to keep her voice quiet.

"I know—holy shits!" I squeaked out through clenched, smiling teeth. I stared at his perfect mane of fluffy curls as all the irony and joke crush stuff fell away, leaving only a real crush. No joke. In that moment of eye contact, this crush had pulled a Velveteen Rabbit and become real. I was going to meet and hump Constantine Maroulis, but the mission to ruin him was aborted. This wasn't a joke anymore. This was real. I wasn't doing this for cocktail banter anymore. With a nod of his chin and a moment of eye contact, I was doing this for real. For life. Forever. We could build a life together based on our mutual love of both performing and our own hair. We could make magic.

"A Night at the Rock Show" closed with "We Are the Champions," the song that made a splash when Constantine performed it on *American Idol* all those years ago. Immediately after the show, a gaggle of women assembled outside the green room door, and Heidi and I agreed that such behavior was pathetic and would probably impede a D-list hump, so we sat down to eat some Mexican food. I needed to chow so that I could sober up before I drove the rental car back to Brooklyn, and we needed to review on the night's events.

"Well, he totally pointed at you and checked you out, so what's the plan now?" Heidi asked as we shoveled guacamole in our faces.

"I don't know. Perhaps I'll play it coy and just tweet something about the show? I mean, I'm not going to stand by the green room door like a tool. He's probably gone by now anyway," I responded. Heidi and I talked strategy for about an hour, then headed out to the parking lot. As we exited MexiCali Live, I pulled out a cigarette so I could smoke before we got in the car. My formerly valuable "smoking while driving" skills had gone down the crapper since college.

At this point, it had been maybe an hour since the show and I was mid–Marlboro Light when who walked out of the venue but my hairy Greek sex god, friggin' Constantine Maroulis! The main event! The reason we were in goddamn Teaneck, New Jersey, on a school night. The master of puppets of "A Night at the Rock Show!"

I took a deep breath, and as Constantine walked by us on the nearly empty sidewalk, I caught his eye and said, "Great concert in there." He acted surprised and appreciative, and Heidi, Constantine, and I had a nice chat about performance and power ballads. He came off as surprisingly humble and sweet, only further convincing me that perhaps I had "finally found the love of a lifetime," just like FireHouse said.

"How did you guys hear about this concert?" Constantine inquired.

"I'm kinda of embarrassed to admit this," I said as I scolded myself from inside my own head, *Selena! If you apologize and act like it's crazy behavior, it becomes crazy behavior! AshWantsToRock never apologizes, and neither should you!* I continued, "But I saw it on your Twitter feed."

"Oh yeah, I'm trying to do more promotion stuff with Twitter lately," he said. *You sure are, Connie M.,* I thought. *Your Twitter feed reads like a self-promotion deluge and somehow I love it.* "Where do you guys live?" he asked.

"In Brooklyn. We drove out here . . . for this concert . . . it's not too far," I lied.

"Whoa—you guys came all the way out here to see me!? A D-list celebrity!" he said.

Stop the record—did he just call himself a D-list celebrity? His self-awareness was both refreshing and worrisome. I looked at him, tilted my head, and tried to peer into his subconscious. I had been jokingly referring to Constantine on my Facebook page and Twitter feed as exactly that—"a D-list celebrity." Did he somehow know? Could he tell that I'd been reading his every tweet for the past few months? Did he know that I'd spent many a drunken night typing his name into Google images and scrolling through photo after photo of his smiling face and sick weave? Or maybe this is just how he charms the ladies—with self-awareness and good hair.

Perhaps all the gossip I've ever heard about him is wrong, I thought, *and he's not a complete douchewad cheesedick after all. Maybe he's just completely misunderstood and I'm the only one who gets him.* This belief was only further compounded when Constantine not only gave me his email address but also his phone number. Yes, my friends, *digits.* This exchange didn't just come out of nowhere—we had some laughs, talked about comedy and performing, established that I'm from Boston and he's been there. We made some serious connexies, people!

"Send me an email about your comedy show sometime," he said as I typed his email address into my old-school flip phone. "Whoa—nice phone! Haha!"

"I know—I have a whole standup bit about how I'm a Luddite and I hate technology and I still carry a Discman because I'm like a Pilgrim."

"That's funny stuff—here, why don't I give you my number?"

he added, and ten digits rolled off his Greek tongue into my millennium-style phone, and my hands shook with excitement and surprise.

By then, his "roadies" (the other guys in the band/his friends) were finished loading the equipment into a lame-looking van, so he had to get a move on. Heidi and I hugged and cheek-kissed him good-bye, then crossed the street and walked into the parking lot.

"Holy shit, holy shit, holy shit!" Heidi whispered as I took deep breaths.

"No freaking out until we're safely in the car," I spit out as I nearly hyperventilated. Once we were safely inside the sealed pod of the rental car, I commenced shrieking, "HOLY FUCK, I JUST GOT CONSTANTINE MAROULIS'S NUMBER! HOW YA LIKE THEM APPLES!? I GOT HIS NUMBA! HAHA! OMG OMG OMG!" Heidi and I hugged and stared at each other, attempting to digest the gravity of the night's events.

"Selena—you amaze me!" Heidi blurted out. "You've proven that anyone can achieve his or her dreams, no matter what they are. Obama didn't prove that—*you* did! You did it! Yes, we can!" she shrieked. I went to bed that night floating on air. It was as easy as that. You *can* achieve your dreams. Heidi was right. I proved that. I did.

Or at least it seemed like I did until I texted him the next day.

I had a standup gig in the homosexual haven of Fire Island, New York, the next night, so I spent the day after "A Night at the Rock Show" in transit, just like so many rock-and-roll bands on the nights after *their* rock shows.* It's a sign, right? Getting to Fire Island is like *Planes, Trains and Automobiles*, but I was

---

* Just like Bob Seger crooned about, "Here I am . . . on the road again."

floating on a cloud of euphoria the whole way, so it didn't bother me. Constantine Maroulis was to be mine, and I loved sharing the story with my two fellow standup comedian travelers, Leah and Danny. I was the token hetero on this road trip.

"I'm going to text him now so that we keep the momentum going from last night and he doesn't forget me," I explained to Leah and Danny on our way to Fire Island. On the train, they had dutifully listened to the entire story from start to finish. I was unrepentant in my willingness to dominate conversation with the saga that should have been nicknamed "Hair," but with less body odor and more cheap cologne. And so once we reached our hotel on Fire Island and had time to kill before our show that night, I fired off my first text. Light, witty, and awesome, just like me.

"Hey, this is Selena. I put a gerbil in a wheel to generate enough electricity in my old-school phone to send you this text. Great to meet you last night!"

I was a hilarity machine . . . but was Constantine ready for this jelly? What guy wouldn't fall for this witticism? Apparently a random schmo who wasn't expecting a text.

"617—is this Boston?" was the response.

Huh. That was weird for a guy with whom I talked about Boston *last night*. No matter. We were going to fall in love, and this was simply a bump in the long and winding road. Someday when we were sitting on rocking chairs on our wraparound porch while our grandkids climbed trees, we'd laugh at this exchange.

"Yes—I'm a Masshole through and through, so I keep it real with the Boston digits."

"Nice, mami."

Hmm . . . I'd only heard the word "mami" used by the

Mexican guys who hung around outside of New York City bodegas. That didn't sound very Greek to me, but then again, Spanish is like Greek to me.

"Not as nice as a Greek Idol, am I right?" I tried my hardest to will whoever was on the other side of the phone to be my Greek lover.

"You sound hot hahaha" was the response. Huh!? What was going on here?

"Selena, you need to put the phone down," my homo amigos instructed me. Lesbian Leah and gay Danny had been listening to the Constantine saga unfold all day, and they were understandably sick of it.

"To be honest," Leah said, "it seems like either you took down his number wrong, or he is a jerk and he gave you a fake number."

A fake number? But would my Constantine do such a thing? He pointed at me in the concert. We spoke after the show and joked around. He offered *me* the digits! I didn't ask for anything!

"Do you have another way to reach him? I mean, can you email him so that you don't keep texting with this random Latino kid in Los Angeles?" Danny suggested.

"*Yes!* I have his email address! I can email him, make a joke of all this, and then finally we'll be in communication and our love can begin."

Leah and Danny gave each other a look.

"I'll just need to borrow your smart phone, Leah"—because my old-school flip phone could barely send a text, much less an email. Leah handed it over, and I began slowly typing my message on her miniature QWERTY keyboard.

"This is a pain in the ass," I exclaimed, "but I'll do it for Connie." We laughed.

Hey Constantine—
I must have taken down your phone number wrong, unless
you're into calling ladies "Mami" and doling out compliments
such as "You sound hot." Either way, I wanted to give you
the information about this standup comedy show I run on
Wednesday nights.

And then I did something to the tiny, elfin keyboard that
made the email send.

"Nooooo!" I shouted as I flailed my body around the filthy
hotel bedspread that was probably covered in dried semen
and tears. "This can't be happening! It just fucking *sent*, and
I didn't want it to! I hate your phone! What the fuuuuuuck!?"
I wailed.

Leah quickly opened the paper-thin accordion of a bathroom door, which gave the illusion of privacy without actually
blocking the sounds of tinkling. "Let me see what you did," she
scolded and grabbed the devil phone from my shaking hands.

"Huh. Yeah. It sent." She put the phone down on a tiny bed-
side table.

"But I didn't even give him the information! I need to send
him another message! I look like a psycho! Oh man, this is just
like Jon Favreau's character in *Swingers* when he keeps leaving
the voice mails on his ex-girlfriend's answering machine and
they keep getting cut off because he's rambling, so he has to
keep leaving messages," I lamented. "But I have to! I have to get
him the information—otherwise I look crazy," I decided.

"You think that if you don't give him the information, *that* is
what will make you look crazy?" Leah tried to bring me back
down to earth, but I wasn't having it.

"I just need your phone for *one* more message. Just one more, then I'm done, I promise!" I begged like a drug addict.[*]

"You're only allowed one more!" Leah implored and handed me the devil phone.

> Whoops! That sent before I was ready. Anyway, so the show is on Wednesday nights at Luca Lounge[†] on Avenue B between 13th and 14th streets in the East Village. It's standup and storytelling and always a good time. Come by some Wednesday and I'll buy you a beer. —Selena

OK.

When I didn't hear back from Constantine after twenty-four hours, I figured that he probably doesn't check that email address very often so I should tweet him. He said himself, he's trying to do more on Twitter. And if he's willing to tweet and retweet with AshWantsToRock, he'd *better* be willing to throw down some 140-character love notes with me. I had already baked this cake of crazy, why not frost it?

> @ConstantineM Such a blast at MexiCali Live last night! Great concert, great time!

And then I waited. For him to RT it or at least thank

---

[*] I would insert a joke about Ke$ha's song "Your Love Is My Drug" here if she didn't make me turn into a curmudgeonly old lady. Ke$ha needs to stand up straight, stop dressing like an asshole, and not end a hit song with a silly throwaway line such as "I like your beard." Got it, young lady!?

[†] Note: This venue is no longer there, so don't go trying to visit that venue in your tour of my backroom comedy shows.

@SelenaCoppock. Or, even better, for Connie to organically tweet about the show and how he *loved* the blonde chick in the crowd.

Alas, there was nothing. No mention of the show, no mention of meeting two hot comediennes outside the venue, no nothing. Just a fat Heisman in *my* face instead of his. How did this go so wrong!? This was a *joke* crush! It was a joke, and somehow I felt completely rejected and embarrassed nonetheless. I was supposed to eat him alive, not the opposite. This was pathetic. The only thing more pathetic and sad than a person who earnestly, genuinely loves a D-list "celebrity" and *American Idol* reject is a person who ironically, jokingly loves a D-list celebrity and somehow still ends up heartbroken.

The heartbreak that day and in the weeks and months after was soothed by the knowledge that it never would have worked out with Constantine anyway. The rule—don't date a guy who is as hair-obsessed as you are—exists for a reason. It simply won't work. Sure, he has great hair and I have great hair, but when we eventually got serious enough to cohabit, where would we store our combined collection of hair products? There's not a bathroom big enough in this world. My root boost spray will never be stored next to Constantine's curl-separator serum, and that's OK.

CHAPTER 5

RULE: *Have a Blonde Mentor*

Hair-wise, kids are sitting on a gold mine and they don't even know it. Or rather, a gold mine is sitting on their heads and they don't know. Children often have phenomenal natural color and exquisite natural highlights, yet they can't even begin to appreciate those gifts because they don't understand the intricacies of hair color and hair care. George Bernard Shaw said youth is wasted on the young, but I think a more fitting phrase is that good hair is wasted on the young. Due to this childhood ignorance of hair products and proper application, a hair mentor is a crucial ally for a young person.

I've been fortunate that throughout my life, I have received hair guidance and support from a blonde mentor: my mother, Susan. My two sisters, Laurel and Emily, are brown-haired, like my father, so my mother and I always had a blonde bond. Laurel, Emily, and my dad just couldn't understand my mother's and my addiction to pale-blue shirts and purple shampoo. Throughout those rough years of adolescence, my mother taught me a lot about life and also, more importantly, about overconditioning. During sixth grade I was addicted to Salon Selectives products, and I'd use dollops of shampoo and conditioner in equal measure. My shower routine was that I'd shampoo my full head, then condition my full head; then, once I dried my hair post-shower, it would appear to be filthier than it was before I even began the whole exercise. My mother was flabbergasted as to how my hair could look perpetually dirty (those were tough times in Selena hair history), and I was clueless about the nuances of conditioner and fine hair. Finally, she sat me down and asked what I was doing in the shower—how was it possible that I could wash my hair and yet be unable to clean my hair? I explained my system and my mother imparted some brilliant advice: Slathering your head with conditioner, from root to tip, will undo any washing that you just did.

"But I want my hair to be soft and conditioner makes it soft," I explained.

"But this is too much of a good thing. What you have now is beyond soft and downright dirty all over again." Aha. I, the young ninja, finally understood the prophecy: condition, but only on the ends of your hair. My blonde mentor mother had saved the day by saving my hair.

Every young blonde should have a blonde mentor to keep her away from Sun-In and school her on the intricacies of proper conditioner application—that is, a blonde mentor to keep a young towhead on the proper platinum track. My beautiful mother is an ashy blonde contrast to my brassy blonde ways, and she has always provided me with essential balance and crucial hair care advice.

My mother was something of a hair chameleon throughout my childhood: different cuts, occasional perms, but always ashy blonde highlights. Still, her exemplary hair record includes a few catastrophes since she herself lacked a blonde mentor (her mother was an auburn-haired knockout who didn't understand Susan's ashy-haired aspirations). My mother gave me a breakdown of her worst blonde incidents and I share them here, in Susan's own words.

1960—*Peroxide Portside*

My parents gave me a present of a seventeen-day cruise from Venice to New York City when I was sixteen. Since I was alone, it was not much fun and rather scary. But I thought that I would make the trip more interesting if I became a blonde. Since my redheaded mother would not have understood this at all, this trip was the perfect time for me to experiment without her presence. I bought a small bottle of peroxide, and in the little sink in my stateroom, I poured and dabbed it on my hair, thinking that somehow the dabbing would be enough and transfer blondeness across my entire head. In my fantasy, I would turn into Marilyn Monroe instantaneously. In reality, my hair was still mousy brown with splotches of white here and there. I looked like I was wearing a polka-dot wig. Even I knew that this experiment had not gone according to plan.

When my parents met me at the ship, my mother had a predictable reaction. There was no screaming, just a set mouth and a determined manner: "Tomorrow I am taking you to my hairdresser, who will straighten out this mess." Mother went to a small salon on the West Side to get what she called her "touch-ups." They covered her white roots with auburn hair color so that she could once again become a youthful-looking redhead.

Dad called Mother's salon "the Cell" because he laughingly accused the owners and the clientele of sympathizing with all things Communist. So I dutifully went, listening for subversive talk but hearing none. But my hair did return to its mousy-brown natural state.

1967—Streaking in Montreal

I was in Montreal working at Expo 67, the World's Fair. I had seen pictures in magazines of models with beautifully streaked or highlighted hair that looked natural and subtle. I thought that I explained adequately what I wanted at the salon, but **les mèches** *(the highlights) that I got were true, thick stripes of light- and dark-GRAY hair. I looked like I was wearing a gray pinstripe suit on my head. This experience gave me a scary preview of what I would look like in forty years—if I let nature take its course, which I had no intention of doing. Not after what I had seen! The remedy for incidents one and two was to have my hair dyed brown to cover the blonde and gray errors. Grrr—thwarted again and again in my attempt to be a blonde.*

1969—Cambridge Ring Around the Roots

Once again I thought that I had explained what I wanted, even going so far as to show a picture: "See! See! This is what I want." Well, you know what is coming. This time my hair looked like straw with an interesting orange corona around my face. I felt like a medieval monk with a bad tonsure, thinking weighty thoughts like, "Where can I hide my head so no one can see me?" After that incident, there was nothing to do but wait. My hair was too damaged to dye it some more.

Thankfully, after that Cambridge "monk look" debacle, my mother met a good colorist and then, in short order, a good man (my father, Michael).* My mother did her best to help me through the trials and tribulations of life as a young blonde, destined to be awarded "Best Hair" from Weston High School in 1998. She did make a few missteps, though, when she caved into my and my sisters' childhood pleas and let us get perms. Many, many perms. The worst of which was something called a "nonchemical" natural perm. (Umm . . . if you're not going to use chemicals to will this straight hair curly, then exactly what are you going to use?) Laurel, Emily, and I lined up for that new type of perm, hoping to have bouncy, 1980s-style curls, but what we got was much worse. "It took all of the shine out of your hair," my mother recalls. "It looked like something was dead on top of your head." My mother got a bad perm at the same salon herself. She went in for a regular perm and came out with an Afro puff, which prompted my father to call the salon and yell at them, asking, "How could you do this?" What can I say? The Coppock family has a lot of hair drama.

It's nice to know that even my blonde mentor experienced some bumps and detours along the way to hair glory. My mother doesn't have time to act as your personal hair mentor, dear reader—she's got her hands full keeping me away from overconditioning. But she's willing to share some of the tips that she has learned over the course of a lifetime of blondeness.

---

* They dated for two months, then got engaged. How amazing is that? They've now been married forty-plus years. Thank God she found a good colorist when she did!

- Don't be afraid to have one hairdresser cut your hair and another hairdresser color it. My mother has almost always had one person who does her cut and another who does her color. She has honed in on the specialty of a hairdresser and shopped around to get exactly what she wants. Sure, having one hairdresser do the cut and a colorist at a different salon do your color can be a time-consuming and expensive endeavor, but do you want good hair or not?

- Try, try, try to explain ashy vs. brassy so that you don't end up on the wrong side of the blonde spectrum. As I mentioned before, my mother's mother was a natural redhead—auburn hair and porcelain skin—so my mother has a lot of red in her pigment already, which can lead to brassy color if the colorist isn't careful. If the color is too warm, my mother insists that her head looks like orange-yellow Velveeta cheese—not the look she wants. She likes her hair to be a sleek whitish blonde (unlike my preferred brassy shade), and when she tries out a colorist for the first time, she makes it a point to explain this difference and her own knowledge of her red pigmentation. When the colorist makes her adequately ashy, she looks fantastic. When the colorist somehow leads her to brassiness, poor Mom has a mac-and-cheese head.

- Bring a photo. Don't feel corny pulling out a photo or magazine cutout. If you were having a pair of shoes dyed to exactly match your dress, you would bring a fabric swatch of the exact color, wouldn't you? Well, your hair is no different—bring a point of reference. Also, please never do that matching dress-and-shoes combo—the 1980s are over.

- Follow a good hairdresser wherever he/she may go. Even if

he/she talks too much. Finding a hairdresser who does your cut or color just the way you like it is a herculean task. So if you're fortunate enough to find a good hairdresser, stick with her. Even if she chats more than you'd like. Even if she moves to a salon that's an hour drive from your home— make the journey. Do you want convenience, or do you want hair that makes people do a double take? Once you find a good hairdresser, follow her to the ends of the earth.

- Don't snap your gum. Doing that makes you look trashy. (For more of these gems, check out Chapter 11.)

Heed the wise words of my mother, Susan—a lifelong blonde, my icon of blondeness, and my invaluable blonde mentor.

PART TWO

Blonde Maintenance

CHAPTER 6

RULE: *Natural Blondes Must Wear Sunscreen*

The California girl archetype is deeply entrenched in American pop culture history: She's lean, tan, laid-back, and topped with a head of naturally sun-kissed blonde hair. The Beach Boys built an empire on this character, and *Baywatch* sold it to the American public and beyond (Germans love their Hasselhoff). If there's one thing that the 1980s taught us, it was the crucial lesson that to be a desirable blonde, you had to have a great tan and a pair of red pumps (if every hair band video is to be believed). The nerd archetype, on the other hand, is grounded in that character's complete inability to achieve a tan. The *Police Academy* films, the *Revenge of the Nerds* franchise, and '80s teen films with poolside scenes almost always featured a pasty nerd character whose gangly arms were adorned with water wings and whose nose was covered in zinc oxide. The message of '80s cinema for adolescents was clear: Nerds wear sunscreen and are clueless about aquatics; cool people tan and swim well.

I grew up watching *Baywatch* somewhat religiously and

viewing an inordinate number of tan blonde women running down California beaches in slow motion. These tan blondes were either running in slow-mo to make a rescue (Pamela Anderson, Nicole Eggert, Donna D'Errico), or they were making bad decisions beachside (only to be saved by David Hasselhoff's legendary character, Mitch Buchannon and that one brunette lifeguard lady who had A cups and actual lifeguard skills). Thanks to *Baywatch*, my young mind eternally linked blonde hair and tan skin. Blondes were tan—that's simply how it went.

Throughout my childhood summers, every morning before day camp, my mother would dutifully slather me in SPF 15, ruining my chances of ever becoming a tan, slow-mo-running *Baywatch* babe. (Note: This was before parents started coating their kids in SPF 600 to the point that now kids have vitamin D deficiencies. SPF 15 was considered pretty hard-core during the era of *Kids Incorporated* and Milli Vanilli.) I needed my mother to ease up on the sunblock application so that I could achieve the sun-kissed look that I saw on TV and desperately wanted to mimic in my own life.

"Mom, I have blonde hair. I shouldn't wear all this sunblock. I should be getting tan like the women on *Baywatch*," I would explain, using the brilliant logic of an eight-year-old who just wants to stop being teased with the nickname Whiteout.

"Selena, those women aren't natural blondes," she'd respond. She then leveled with me as to why I possessed natural blonde hair and the pigmentation of a corpse as I clutched my jelly bag and stood there, quaking in my jelly shoes.

"Our family is Irish, English, and Scottish. We are fairskinned and have light hair and blue eyes, and we'll never get tan like the women that you see on TV. They're probably Italian or Greek and color their hair blonde, but their hair is really brown when they don't color it," she said.

Huh? The women on *Baywatch* weren't paragons of natural beauty? My young mind couldn't come to grips with this harsh reality. First I learn that Santa's not real, now the cast of *Baywatch* is revealed to be bottle blondes! Next you'll tell me that their breasts have been surgically enhanced or something completely inconceivable and insane like that! Is nothing sacred? I didn't understand it. In my mind, blonde hair and the ability to become tan were intertwined. One went with the other, just like peanut butter and jelly, or Laverne and Shirley, or water parks and the unwashed masses. Getting my nascent brain around the fact that these women were completely fake and that tan skin and blonde hair weren't naturally correlated was like trying to explain existential philosophy to a toddler. It just didn't compute.

But my fair-skinned and fair-haired brethren should not be ashamed of their look—the stereotype of the bronzed blonde is unrealistic for many natural blondes, as I eventually realized. Pasty ladies should be proud of their porcelain complexions and not feel like they must submit to the platinum-haired, tan-skinned, California girl stereotype. There are multitudes of fair-skinned knockouts in entertainment and fashion: Amanda Seyfried, Scarlett Johansson, Robyn, Taylor Swift, Dakota Fanning, Michelle Williams, Cate Blanchett, Emma Stone, Courtney Love, and many more. These ladies are gorgeous, possess porcelain complexions, and wear their fairness with pride. They don't layer on bronzer and tanning cream to fit in with the characters from *Jersey Shore*. They cover up on the beach, slather on the sunscreen, and almost never wrinkle. For their inspirational self-acceptance and confidence in the face of a bronzed world, I admire these porcelain princesses.

However, I am unable to be like them. I cannot resist the siren call of the "healthy" tan, and so I have perfected a method to make even the pastiest, palest blonde a bronze, blonde goddess (or at least a less-than-paper-white goddess). You need not be banished to a life as an assumed Goth kid who is allergic to sunlight. My naturally fair-haired brothers and sisters, I decree that you can still wear some sunblock and get a bit of color nonetheless. My blonde bestie, Suzanne, and I developed a strategy for maximizing melanin. Hold on to your socks.

How to "Tan" as a Pasty Girl

I don't like the nickname, but I have been called a pasty girl on more than one occasion. A few years back, Suzanne and I took a trip to Las Vegas, where we befriended a bachelor party over drinks at the Palms Casino Resort's Playboy Club. They were nice guys, but they promptly nicknamed us "the Pasties" (and it wasn't a reference to nipple covers). The guys said that it was a term of endearment, but if you've ever endured playground teasing about your fair skin, you know how harsh that nickname can feel. We rolled with the punches, though—hell, this crew was buying drinks and spending money like finance guys circa 2007. But Suzanne and I knew what we had in our back pocket on that trip: an extensively researched sunbathing formula to fight that nickname and be, in fact, less pasty.

People will tell you that on vacation, you should slather on the SPF 30 or SPF 60, wear a hat, not hit the beach between the hours of eleven a.m. and two p.m., and generally have your "beach vacation" include as little beach time as possible. This need not be the case! Do not listen to these losers!* You should not return from a tropical island looking like you spent a week in front of a computer beneath fluorescent lights, working eighteen-hour days of computer programming. Ladies and gentlemen, I shall now reveal my secret weapon: SPF 8.

You're thinking, *SPF 8? What, is this the 1960s and people are using reflective mirrors and baby oil to maximize their tans? This author may have a sick weave, as I saw in the author photo, but what is she thinking?* I'm thinking that everyone looks healthier with a bit of color, unhealthy though it may be. I'm thinking that when I was a kid, my rich peers would go to the Caribbean during February school vacation (while I spent five straight days putzing around our local mall) and come back oozing a sense of relaxation, health, and wealth. I'm thinking that there is no reason to act like you are allergic to sunlight. (Unless you really are allergic, in which case, please skip to the next chapter and *do not* heed my advice. I have no idea what I'm talking about, OK?. . . Are those pasty sun allergy kids gone? Good, now *listen up!*)

SPF 8 is like manna from heaven. It usually comes in a brown bottle (because it technically qualifies as "tanning lotion" on the sunscreen continuum), which looks a hell of a lot cooler in your beach bag than a stark white bottle of SPF 3000. You're getting cooler by the minute, reader! Sunblock should never be applied beachside or poolside, if possible. It's much easier to get a uniform layer of sunblock on your entire body if you apply it while you're still indoors, before you go out in the

---

* Perhaps this is obvious, but this book is not on the "favorites" list of the American Cancer Society.

sun. That way, you can spread the sunblock on your entire body and not worry about missing spots or getting burned near your bikini straps or edges. Also, if it's done in private, strangers don't awkwardly observe you rubbing down your entire body (back of thighs! ears! tops of feet!). Private application is a win-win for everyone. Once you're coated in SPF 8 and have assembled the requisite beach accoutrements—chair that can recline (to avoid tiger stripes on your stomach), *Us Weekly* (*People* and *In Touch* are also acceptable, but NOT *Time* or *The Economist* or anything remotely informative), snacks, and iced Dunkin' Donuts coffee* you are ready to hit the beach.

So you're on the beach—what now? First things first: chair placement. Do *not* face the water unless the shadow permits it. Some people place their chairs facing the waves no matter what. That's a nice view, but do you want a nice view, or do you want to achieve a bit of a tan and drop the albatross of pastiness once and for all? No pain, no gain—or more appropriately: If you sit at a weird angle with your beach chair casting a shadow on your thigh, you will end up with a half-tan, half-pasty thigh. I'm trying to save you from yourself! So place your chair with the shadow casting directly behind you as you face the sun and rotate that chair to follow the sun as the day unfolds. Whoever said that what you learned in eighth-grade Earth Science would never come in handy?†

If you're at the beach with a pasty friend who isn't intent

---

* I'm not even being paid by DDs to push for their coffee—I genuinely love it. But if a Dunkin' Donuts executive is reading this, please make me your spokeswoman! I adore your coffee so much that I call it "Deeze Nuts" or just "the Deeze" and drink at least one cup a day.

† My eighth-grade science teacher, Mr. Stasik, would be so proud of how I'm using his brilliant lessons. To teach people how to get tan!

on escaping pastiness, she'll probably encourage you to reapply your sunblock as the hours tick by. *Do not listen to her.* She knows nothing. Much like how the infamous dating book *The Rules* tells you not to talk to your therapist about *The Rules*, do not talk to pasty people about your attempts to escape the pasty prison.* They want you to stay with them, looking paper-white and ill, but you're blowing this proverbial popsicle stand and you're going to get some color. If you reapply sunblock, even SPF 8, you will undo all the hard work (careful initial application, chair rotation) that you've put in. So resist the urge to reapply and instead, go get another delicious Dunkin' Donuts iced coffee.†

Once you have read through all of your magazines, chatted with your beach crew about every possible topic of conversation, polished off a few iced coffees, and generally had your fill of the beach, stick it out for thirty more minutes. The sun needs to work its magic, and if there's one thing that we know about the sun, it's that it doesn't move quickly. Well, it doesn't technically move at all—rather, the earth orbits around it—but you know what I mean.‡ When it comes to getting color, patience is key.

Head home and wait for the fantastic results to blossom in four to five hours. In the meantime, you should definitely shower since a day at the beach leaves most people smelling extremely funky. If possible, don't shave your legs after that day of SPF 8 experimentation, as I have a scientifically unproven belief that you will shave off whatever color you just got. Post-shower,

---

* In this life, we're each on our own path. And this path is going to lead you to hotness.
† Ya like that, imaginary Deeze Nuts exec? I'm not afraid to throw in *two* references to your coffee. *Give me that job as your spokeswoman!*
‡ This isn't a friggin' Earth Science textbook.

you will enter the second phase of the quest for tan, and it's a step that is even trickier than the previous one: Apply bronzing lotion.

When most people think of bronzer or tanning lotion, they picture Christina Aguilera on the red carpet, looking like a transvestite cinnamon stick that has been dusted with glitter. She's an example of bronzer gone wrong—you need not look like an orange disco ball with a wig on top. Other examples of bronzer abuse include George Hamilton, Valentino, and everyone on *Dancing with the Stars*. Thankfully, great advances in bronzer technology have been made in the past twenty years, and now even the pastiest pasty can achieve a subtle tan thanks to bottled sun. Said sun can either be self-administered at home (using a tanning cream) or by a trained professional in a spray tanning salon (using what resembles a backyard hose filled with filthy water). Since I am a believer in the pioneer spirit (and I'm usually broke), we'll discuss the at-home bronzing process because every wannabe tan gal should know how to take care of her own business.[*]

Let's do what Fraulein Maria of *The Sound of Music* taught us in the opening of "Do-Re-Mi" and start at the very beginning, a very good place to start. (After all, when Maria was played by Julie Andrews, she had a sweet bowl cut of blonde hair, so she can definitely be trusted.) With bronzer, starting at the beginning means shopping for the proper tanning product. You don't need to drop a ton of money for a good result—you just need to be informed. From age eleven to fourteen, I regularly stole my mother's antiquated tanning lotion from her bathroom

---

[*] That's not a reference to masturbation, I swear!

and conducted bronzing experiments on my own body.* Back in those heady days, most tanning creams emitted a distinct and foul odor and took hours to develop. Not so anymore. It's the new millennium, and soon we will be placing our fake-tanned bodies on hoverboards to ride over to the floating Zipdorp shop.† In the interim, we should all achieve bronzed perfection by using a product that changed my life: L'Oréal Sublime Bronze in Medium. This product harkens back to the carefree days of the late 1990s, when every major cosmetics company released some sort of bronzer product for the summertime. This L'Oréal product is the best of the bunch, and its staying power in the marketplace proves that superiority. The dark shade of the bottle and bold, dark shimmer of the product might intimidate some tan-seekers, but there's no reason to fret, my pets. If the bronzer is too bronzed for you, simply cut it with any old lotion for a less severe look. Simple as that. Just as you might overseason a curry dish and then dial it back with some shredded coconut for balance, body or face lotion can be added to the L'Oréal solution to exactly match the shade you are seeking. In the wintertime, you probably want just a touch of color to remind others that you aren't a zombie dancer from Michael Jackson's "Thriller" video. In the summertime, you probably want to let it rip with the bronzer so that strangers will think that you're a relaxed, laid-back beach bum who spends her Saturdays in the sun, not at home crying while clicking through her ex-boyfriend's Facebook photos (or whatever).

Since bronzing lotions have grown into a multimillion-dollar

---

* This is the closest that I will ever come to donating my body to science. Sorry, scientists.

† Product not available until 2074 and comes in flavors Wicked Awesome, Banana, and Polka Dot.

industry (and yes, I feel like I am something of veteran of the bronzer world), every cosmetics company has gotten in on the action, with most offering three bronzer options: a fair/light bronzer, a medium bronzer, and a dark bronzer. Don't bother with the fair/light option unless you are allergic to the sun, as I mentioned before, though I must ask why you are still reading this chapter, little sun allergy buddy—I already asked you to skip to the next chapter. Move along! The fair/light rarely produces enough tan to justify the expense, so jump into the deep(er) end with either medium or dark. Remember, you can always cut it with lotion to lighten the bronzer hue.

If you start using a bronzing lotion or gel regularly, you will definitely want to be exfoliating your skin regularly, too. Bronzer can build up in weird places and you need to slough off old, bronzed skin cells to have a clean palette for the next application. Also, after you apply your bronzer-lotion combo to your face or body, don't forget to wash your hands right away. Lindsay Lohan forgot this crucial step once upon a time, and the paparazzi were all over her orange hands. Don't be that girl—scrub your hands right away and be sure to focus on cuticles so that you don't end up with creepy orange nail beds. If you are putting bronzer on your body (arms, legs), be careful not to end up looking like a tan girl wearing white gloves—I told you that bronzer application was a tricky science! After you have applied tanning cream to your arms, you should wash your hands, then go back to your plain lotion and squeeze a bit into your hand. Rub your hands together and rub the lotion into the top of your hands, blending from wrist onto hand. This way, your tan arm will blend into your more white hand and you won't have a distinct boundary showing the edge of the washed hand (the "white glove" look). Rub any additional plain lotion along the soft underside of your arms, where nobody gets tan anyway.

The final step in looking like a tan blonde (despite being a natural blonde who can scarcely tan) is thoughtful clothing selection. Wearing a white bikini on the beach can be a hot look because it makes you appear quite tan, relative to the bikini. The careful use of white need not stop there, though: In the summertime, I've been known to rock a white bikini, white jeans, and white purse. While rocking this look, I've been told that I look like an extra from a Warrant video, so brace yourself to deal with some haters who can't handle your hotness. And screw the haters—you look *dope*!

Keep the light clothes in mind when selecting outfits for work or socializing—white attire can beautifully showcase your tan, however subtle that tan may be. But ladies, I must make a request: Please stop wearing clothing that exactly matches your flesh tone in color. When viewed from afar, too much flesh tone gives the look of complete, sexless nudity, like that weird 1980s TV show with the exposed-organ-and-skin-suit guy, Slim Goodbody (minus the organs—at least those break up the uniformity!). This "ball of pasty flesh" phenomenon occurs mostly on white women—you often see fair-skinned celebrities on the red carpet wearing delicate dresses that match their skin tone, as if a new Pantone called Eastern European Heritage Plus Vitamin Deficiency were created just for that dress. This trend isn't doing anyone any favors, and every time I see a white lady on the red carpet wearing a getup that Steven Cojocaru calls "petal pink" or "flesh tone" or "beige," I want to vomit.* Same with darker-complexioned women—when they wear a color

---

* The brilliant Tim Gunn is with me in this opinion. (See his wonderful book *Gunn's Golden Rules*.)

that's quite different from their skin tone (say, a bright pink or yellow), it really pops, but when they stick too close to their flesh tone, the entire look becomes too uniform.

A final step that isn't required, but is encouraged, is to maximize whiteness of your white features—eyes and teeth. This is done using the stoner's favorite tool, Visine eye drops, and the beauty queen's favorite tool, Crest Whitestrips. Yes, this might seem a bit overboard, but achieving the illusion of a sick tan has a lot in common with fundraising for Heifer International: Every little bit helps. Making your teeth and eyes extra white will make your skin, by contrast, seem more tan, and the wheel of pasty shame and self-hatred keeps on turning and turning and turning.*

Props must be given to celebrities who are fair-skinned and wear their pastiness with pride. I really admire Julianne Moore, Tilda Swinton, Nicole Kidman, Gwen Stefani, and Cynthia Nixon for their willingness to buck the trend and not worship the sun—they are stronger women than I. My bronzer addiction isn't quite as rampant as it used to be in my teenage years, but it still persists. And so I have developed the previously described rituals for "getting color" in the summertime.

Let's review your "getting color" checklist:

- SPF 8
- Beach chair
- *Us Weekly* (or *In Touch* or *People*)
- Dunkin' Donuts iced coffee

---

* Nothing's disturbing the way it goes around. Where are my Edie Brickell & New Bohemians fans at?

- A free afternoon
- Bronzing lotion
- White bikini or white purse or white pants
- Eye drops and Whitestrips

I've accepted that I'll never be a slow-motion-jogging Los Angeles County lifeguard who is bronzed to perfection. But with the help of SPF 8, hours of beachside activities, L'Oréal Sublime Bronze, and white clothing, I just might be mistaken for someone who can tan naturally and who dyes her hair blonde.

CHAPTER 7

RULE: *Know How to Work the Weave*

At some point in their lives, 75 percent of American women color their hair, whether at home or in the salon.* Around 20 percent of women are born blonde, but as they age, their hair is likely to turn darker. This means that plenty of natural blondes fall within the 75 percent of American women who color their hair, as blonde highlights are a common request in salons across the country. So coloring and highlights are a big part of blonde culture, even for natural blondes.

Perhaps you wish to join that posse of women who get a boost from a box of Clairol or a colorist but you aren't quite sure of the correct name for the style that you're seeking. What's the difference between highlights and lowlights? Where does brassy end and ashy begin? If you have red undertones, should you be careful of certain potential problems in going blonde? If there is one

---

* "How Hair Coloring Works" by Marshall Brain on TLC's *How Stuff Works* blog.

thing I have learned in my experiences with blonde dye and re-sultant color catastrophes, it's that one needs to know the jargon of hair color change. Along with knowing the lingo, it can't hurt to bring a few photos to the hair salon—hues that you like, colors that you don't like. Just as my mother advised earlier, don't feel silly bringing along pictures of celebrities, friends, family, or yourself in earlier eras to show the colorist, especially if you're popping the cherry with a new colorist. Would you rather feel silly for five minutes before the dye hits your head or feel that horrific pit-in-stomach anxiety as you choke back tears upon realizing that the colorist has given you purple hair?

Hair color is a mad science that combines many variables: your underlying pigment (your natural or "virgin" hair color), the color that you are seeking, the porosity of your hair (how well your hair will absorb and hold color based on how damaged your hair is), the level of developer used (this is what opens up the cuticle and activates the color), the color itself, and the length of time that both the color and the developer are left on your head. After all of those issues are accounted for and calculated, sometimes you *still* "can't get there from here."

To whip up this layman's guide to going lighter, I met brilliant NYC-based colorist and friend Michael Robinson with the Antonio Prieto Salon. Michael is a gorgeous blonde lady, despite the fact that she shares a first name with my brown-haired father. Most important, Michael is a talented and friendly colorist, so she didn't mind answering my multitude of ridiculous hair questions. She gave me a crash course in color and taught me that hair color might seem like a nebulous world filled with buzzwords such as "champagne," "ashy," and, "hot roots," but it's actually grounded in empirical logic: numbers and the color wheel. I hadn't thought about a color wheel since sixth-grade art class and I have a severe aversion to math,* so I threw myself at Michael's feet and begged for enlightenment . . . and a root touch-up while we talked.

The hair color industry organizes natural hair shades on a continuum that goes from 1 to 10. The 1 ranking signifies dark black, usually Asian hair, and 10 is the lightest color that can occur in nature (think Scandinavian blonde beauties). Of course bright blonde is a "Perfect Ten," natch. All natural hair colors can be found somewhere in this range of ten.

When thinking about this ten-pronged color continuum, something struck me. "Wouldn't a Marilyn Monroe platinum blonde be more of a 10 than a random Scandinavian blonde? That is, isn't an almost-white blonde considered blonder than a yellowish blonde?"

"Oh no, that platinum, almost-white color that you see on some celebrities—that is outside the 1-to-10 scale. It's considered a 12, and those women are called Special Blondes," Michael explained as she gave me autumnal highlights. She reminded me that the 1-to-10 range is for purely *natural* hair colors. That 1940s-style white blonde is certainly not a shade that occurs in nature, thus its categorization off the scale as Special Blondes or Special 12. This shade is the ashiest that you can go—it's practically white. Modern-day examples of this include Gwen Stefani, Elisha Cuthbert, Christina Aguilera, and Michelle Williams.

"So if the range is 1 to 10, and you have Special Blondes that

---

* The few positive math experiences of my life were in geometry, which is an exciting form of math because it's all about shapes and degrees and assorted other things that I can see and that actually exist, and in a class called Explorations in Math during my freshman year in college, where I rubbed elbows with the football and hockey teams.

are 12, then what color is at 11? A blonde that is really light, but not quite 'Special Blonde,' but blonder than a natural blonde?" I inquired.

"There's really no 11 on the official scale. Sure, you could make a color that I suppose is considered an 11, but it's just not recognized in the system." Huh. So this one *doesn't* go to 11, unlike Spinal Tap's amplifiers.[*]

Special Blonde or 12 coloring often requires a double process, when the hair must be completely bleached to the scalp to remove all pigment. Oftentimes that process must be administered twice to achieve that platinum hue, thus the moniker "double process." A single process is half of a double process (fun with fractions!), and it's a way of achieving the wanted hair color with only one step. When a single process is done, all of the hair is painted with one solid color so the hair color becomes uniform and every piece of hair receives color. It's mostly used with women who have red hair or dark hair, or are doing gray coverage. Technically, a single process can be done at home or in the salon, but the at-home application of one color all over is what I tend to think of when I think of single process. A double process, which is much more complex and dangerous, should not be done at home. Beware the double process because you might end up with a "chemical cut," which is what happens when hair is so damaged and overprocessed that it simply breaks off because of the trauma. Sounds horrifying, huh? You go into the salon for some exciting color on your beautiful, long mane, and you emerge looking like G.I. Jane or buzz-cut-breakdown-era Britney Spears. I've definitely seen a few gals

---

[*] If you are not familiar with *This Is Spinal Tap*, Rob Reiner's brilliant rockumentary, please update your Netflix queue immediately.

with chemical cuts, but I thought they just had exotic taste and fancied themselves Halle Berry look-alikes who could pull off such an unforgiving look. Turns out my assumption was incorrect and they were just trying to get some color, but things went way wrong.

But back at the natural color scale, let's explore an example. Say you have a woman who is a natural 3 (medium-brown hair) who wants to try her hand at blondeness (try her *head* at blondeness, really) and is shooting to end up at an 8. If she's smart, she'll make that type of drastic jump at the salon and put her hair in the hands of a trained professional. In my estimation, 99 percent of at-home, brown-to-blonde coloring sessions result in orange hair. Remember Brenda Walsh's orange dome from *Beverly Hills, 90210*? At least that was a realistic portrayal of what can happen. That's more than I can say for *The Smurfs*. When Gargamel first "created" Smurfette (creepy?), she had black hair. It wasn't until Papa Smurf stayed up all night making her into a real Smurf that Smurfette become blonde. Apparently, in the Smurf world, "stayed up all night" means "executed a feat of hair color change that can never be done anywhere outside of the drawing room at Hanna-Barbera Productions." Don't follow the lead of Papa Smurf and attempt to change black hair to blonde both at home and overnight. Put yourself in the trained hands of a professional: a colorist. Colorists are trained in assessing the underlying pigments of your hair; knowing what can and cannot be accomplished with peroxide, glaze, and timing; and memorizing which color combinations create other colors. They must regularly refer back to the color wheel and the range of 1 to 10 in which they are constantly creating colors.

Another piece of hair color jargon that indicates less-than-desirable results is "hot roots." The label "hot roots" sounds more like a reality TV show in which successful supermodels return to their humble hometowns, but it's actually used to describe the phenomenon of the root part of the hair strand becoming brighter and more vibrant in color than the rest of the hair. Your head naturally emits heat, and when hair color is applied to the full strand, the section that is closest to your hot dome will sometimes absorb color more quickly that the rest of the shaft. This is why colorists usually pile all your hair atop your head and stick you under a heater after they apply color—so all of the hair is evenly heated and thus develops uniformly and you don't get hot roots.

I asked Michael about the two types of blondes: ashy and brassy. She told me that the industry standard is to refer to these as "cool" and "warm," respectively. "Cool" (or what I still like to call "ashy" because I'm like Sinatra and I'll do it my way, thank you very much) is synonymous with champagne- or platinum-blonde hair. One also might hear descriptors such as "soft beige," "soft silver," and "lilac champagne" to describe levels of cool blonde. Michael has heard this referred to as "Upper East Side blonde," and it's naturally found on white people with fair skin and light-blue, gray-blue, gray-green, or blue-gray eyes, who sunburn easily and look best in silver (instead of gold). The natural hair colors that are considered cool include blue-black, dark brown, medium ash, ashy blonde, and light brown. Regardless of what color they have naturally, women who want cool blonde hair are oftentimes a bit older and from the Upper East Side of Manhattan or somewhere equally WASPy. Older blondes who regularly get cool highlights can stumble into purple quite easily because they are adding ashy tones to gray or white hair. When hair is gray, there is no pigment, so colors can end up being very bold because the hair is a pigment-less vessel of display. Check back to your handy chart in Chapter 1 for reference.

"Warm" (or what I call "brassy") is the golden California blonde that is quite popular in Texas and Los Angeles. "Honey caramel," "butter pecan," and "bronze" are adjectives often used to describe a warmer blonde tone. A warm blonde occurs naturally in people with a golden or yellow undertone to their skin and green, hazel, brown, or amber eyes; whose hair is naturally red, brown, strawberry blonde, or golden brown; who can tan easily; and who look better in gold than silver.

We've talked plenty about going blonde, and any colorist will tell you that it's always safer to go lighter. Highlights are an easy, low-commitment, and flattering way to play with hair color. The request that gives pause to most colorists is when a blonde client comes into the salon and asks to be made a brunette. "That's when you get into the emotional needs of the client," Michael explained. Every colorist with a few years of experience has witnessed a client have a blonde-to-brunette freak-out. As I did back in 2000 when I followed the lead of Cameron Diaz (circa January 2000 when she went bold brown for a minute) and became an almost black-haired lady (more on this dark period in my life can be found in Chapter 10). I forced my mother's beloved colorist to make me a dark, severe brunette, and I regretted it within forty-eight hours.* Make no mistake: Blonde to brunette is a major adjustment. Every fall and winter

---

* Though now, in retrospect, I think it was a fantastic exercise. Every blonde should spend a few months on the dark side, just to see what it's like.

when I would mention lowlights and toy with the idea of going light brunette for a bit, my old colorist Reinaldo would just nod, smile, and mix more caramel-hued dye for my highlights. He knew that I'd ultimately hate darker hair, and he was right.

Michael went on: "When a client comes in asking to go darker, you spend a while talking them out of it. You walk them through every step: what you'll do to take them to brunette, then what you'll have to do to correct it or undo it. The time, the process, the potential for doing a color removal (which just completely strips the hair of applied color)—it's a lot to take on. And even if they push-push-push and insist that they want to go brunette for a change, most of them freak out and want it undone within a few weeks."

There are plenty of hair color phenomena that are more quotidian than hot roots, chemical cuts, and dramatic color changes. You're probably familiar with a partial foil, which is when highlights are applied using tin foil to isolate the pieces. This is done over half of the head—usually just the crown to the ears. A full foil is the same thing across the entire head. Other options when it comes to foils are T-section (when foils are applied in a T formation on the head—the top and sides receive foil packets) and Starburst (which isn't an overrated, waxy candy but rather when five to seven packets of foils are applied on the top of the head). Highlights are streaks used to subtly lighten you color, and in contrast, lowlights are streaks that darken your color. The same method of application is used for highlights and lowlights, though—small sections of hair are painted, then wrapped in foil to isolate. A solid or uniform color is one that doesn't have highlights or lowlights—it's very monotone in hue. This is what lots of Special Blondes are: Their hair is entirely one uniform shade, and there aren't other colors woven in for depth.

Michael's training and expertise has given us a strong base for what to expect in the salon with hair color. But what about at-home tricks and tips? This is where my lifelong hair obsession finally comes in handy. Throughout my childhood and teenager years, I engaged in a lot of trial by fire with hair color, assorted hair products, and hairstyles. Finally I can feel like the ugliness of those years (and years) of perms was not in vain. I can share my lessons with you, dear reader.

Personally, I have fine hair, as do many natural blondes. Just look at the three daughters in *The Brady Bunch*—all had very fine, occasionally limp hair. How do you care for hair like that, living in this crazy world of shampoo and conditioner? I'll tell you the key for fine-haired ladies: Don't overcondition. Conditioner is alluring and silky, and it calls to us, just like it does to Adam Sandler in 1995's *Billy Madison*. "Conditioner is better. I leave the hair silky and smooth." Conditioner can be great (especially during dry winter months), but it should be used sparingly and only on the ends of the hair—away from the roots. I recommend shampooing your hair like a normal person (using a color-protecting shampoo or a purple shampoo, as necessary), then putting conditioner just on the ends (*not* the roots) and letting it sit there while you shave your legs or belt out a few power ballads in the shower. Then rinse. As you are brushing through your damp hair post-shower, if you are having trouble getting the brush through, feel free to spray some leave-in conditioner onto the middle and ends of the hair (again, away from the roots). If the opposite occurs and your hair feels overconditioned and floppy (like the hair of Janice the hippie chick in the Muppet band), simply brush through it and compensate for that silkiness with extra quantities of products that will give you back some body: gel, mousse, or hair spray.

Many people flinch at this laundry list of hair products. The words "hair spray" make them picture a cheesy girl with giant "mall bangs," a New Kids on the Block T-shirt, and pegged jeans circa 1990. But hair spray can be quite useful, and it should not have a horrible connotation. In fact, contrary to popular belief, putting product in your hair is a good thing because it coats the shaft and protects your hair from hot styling implements such as curlers and irons. With a few exceptions, hair products such as gel and mousse shouldn't be applied to dry hair or you'll end up with sticky, gunk-filled locks. You can do a lot of useful hair product application during that precious and precarious witching hour when the hair is still damp, before you use the blow-dryer. Applying gel or mousse during this window of opportunity, while hair is still damp, will give you the body that you crave but permit movement and bounce.

I just got lost in a mystical window—where were we? Oh yes, fresh out of the shower with a wet head of tangles. Perfect. After you brush through your hair, you may wish to spray it with a bit of water or wet your hands and run them through your hair if your hair air-dries insanely quickly, as mine does. I know that it seems counterintuitive to towel-dry, then re-wet your hair, but just trust me: I'm a genius with dope hair. Once the hair is untangled and damp, you should put some gel on the palm of your hand (a quarter-size drop at minimum) and run it through your hair to coat the shaft and add body and thickness. If you have accidentally overconditioned your hair, use more gel than normal. You also can use mousse, if you prefer that. Then you might wish to use a root boost spray or a spray gel on the roots. This ensures that the weight given to the rest of the hair (from the gel that you just applied) won't weigh down the roots—they will be boosted up, too. Like a Wonderbra for your dope hair.

As far as specific products or labels, I'm no snob. I generally use any L.A. Looks gel—they come in an assortment of colors (fear not—the funky color of the gel doesn't show up on the actual hair) and all are good. Also, Garnier Fructis has some fantastic products, and Herbal Essences has some wonderful shampoos, conditioners, and products—their Body Envy mousse is a personal fave.

If you are a bronzer addict like me, at this point you might want to clip up your hair off your face and back (I recommend a small hair clip with plastic or rubber texturing on the inside edges of the clip as it gently grips wet, slippery hair) so that now you can apply lotion to your body, and a nice bronzer cream/lotion mix to your face. It's quite a ritual. Once that bronzer cream/lotion mixture has had a bit of time to sink in, feel free to take your damp hair down to let it air-dry a bit. But not too much. Don't go calling a friend during that window of time because it's a very limited phase and you can't be yammering. The hair is drying, but you cannot let it dry completely or all your hair work will be for naught.

Once your damp hair has dried a bit, it's time to blow-dry. My best friend, Suzanne, somehow managed to get a wicked case of carpal tunnel syndrome from blow-drying her hair. No joke. She saw her doctor to get to the bottom of it, and he was able to identify the offending behavior that was causing her wrist problems. He had some wise words that we all should heed: When you're blow-drying your hair and you have the dryer in one hand and a brush in the other, keep them moving around the head. Don't get stuck in one spot doing the same motion continuously. In this way, blow-drying isn't unlike childhood bike riding: safety first. Everyone has his or her own way to blow-dry—some people separate the hair into sections to isolate the sections that they are working on, other people only blow-dry with their heads upside-down, others start with their bangs and move back, and still others start at the back and work their way forward. All are correct. Much like the Hard Rock mantra of "Love all, serve all," when it comes to blow-drying your hair, "Love all, dry all (strands of sweet hair)." I personally start at the back and bottom and get that settled, then work my way up and forward. The toughest section is the hair that frames the face. Cowlicks can muck things up, and it's often hard to get the hair to point where you want it to point and hang how you want it to hang, right off the ol' dome piece. When I'm blow-drying, I simply focus on getting the hair dry and straight, and I leave the specific styling and pointing of hair to later.

"Later" comes quickly when you have fine hair, so now it's styling time. At this point, when the hair is completely dry, gel and mousse are verboten but a touch of hair spray and styling wax is permitted. Part your hair how you wish to part it (I love a good diagonal side part—a flattering look on most and a nice way to balance things), then lock in the style by giving it a quick spritz with hair spray from an aerosol can. I know, I know, environmentalist blondes reading this book are thinking, *She's a terrible person, and aerosol cans are the devil. Aerosol cans cause rips in the ozone layer, and this jerk is slowly killing our planet because she needs to lock in style.* Don't blame me! Blame the scientists who have yet to create a hair spray application device that is as good as aerosol but without the environmental repercussions! You just can't beat the light spray that an aerosol can emits.

Earlier I mentioned styling wax. It's not just for the boys and the lesbians anymore! Styling wax should be used in moderation because a little goes a long-assed way. Don't make the same mistake that I did when I first dabbled in styling wax and apply it to wet hair post-shower. Again, that damp time is for mousse, gel, and root boost spray, but not for hair spray or styling wax. If you apply styling wax when the hair is damp, your hair will dry and look filthy all over again. Styling wax's purpose is to control hair and rein in flyaways at the final step of styling. I use a dab of styling wax if I'm parting my hair for an updo or pigtails and if I have flyaways that I need to smooth down. Be warned, though: Styling wax can be quite thick and heavy, and you should only use a pinch between your fingers and apply it to a specific spot. If you have flyaways all over and need to smooth things out (perhaps you didn't use enough conditioner and/or it's wintertime), don't use styling wax in this situation. It's too heavy for all-head application. In this circumstance, I used to use a product called Secret Weapon, but it was discontinued a few years back. That was what I call my own personal D-Day (discontinuation day), and it was a dark day for both me and Suzanne, who was hooked on Secret Weapon, too. You can replicate the effect of Secret Weapon with any old hand or body lotion. I learned this trick from some black friends who swear by it to smooth their flyaways.* Simply squeeze a bit of lotion onto your hands and rub them together; then, once the lotion has dissolved a bit but while it's still somewhat tacky, gingerly run your hands either over your hair (if it's parted) or through it (if you're foregoing a part and shooting for a loose style that you will toss around).

But that's just my system—yours might be quite different. I have a blonde friend who possesses super-thick hair and needs

---

* Hair brings people of all races together! If I ever run for office, I will run on a hair-focused platform and I'll score a wide array of supporters, mark my words.

to slather on conditioner before spending twenty minutes with a high-intensity hair dryer. I have another pal who conditions and combs her hair in the shower, then must carefully let it air-dry and cannot run a comb or brush through it once it has dried. You'll want to conduct your own experiments to find what works for your hair, and explore different hair products using trial by fire.

For quick reference, let's recap the hair jargon we just learned:

- Underlying pigment: the color of virgin, or never-colored, hair
- Porosity of hair: how well hair will absorb and hold color
- Developer: the liquid used to open up a cuticle of hair and activate color
- 1-to-10 continuum: the way that colorists chart natural hair colors, with 1 being the darkest and 10 being the lightest
- Special Blondes/Special 12s: platinum blondes, a color that doesn't occur in nature
- 11: the level that Spinal Tap's amplifiers crank up to, oddly not a position on the hair color continuum
- Single process: a uniform color that is spread across all hair (mostly used for dark hair, red hair, and gray coverage)
- Double process: when a single process must be administered twice in order to remove old color and achieve new color (mostly used for platinum blondes)
- Chemical cut: severe hair breakage caused by overprocessing
- Hot roots: when the roots are brighter and more vibrant than the rest of the shaft

- Cool (ashy): blonde that is platinum or silvery—also called Upper East Side blonde
- Warm (brassy): blonde that is yellow or golden—also called California blonde
- Color removal: a process that can be done at home or in the salon, when a hair color is stripped from your hair— used only in hair color emergencies
- Highlights/lowlights: painted pieces of hair that are either lighter than the rest of the hair (highlights) or darker than rest of hair (lowlights) and add dimension
- Full foil: when highlights are painted on and sealed with foil packets across the entire head
- Partial foil: when highlights are painted on and sealed with foil packets, but only from crown to ears
- T-section foil: when highlights are painted on and sealed with foil packets, but only on the top and sides of head
- Starburst foil: when highlights are painted on and sealed with five to seven foil packets on the top of the head
- Purple shampoo: used to counteract brassiness in hair that has been colored blonde
- Good products: gel, mousse, hair spray, root boost spray, L.A. Looks gel, Garnier Fructis, Herbal Essences' Body Envy line, hair clips, styling wax

That's a comprehensive overview of in-salon color, at-home color, and at-home styling. Phew. I hope that you have learned something new courtesy of the trained professional, Michael, and the hair-obsessed writer, me. I shall close this chapter with one word of advice: When it comes to styling, no tendrils. Dear

Lord, no tendrils—ever. Please. If you're thinking, *What is she talking about? What are tendrils?*, then I assume that you never attended a wedding or prom in the 1980s or 1990s, and you should consider yourself lucky. For the blissfully unaware, tendrils are pieces of hair (usually framing the face) that are deliberately left out of an updo to make the look appear less severe. They are often curled (by cheesy people) in a very small barrel curling iron so that those few strands ostensibly frame the face. Unfortunately, these tendrils fail in their mission to frame the face and instead make the wearer look like a grape arbor, with errant crap dangling down like vines or bougainvillea. It's not a hot look on anyone, but especially not on blondes—I expect more from you.

CHAPTER 8

RULE: *Don't Try This at Home:*
A Cautionary Tale

Dolly Parton's character in *Steel Magnolias* put it best: "I don't trust anyone who does their own hair. I don't think it's natural." Certain types of ablutions and personal care cannot and should not be self-administered at home. These include back massages (you can't give yourself a back massage, no matter how much you brag about your flexibility thanks to yoga), plastic surgery (not even if you find yourself in an Aron Ralston–*127 Hours* situation), and most hair color changes. All thoughts of at-home hair color change should be accompanied by a helpful public service announcement: Don't try this at home. The only hair coloring that can be successfully self-administered at home is a single process (which I discussed in Chapter 7) used for darker hair (gray coverage), redheads, or completely uniform color. Otherwise, heed the advice of the guys in *Jackass*, and don't try this at home.

There was a time when I swore by self-administered, at-home hair color. This time was called "when I was broke and didn't quite know how hair color worked." This segment of my life overlapped with my first year after college, when I lived in Chicago and earned a pittance while working as a paralegal in the grayest office ever. It was an office so bland and drab and gray that I wondered if the partners had taken the set of *Office Space* and spent a small fortune moving it from a soundstage to Chicago. I had been drawn to the lovely city on the lake because my sister Laurel was living there and it had (and has) a bustling comedy community. My dreams of improv comedy brilliance were dashed by an exhausting work schedule that left me without enough energy to do much more than eat dinner and fall asleep after work.

In most offices, the employees who occupy the lower-level jobs band together and become a friendly team. They are brothers-in-arms pitted against the wholly out-of-touch and usually moronic higher-ups who make business decisions with no idea how anything will actually trickle down to the client or customer level. At almost every job I've ever had, I've made fast friends and gotten along swimmingly with all of my coworkers. During high school summer vacations, I'd serve as the token white girl in a Boston law firm's mailroom, where I quickly became buddies with everyone. We'd crack jokes, listen to dancehall reggae music by Beenie Man played far too loudly (not my choice), and keep our eyes open for free leftover food in the conference rooms. During the academic year in high school, I worked as a sandwich maker at Bruegger's Bagels in downtown Weston (blink and you'll miss "downtown" Weston). Again, I was pals with everybody—managers, fellow sandwich makers, and even the troll-like guys who were there just to cook the bagels in a giant cauldron. At that job, I initiated a fun game called "the Hottie Tally" wherein we would keep a record of how many hot guys came in each day. Our record was a mere three—not much talent in downtown Weston's foot traffic, sadly. I've fit in at every job I've had except one: at that damn law firm job in Chicago.

I was a paralegal, which was just a way of saying "administrative assistant" that made you feel like you hadn't just wasted four years studying English literature at a liberal arts college. The salary for this job was about half of what it cost to attend my college for one year. So after paying rent and a few bills, I was perpetually broke. Like a stray cat (minus the strut), I was living on hard-boiled eggs and cans of tuna. The paralegal gig paid horribly, and even worse, my coworkers seemed to hate me, thanks to one girl at the firm. Kristy had been the "cute blonde" at the office until I arrived and unwittingly dethroned her. My apologies.* I have great hair and tolerable features: I was born this way.* Kristy wasn't doing much to earn the title of "cute blonde," but as the only blonde at the firm she was, by default, the cute one, I suppose. This same logic can be used to declare Latvia the most developed and stable of the Baltic states. It's still not saying much.

Nonetheless, blonde "cutie" Kristy definitely would have benefitted from a root boost spray (sprayed on while the hair was still wet, of course), a bit of gel (to coat the shaft and build body), and a good blow-dry. But I wasn't about to share my gems of hair brilliance with her. Not after how she treated me.

Kristy took it upon herself to organize paralegal outings to a nearby bar after work on Fridays. This would happen with enough regularity that it didn't take long before I realized that

* Lady Gaga's hit song "Born This Way" is an anthem for the gay community that can fit quite well for being dope.

I was being left out by her, perhaps deliberately and very frequently. I hate to pull out the pithy "don't hate me because I'm beautiful" line, but seriously, gurl, don't hate. On me. Because of my dope weave. I'd like to give you some tips if you'd stop blatantly excluding me and pretending that you don't care about me. The opposite of love isn't hate, Kristy; it's disinterest.

Fortunately, I had one ally at the office: Dmitry, the Russian paralegal who collected kitsch. Dmitry's cube was filled with ripped-out magazine pictures of Liza Minnelli and David Gest's wedding (specifically the photo in which they are flanked by Michael Jackson and Elizabeth Taylor), posters of kittens, macramé crafts, and other such oddities. The no-nonsense black woman from Chicago's South Side who served as our office assistant was completely bewildered by Dmitry's cube, but I loved it. His cube cracked me up, he cracked me up, and he had my back. Thank God I had him because, thanks to Kristy's manipulations, I wasn't exactly winning the company popularity contest. Almost every day, Dmitry and I would eat lunch together in the conference room and troubleshoot the latest office gossip. Dmitry had moved back in with his parents (to the suburbs north of Chicago) after college, so he'd spend lunchtime munching on his traditional Russian food prepared by his mother. I'd chow on my lunch, which consisted of a tuna salad sandwich (brought from home because I was broke), Doritos (also brought from home because it's cheaper to divide up a big bag of Doritos than it is to buy small individual bags), and water (one of the few things the law firm supplied—a community bubbler). That exact meal was my lunch every day for six months. I was probably walking around with a wicked case of mercury poisoning. We'd discuss our fellow paralegals, the Goth kid who ran the file closet/photocopy room, the bizarre assortment of lawyers and their eccentricities, and what we'd done the night or weekend before. Dmitry would tell me stories of suburban family life—eating dinner with his Russian-born parents and younger brother, watching TV, borrowing the car. My conversational contributions would be updates about my nights and weekends: visiting the gay gym in my neighborhood (the Body Shop) where I would be wholly ignored by buff men, eating dinner alone in my apartment, or drinking at Wrigleyville bars with my two friends Ginny and Kate.

As if earning a barely livable wage wasn't prize enough, I was assigned to work for one of the lawyers who was a Jekyll-and-Hyde-type woman with a JD from a subpar law school. I can tolerate working for an asshole as long as I know what to expect. That's fine by me. But if I hear the click of your shoes and I don't know whether you're coming to ask me "what the fuck" I was thinking when I failed to make a third photocopy of a client's passport even though we still have the original inside the file folder* or to inquire about my family reunion in Idaho (despite the fact that I'm not from Idaho and I clearly told you that I was going away for a weekend with my family in Boston), then I'm going to hate you. Just be consistent with my fragile sensibilities, would ya? Much like a child who is learning how to trust and other such shiz from Maslow's hierarchy of needs, I just need consistency, dammit.

Thanks to my attorney assignment, I spent many hours at work in the bathroom crying and many hours after work at Pippin's (a bar with peanut shells covering the floor and eight-dollar pitchers). I was too broke to afford much hair upkeep, save for a basic trim at Supercuts every so often. Those were the days

---

* Actually happened. Verbatim. Professionalism at its best!

where I'd wait for a haircut in a long line of men (who needed a foolproof buzz cut), then receive my haircut within eyeshot of said men. They'd watch the hairdresser spray my hair wet (no shampoo), then cut it straight across. The glamorous life!

The haircut situation was degrading, and there was no way I could afford any sort of salon hair color. I could hardly afford to ride the bus, much less drop a hundred dollars or more on a nice set of partial foils. My sister (who was my roommate at the time, though our living arrangement was more like "ships in the night") told me about an Aveda training salon that was only a few blocks over from our apartment. You could make a reservation, show up at the Aveda training salon obscenely early on a Saturday morning, and get your hair done for free by a hairdresser in cosmetology school. You only had to pay the tip—fantastic! I promptly made a reservation, and on the appointed Saturday morning I used free transportation (my legs!) to get to the Aveda training salon, which was housed in a near-abandoned mall. Finally I'd have a day of relaxation and self-improvement, and it would be free of charge, too! I was elated.

"Selena Ko-pock?" a young wannabe colorist shouted in the crowded waiting room.

"That's me!" I popped up and followed her to her client chair, where she sat me down and we talked. I explained what I wanted: blonde, blonde, blonde. Take me there however we have to get there—just take me there. Take the scenic route, take the long way home,* whatever you gotta do—I just need some fresh blonde on my dome. Summer had arrived, and I had decided that some nice highlights were just what I needed to pull out of this Chicagoland depression. It's that simple, right?

---

* Is Supertramp underrated as hell, or is it just me?

A job that hardly pays a living wage and feelings of inescapable loneliness and alienation might persist, but blonde highlights will turn this boat around! I was quite chatty with the young colorist, and I thought we were connecting over a shared vision: a blonder, happier Selena.

The colorist washed my hair (which in retrospect makes *zero* sense if you are going to color a person's hair, but perhaps washing hair was standard operating procedure for the first step at the training salon—after all, you never quite know who is walking through that door for free services or how often she showers) and then began brushing it out. As she was brushing my hair, she began frowning. What was wrong? Why was she staring at my hair and frowning? Did she hate the cut and color? So did I! You're preaching to the choir, my new beauty school friend!

"Your hair isn't in very good shape," the colorist informed me.

"Yeah . . . I'm kinda not surprised. I haven't really had money to take care of it or get much done."

"I'm going to get my instructor—hold on," she said and disappeared. My chair was positioned with a view out the window of the basement-level training salon and into the ventilation shaft of the building. The building's center shaft was quite big and must have been built to be a central courtyard, but it hadn't been completed. The ground was cement and the would-be courtyard was empty and shadowy. I just stared and wondered what would happen now. Could they refuse to color me? Is that what hell feels like?

"Hi there." The instructor introduced herself curtly and stood next to the colorist-in-training as they looked at a chunk of wet hair on the back my head.

"See what I mean? It's stretching. She wants to go blonde, but this stretching worries me," the young colorist explained to her teacher. I felt like a show dog with a defect. The judges were talking about it right in front of me, as though I couldn't hear or respond (unlike show dogs, I know).

"Is something wrong?" I inquired, reminding them that I had both ears and a mouth (and that I don't sniff butts, dog style).

"Yes, your hair is quite damaged," the instructor explained. "You see how it's pulling a bit? Stretching here, you see? When hair is damaged, it stretches when it's wet, see?" She showed me pieces on the side of my head that did seem to be stretching a bit. "It would be unwise to dye hair if it's damaged like this," she continued, but I had stopped listening. I wanted to scream, "Just dye my friggin' hair, would you? I got up *so* early for this, and one of the only pleasures that I have *in life* is sleeping late because it's free. My hair can handle it—trust me. My hair is tougher than it looks. When I was a kid, I got perm after perm after perm because of Jennifer Grey's awesome hair in *Dirty Dancing*, and my hair never fell out, even after all those stinky chemicals. My hair can handle it, trust me. Just sweet Lord, please make me blonder. I need this."

"OK . . . well, if you won't dye my hair, I'll just walk down the street and buy an at-home dye kit," I said. I'm nothing if not reactionary and honest.

"I wouldn't do that," the teacher advised me.

"Well, I'm going to." I unbuttoned the Aveda training center smock and reached for my purse. "Ummm . . . thanks?" I wasn't about to give a tip to a girl who had washed my hair and then refused to do anything more, so I simply walked upstairs and out to the street with a wet, half-brushed head of hair.

What the fuck? I thought as I walked. Almost immediately, hot tears began flowing down my face. *I just want blonde hair! I don't care if it's damaged! Just give me what I want! I got up so damn early for this!* I was muttering to myself as I walked by a Caribou Coffee shop. Since I hadn't given the colorist a tip, I had some cash on me, and a flavored coffee was just what I needed. Unkempt, wet hair be damned! The coffee soothed my soul, and then I walked back to my neighborhood. I walked past the tanning salon where I had befriended the owners—a chatty gay couple who took a shine to me when they discovered that my birthday is only a day off from the birthday of their beloved Barbra Streisand (and yes, they gave away free tans to everyone on April 24 to celebrate Babs's birthday). I trudged over to the Walgreens on the corner of North Broadway and West Belmont, where I purchased an at-home highlighting kit. Then I walked back to my apartment, past Pleasure Island (a sex toy store), Reckless Records (a hepcat record store), the theater where *Puppetry of the Penis* was playing, and a sushi restaurant that I could never afford to visit. I took my building's stinky, antiquated elevator up to the fourth floor and walked into my perpetually empty apartment.

I locked myself in my bathroom and took matters in to my own (rubber-gloved) hands. Screw those jerks from the Aveda training salon. I was going to reach my dream of being blonder, even if I had to do it in my own bathroom. A bathroom that boasted two sinks but a layer of grime that no amount of bleach would eliminate. After a certain number of tenants precede you, there's just no getting that tub clean. I started in on the steps outlined by the home blonde highlighting kit. I tried painting thin streaks of bleach onto small bunches of hair and then placing them down on my head, but the bleached sections of hair began bleeding onto other hair. Finally, my patience wore thin, and I couldn't be bothered to carefully paint each thin section of hair. It's impossibile to do quality highlights at home without those aluminum sheets (foils) that professional colorists use to isolate small sections. I noted this and decided to just go for broke with thick, bold highlights. *It's summertime!* I thought. *Bold highlights will mimic the natural effects of the sun and give me a sunnier disposition!*

Alas, the sun doesn't lighten hair in tiger-stripe-like swaths of brassy color just above your ears. And it didn't take long for my Jekyll-and-Hyde lawyer to notice the color change.

"Oh, did you get your hair done?" she inquired at work that Monday as she handed me a stack of files to process and prepare so that she could sign the letterhead cover letter and then bill the client another $450 an hour.

"How nice of you to notice. Well, yes, I do indeed have some fresh 'highlights,' if you will (will you?), on my dope weave (and I use the word 'weave' facetiously as my hair is actually all my own and I think that weaves on white women are quite suspect), but no, I didn't 'get it done' per se. I didn't go into a hair salon and enjoy a glass of complimentary champagne (though the imagined drink probably wouldn't technically come from the Champagne region of France, so it wouldn't technically be 'champagne' so much as bubbly white wine), a scalp massage (though I would love one of those as I fear that I am becoming aphephobic, that is afraid of touch, from lack of human contact), and a pricey cut and color. No, the wages that you are currently paying me do not permit such luxuries. I earn practically nothing for enduring your abuse at the grayest law firm of all time. So in short (perhaps it's too late for that, Jekyll-and-Hyde lawyer), yes, I did color my hair, but I didn't 'get my hair done' because that would imply that I earn a living wage." That's what I wanted to say. What did I really say?

"Yeah—I did. Thanks." And I put my brassy, striped head

down to add 0.25 hours to the bill tally for another client.

But I knew it was bad. Suzanne came to Chicago to visit me (bless her heart), and even she seemed startled by my brassy tiger stripes. You know it's bad when a fellow blonde addict thinks that perhaps your blonde wasn't the best idea. Blondes are like the original five members of Guns N' Roses in their legendary song "Mr. Brownstone" with the lyrics "I used to do a little, but a little wouldn't do it, so a little got more and more. I just keep trying to get a little better, said a little better than before." It's always just one more bottle of peroxide, one more at-home highlighting kit—blonde perfection is just one more process away. Blondes are like people who become addicted to plastic surgery. They need just one more surgery to fix this one thing, then they'll stop—promise! And perhaps blonde nirvana truly is just around the corner, but please leave that transformation in the hands of trained professionals. Take it from a girl who suffered through a summer living near Detroit Tigers fans and joking that the tiger stripes on my blonde head were a tribute to the baseball team. At least Dmitry got a laugh at that over lunch.

CHAPTER 9

RULE: *Heed True Blonde Confessions*

Every blonde has been there: You're struck by a bolt of inspiration and you simply must change your hair color and it must be done right away. *What could go wrong?* you think as you embark on an odyssey that will cost you many hours and lots of money, and eventually answer that very question. A lot—a whole lot can go wrong. A few of my blonde friends were willing to share their tress tales of woe.

~~~~~~

Suzanne T. (platinum
perfection, my lifelong bestie
and partner in crime)

What's your worst hair disaster?
Where do I begin? . . . As far as isolated incidences, it's a

toss-up between when I was given an adult bowl cut* (in 2000 as a junior in college) after being told I would look like Cameron Diaz and the time when I went essentially brunette. The lowlights got a touch out of hand that winter, and I never felt like myself. As far as everyday disasters, nothing is worse than humidity or having an amazing hair day when you have nowhere to go (shallow, I know).

When did you first go blonde?

I'm proud to say I have always been a version of blonde. However, it was freshman year in high school (age fourteen) when I was allowed to play with blonde highlights, which helped me get out of the dirty-blonde category and subsequently changed my life forever.

Do you have a colorist in your life, or do you color at home?

I dabbled with the world of at-home root coloring for about three years under the guidance of a wonderful blonde roommate, none other than Miss Selena Coppock. I was able to save money and look fabulously blonde. About four years ago I went back to having my hair professionally colored in preparation for my wedding (for fear I'd be too brassy in photos). I have followed three different colorists since then. Each one does his or her own version of blonde, and sometimes I like to switch it up.

Do you love life as a blonde?

I don't even have to think to answer this—yes, yes, and yes.

---

* Note that what Suzanne refers to as an "adult bowl cut" is something that I perceived as a mullet. For more on that, see Chapter 10.

Alison S. (California blonde, world traveler)

What's your worst hair disaster?

Living in Italy, I was frequently referred to as La Bionda. *I liked to refer to this notion as "the importance of being blonde." The attention I received thanks to my hair color was everlasting and I relished every moment—well, almost every one. As a natural* bionda, *I would add just some shimmering, sun-kissed highlights every few months to my dark-blonde base. That, plus a beach tan, was my greatest weapon with the Italian men. However, one time, I decided that I wanted to be more natural, more organic, more* biologico, *as Italians call it. I had been dabbling with using chamomile shampoos and lemon-juice-infused conditioners with great success. A thought occurred to me:* Why not try chamomile flowers for highlights? *I envisioned these beautiful golden locks, like little baby flowers flowing from my crown. My friend accompanied me to the* farmacista *(the pharmacies in Europe are a fabulous cross between an apothecary, pharmacy, and beauty supply shop), and I bought a little box of chamomile flower hair dye. At home I mixed the flowers and stems along with water for a thick paste and lathered my hair. After letting the flowery mix set for about forty-five minutes, I washed, rinsed, and blow-dried. I took a look in the mirror. Not much difference. My hair looked a little changed, but I couldn't really tell. In fact, it might even look a bit darker? No, that couldn't be! So I convinced myself that there really wasn't any difference . . . and then I had a snickering little thought:* My hair was probably already becoming so blonde naturally from the sun that even chamomile wouldn't work anymore! I had achieved a new height in natural blondeness!

That afternoon, I set out to see some university friends in the piazza. Our normal habit was to have lunch in the huge square in the center of the city. Generally there were about thirty of us hanging out and chatting about our day. I sat down in the warm, golden sun . . . and that's when it started. A girl I knew who we referred to as Buja *(and which I later found out was not a very nice nickname, as it's a derivative of liar) yells out and says, "Alison, che cosa hai fatto ai capelli?"—translated, "Alison, what did you do to your hair?" Everyone whirls around to see what* La Bionda *did to her hair. I smiled questioningly.* What the hell did she see that I hadn't? Had she noticed it had gotten darker? Did I leave traces of chamomile stems on my scalp and golden tresses? Did my hair smell bad from the chamomile mixture? Goddamn it, that guy Angelo I am in love with is here too—run! *As Buja came closer, everyone stared deeply into my skull. And then she let it fly: "Ma sei VERDE!!!!" Translation: "You're GREEN!" And that's when it hit me like a ton of bricks: The change I had seen in my tiny bathroom, which by the way had no window or natural light but only a little lightbulb in the upper far corner, was not one of a darker color. Instead, the light hinted towards a different color . . . MOSS GREEN! And now the sun, which I always thought was one of my hair's biggest allies, was an added spotlight to this horrible mistake! I was mortified. I spent the next hour defending my hair color and whether I was truly a natural* bionda *to my friends. Needless to say, I quickly made an afternoon appointment with Fabio (yes, the local VIP hairdresser was Fabio) and proceeded to enjoy a very toxic and enlightening dye job, returning my locks to a normal RGB value of blonde.*

When did you first go blonde?

I was born blonde, but I've been doing highlights since my early twenties to give my tresses a bit more glow.

Do you have a colorist in your life, or do you color at home?

I have a new colorist, Marcus, who only uses 100 percent certified organic hair color and products. I've come a long way from the chamomile hippie flowers.

Do you love life as a blonde?

Yes, 100 percent. I've had brief snippets where I thought of going dark brown à la Liv Tyler, but I just can't do it! I'm a blondie, tried and true.

~~~~~~

Kendra C. (platinum blonde, fellow Masshole comedienne)

What's your worst hair disaster?

My worst hair experience was in the tenth grade. I was just starting to branch out from Sun-In (peroxide in a plant spray bottle) and start experimenting with L'Oréal Preference home coloring products, and I couldn't find a box with a picture of the exact shade of blonde I wanted so I decided to mix a few together to get a unique and unusual shade of blonde. It was a failed experiment that resulted in my mother stripping all the color from my hair and sending me off to my all-girls Catholic school the next morning with a head full of colorless hair.

When did you first go blonde?

I started coloring my hair with Sun-In during the summer before the eighth grade. My hair has a lot of red in it naturally, so most of July I was a brassy mess, but by August my hair was such a bright yellow, nobody even noticed my braces anymore!

Do you have a colorist in your life, or do you color at home?

I have a strong relationship with my colorist now. We've been together for over five years. I know her husband. I've moved from salon to salon with her. We've smoked pot together. It's pretty serious.

Do you love life as a blonde?

I love life as a blonde, but I must admit I have always wanted to be ethnic. Olive skin, black hair, body confidence. C'mon, sounds so stress-free.

~~~~~~~~~~~~~~~~~~~~~~~~~~~~~~~~~~~~~

Jackie H. (bold, brilliant bright-blonde businesswoman)

What's your worst hair disaster?

I can immediately recall. I was twenty-five and had just moved to NYC and was busily taking the city for all it was worth. This meant I was spending all disposable income eating and drinking and taking taxis everywhere. I had let my roots grow out to the point where I really couldn't get away with it anymore but also couldn't afford one of the more upscale salons that I was used to. I decided I would go to this random place in midtown, and since I couldn't spring for highlights, I would just do a one-process bleaching of sorts to get rid of the roots. Big mistake. Huge. I emerged looking like the long-lost fourth child from The Simpsons. *When I went to work the next day, it was clear from the response of my coworkers that something had to be done ASAP. You would think I'd learned my lesson. Nope. Again looking for the cheap way out, I headed to CVS to fix the problem on my own. I picked a darker shade of boxed blonde, thinking it would lessen the Simpson-esque hue I was now sporting. To my surprise, my hair instead turned gray. I'm talking Dorothy from* The Golden Girls. *I wandered outside and was walking around my block, crying and trying to figure out my next move when I stopped on a bench to sit. Luckily, since I lived in Greenwich Village at the time, I realized I was sitting outside of a fancy salon. I had no choice. I wandered in and just looked at the receptionist. No words were needed and she sprang into action. I spent the next four hours in that salon, and my hair was so fried they feared it would actually fall out of my head. Eventually the problem was somewhat fixed, but not without a period of slightly orange locks and a costly fee. At that point I would have paid any amount. And that's the story about the time I paid my rent two weeks late because I needed to get my hair done.*

When did you first go blonde?

I was born blonde but gradually darkened to brunette as I aged. Sophomore year in high school I began to reverse this trend—good old Sun-In on a family vacation to Florida. I never looked back.

Do you have a colorist in your life, or do you color at home?

Colorist (see aforementioned story in which I learned the importance of professional color the hard way).

Do you love life as a blonde?

I will never go back, so I guess that means I do.

~~~~~~

Ginny V. (natural blonde with virgin hair)

Here's a formative story about growing up as a natural blonde. I think the realization when I was pretty young that people regularly marveled at the color of my hair made me much more aware of how special it was to be a natural blonde.

My parents and a friend and I went to Benihana for my tenth birthday. We happened to be seated near a table of visiting Japanese businessmen (why they were dining at Benihana in Cincinnati, Ohio, during their travels, I don't pretend to know). Benihana was always an entertaining place, and it was perfect for my birthday at the time. All the knife tricks by the chef, the novelty of a dinner performance—it was all really silly and festive. After we were settled in for a while, my parents noticed that the group of businessmen kept looking at our table, and they were looking intently at me, sitting with my blonde hair below my ears, in an oversize purple wool sweater from Talbots. After lots of gesturing of the international motion for "will you take a picture," we realized they wanted to take a picture of me. In a kitschy tourist restaurant in southern Ohio that can only remind them of a Disneyfied version of home, the real novelty is the blonde American child. We figured out they must not have seen anyone so blonde before in Japan, and it was clearly worth taking home a picture as a souvenir.

~~~~~~~~~~~~~~~~~~~~~~~~~~~~~~~~~~~~~~~

*Alison J. (California blonde,
also a lucky hair color virgin)*

What's your worst hair disaster?

The day someone said my hair was starting to get darker. Those are fighting words in a blonde's world.

When did you first go blonde?

Born with it and will die with it. That's the only way of life for a blonde.

Do you have a colorist in your life, or do you color at home?

Being a natural blonde has its perks—no coloring for me! When my hair darkens in the winter, I spend my summers soaking in the sun to bring my hair back to platinum status. And getting a sick tan. The two go hand in hand.

Do you love life as a blonde?

There is nothing better than being a blonde. It's a way of life that only blondes understand. To my fellow blonde bombshells (and you know who you are), keep on rocking on.

~~~~~~

Stephanie M. (ashy blonde with fantastic body and curls)

What's your worst hair disaster?

In high school, I was curious to see what the world looked like to a brunette. Unfortunately, I let a friend with extreme Goth tendencies choose the color. Instead of auburn, my hair ended up a vibrant eggplant! I spent the next day in the salon instead of school, getting it stripped out of my hair. It took about two years to slowly highlight my way to normal again.

When did you first go blonde?

I was born a redhead, but within a month, all my hair fell out and grew back in the right color: blonde! And it's been that way ever since, with the exception of the brief and traumatic period of high school, mentioned above.

Do you have a colorist in your life, or do you color at home?

I haven't lived in my hometown for more than a decade, but I still flew home to my colorist Elizabeth for highlights until early

*last year, when I finally found an incredible local colorist, Jerami.
I'm now preparing for my breakup conversation with Elizabeth.*

Do you love life as a blonde?

*Yes! I usually am the only blonde in a group, which I love, and
it's also a great excuse any time I do something dumb. The one
thing I'm envious of is dark eyebrows—they look so much better
in pictures.*

Do you have any funny blonde anecdotes?

*The only two people I know who've accidentally opened doors
into their own heads are me and my blonde roommate. (Mine was
luckily not bad, but she gave herself a concussion!)*

~~~~~~~~~~~~~~~~~~~~~~~~~~~~~~~~~~~~

Elizabeth E. (cool, platinum-blonde Cate Blanchett look-alike)

What's your worst hair disaster?

*My worst hair disaster occurred in my early twenties when I
moved to California and discovered that apartment complexes like
Melrose Place really do exist! I was hanging with a hottie I met at a
party one night, and he suggested we take our private party down
to the pool. We stripped down for some skinny-dipping (which
I'm sure his neighbors and the other partygoers totally appreciated), and all was fun and games until it was time to dry off and
rejoin the group. Getting out of the pool, my super-fine blonde
hair knotted up into some serious tangles, and I realized I didn't
have any way to comb them out. My crush playfully tried to run
his fingers through my wet hair, and his hand literally got stuck in
my chlorine-induced snarls. I had no choice but to rejoin the party*

with a swamp mess on my head. From that day on, I've always been sure to carry a brush in my bag!

Do you have a colorist in your life, or do you color at home?

I'm not faithful to any one colorist. I go through phases of letting my highlights lapse because I've convinced myself that I can return to my natural strawberry-blonde color from high school, then realizing I can't and running back to the salon for a new burst of blonde. Vicious cycle.

Do you love life as a blonde?

Yes! Every once in a while I fantasize about going deep red à la Lauren Holly from the '90s and Dumb and Dumber *fame, but I love being bright and blonde.*

Do you have any funny blonde anecdotes?

This happened to me, I'll just come out and say it. I once boarded the wrong plane by mistake. The airline had changed the gate, and I didn't hear the change because I was listening to my headphones. When I did turn off the music and tune in, the flight was boarding. I waited patiently for my zone number (it was the last to board) and then gave the attendant my boarding pass. I made it all the way to my seat at the back of the plane when a panicked announcement came over the speakers: "Attention, passenger Elizabeth E. You have boarded the wrong plane. Please deplane immediately. Repeat—you are on the wrong plane." Mortified, I turned and began making the slow climb upstream back towards the front of the plane, enduring the stares and ridicule from my fellow passengers. I heard one guy snigger, "Figures she's a blonde."

~~~~~~

Glennis M. (blonde who isn't afraid to change it up and experiment)

What's your worst hair disaster?

Worst hair disaster was the pixie cut/orange glow I rocked for a while around age twenty-one. It's still the photo on my driver's license because, as much as I hate that photo, I am way too impatient to stand in line for a new photo. (This is the year my license expires, so you better believe I'll be getting my roots done before.)

When did you first go blonde?

I honestly couldn't tell you when I went blonde. Because my mom's a hairdresser, I've been doing crazy things to my hair my whole life!

Do you have a colorist in your life, or do you color at home?

I have a colorist in my life, and he's the only man for me. Because my mom was a hairdresser, finding someone to do my hair in New York was not easy. I think that's something that a lot of women experience. Why is that? Anyway, my hairstylist does my hair in his home. He's one of my friends from high school who now lives here, and though he doesn't officially do hair anymore, he will always do mine. He's fantastic. Not only do I trust him completely with taking me from dark brunette to light blonde, we sing show tunes after he's done. It's pretty fantastic.

Do you love life as a blonde?

I loved life as a brunette, and I love life as a blonde. Being a blonde turns all eyes to you when you walk in a room, and what's not to love about that?

CHAPTER 10

RULE: *Spend Some Time on the Dark Side*

There exist an inordinate number of quotes about how one must accept and embrace change. These crop up in high school yearbooks, song lyrics, and greeting cards. They inform us that while "everybody's changing and I don't know why" (Keane), "time may change me, but I can't trace time" (David Bowie), and that "that's just the way it is, things will never be the same/somethings will never change" (Bruce Hornsby or Tupac Shakur depending on which version you prefer). Change is inevitable in life, and what better way to embrace it than through personal aesthetics, specifically hair color?

Supermodel Linda Evangelista is the patron saint of drastic hair changes. She's a style chameleon, and while such severe changes initially cost her runway jobs, they have become her signature. When Evangelista was a young model in the late 1980s, she cut off her long hair in favor of a pageboy-style haircut and was promptly dropped from all of her runway shows that season. Within months she was featured on numerous magazine covers, her short haircut garnered a lot of buzz, and Evangelista became a style inspiration to many women. Her natural hair color is dark brown, but she has rocked every cut and color imaginable: fierce red, blonde, light brown, and a more natural red. Evangelista was a member of the first class of bona fide supermodels (the others were Cindy Crawford, Christy Turlington, Naomi Campbell, Claudia Schiffer, and the hugely underrated Karen Mulder) but the only one to play with vastly different looks. No wonder she was tapped to be the spokeswoman for L'Oréal Paris, peddling their myriad hair color kits.

In her wake, many celebrities have embraced the color chameleon life, including Madonna, P!nk, Cameron Diaz, Britney Spears, Gwen Stefani, and Emma Stone. Hair color experimentation has been represented in music, film, and television, too. Who can forget the *Brady Bunch* episode when Jan was sick of just being Marcia's equally blonde and long-haired little sister, so she donned an Afro wig and insisted that this look was "the new Jan Brady." Or in the first *Sex and the City* film, when Carrie goes brunette and says that her "head is in the witness protection program" after her bridal fashion spread in *Vogue* and subsequent break-up with Big. Or in the 1985 Carly Simon song "Tired of Being Blonde."

Moving from blonde life to a brunette existence is not to be taken lightly. As a woman with blonde hair, you are often assumed to be a floozy and a ditz, but when you go darker, you are often perceived as smart and perhaps mysterious.

The hair color chameleon can end up feeling like a fish out of water when she experiments with different hair color, and she may be surprised at her newfound identity and its associated preconceptions. But it is nonetheless valuable to live the experience of the brunette or dark-haired woman, to sympathize with her plight. As a blonde, you are undoubtedly used to getting attention and catching eyes wherever you go, but this life experience isn't universal. It's a worthwhile undertaking to experience life "on the dark side."

You may be thinking, *This book is called* The New Rules for Blondes. *How is a new rule for blonde life to not be blonde anymore!?* I admire your spunk and understand your quandary. My answer is this: It's always valuable to walk a mile in another person's shoes (and by "shoes" I mean hair). While being blonde is a delight, we shouldn't be fearful of experimentation and we should be eager to try out different looks. If you have blue or green eyes, then a rich, dark hair color can make your eyes pop. Additionally, your new hair color and hair-eye combo will allow you to dress in colors that were perhaps unflattering when you were a blonde. I once dallied in a brunette existence, experiencing life through that dark-haired lens. I learned a lot about myself and the world around me. Like a rite of passage that is difficult when you're in the thick of the drama and trauma but ends up being a character-building personal challenge (changing schools, trying out for the sports team, bra shopping for the first time), life as a brunette was something that was tough at the time but that I now look back on with fondness. I learned firsthand that I can navigate through life's challenges whether I'm blonde or brunette, even when one of life's challenges is *that* I'm a brunette.

When I jumped on Team Brunette, it was late 2000 and Cameron Diaz had just dyed her hair dark brown post–*Charlie's Angels.* She appeared on the cover of *Cosmopolitan*'s January 2000 issue (on newsstands in early December), which I found myself staring at while I waited in line at the grocery store. Her sultry chocolate-hued sophistication infected my brain with the flawed logic that "if Cameron Diaz looks good as a brunette, then I probably would, too." It didn't occur to me that this was a magazine cover that undoubtedly had been carefully lit and photographed for maximum flattery and, on top of all that, the photo was inevitably retouched. Of course Cameron Diaz looked gorgeous as a brunette. And so would I, right?

These flights of fancy are dangerous for me, as I tend to think that what's good for a wealthy celebrity is probably good for a civilian like me. Note: This is the goal of advertising in general. Damn you, *Mad Men*! This phenomenon also occurred during the spring of my senior year in college and resulted in a lot of bizarre photos of yours truly. Around that time, I read an interview with our old pal, hair color chameleon Linda Evangelista, in which she explained that she poses and smiles with her mouth slightly open because a photographer recommended that move to her back when she was a young model. It makes sense for her proportions and the shape of her chin and it has becoming something of her signature move when being photographed (like Tyra Banks's signature move of "smizing," or smiling with her eyes). Smiling as if caught in the act, with her mouth every-so-slightly ajar is a fantastic maneuver for Linda Evangelista. I do not have model-like features, and I am not Linda Evangelista (though I loved her work in the video for George Michael's "Freedom"—she was trapped in a virtual jail made of sweater!), but during the spring months of 2002, whenever a camera was pointed in my direction, I was smiling with my mouth open. Because I should do whatever Linda Evangelista does, right?

And so it was with Cameron Diaz in late 2000. I was about to leave the United States for a semester of study abroad in London (and an imminent twenty-pound weight gain thanks to a steady diet of curry fries and Strongbow Cider), and I was ready for a change. Cameron Diaz's blue eyes popped from beneath her new dark-haired locks, so I knew it would make my blue eyes pop, too. And so I drove to Newbury Street in downtown Boston for a visit with a man who served as my mother's colorist, unlicensed recreational therapist, and spiritual guide, John. You know that your family has a hair obsession when your mother's hairdresser is a distinguished guest at all of your family weddings. John's a wise man, and I think he sensed that I wanted to experience life as a brunette, but he knew that I wasn't ready for all that brown-haired life entails (actually being given speeding tickets and not just warnings and flirtation, not being stared at in bars, not being treated like a rare flower, wearing a lot of jewel-toned shirts, etc.). So he pushed me to go light brown and ease into the brunette experience. We got through the time-consuming single process, and I emerged as a brunette, albeit a light brunette. But I wasn't happy. I've always been like Ado Annie from the musical *Oklahoma!* With me it's all or nothing. Let's either be platinum or dark brown, but nothing in between. If you're going to go brunette, go all the way. I still believe this. Either go big or go home. You've got to bet big to win big and all that jazz.

Within a few days, I found myself back in the colorist's chair and John dutifully gave me what I wanted, despite his warnings that bright blonde to dark brown is an extreme change and I would probably, ultimately be unhappy with the severity of the color shift. By nightfall, I possessed a head of dark-brown hair and my friends and family looked me straight in the face and didn't even recognize me. This is a side effect that you must prepare for—post–color change, friends and family will literally make eye contact with you and not quite process that it's you. At the time I thought this might be enthralling—to see what it was like from the other side of things. *This could be fun!* I thought. Immediately, I found that I needed to catch my reflection in every mirrored surface possible to see my new hair—to fully see what the new Selena looked like. *Wow—that's different,* I anxiously thought every time I saw myself. I had a little hitch in my heart and an odd feeling in the pit of my stomach. *Well, Selena, this is the new look that you wanted,* I thought as I tried to digest the fact that the sunlight wasn't hitting golden highlights anymore. I had to go with it, though—I had gone this far over to the dark side—I had made a choice that I had to live with. I'd imagine that my feeling was similar to that of a woman who says yes to a marriage proposal despite some misgivings. She walks down the aisle thinking, *It will be fine. We've already embraced this decision and gotten this far down the track—there is no turning back. It will be fine . . . I hope.* And without quite knowing what was happening, I began grieving the loss of my blondeness.

I fell asleep that night as a brunette for the first time ever. When I awoke the next morning, I cracked my eyes open ever so slightly to see brown hair in my face. You know when you're still half-asleep and not completely aware of what is going on? If you're staying in a hotel, it's the half second during which your brain processes the jump from "Where am I? Huh? This ceiling looks weird" to "Oh yeah, I'm not in my bed—I'm at a hotel." Well, in that half second, in my head I thought to myself, *Ewww—there's a brunette in my bed.* Then I came to and realized: that brunette was *me.** I felt like Tom Hanks when he first gets big in the movie *Big.* He gets exactly what he wished for,

---

* Like a hair color version of a horror movie where the calls are coming from inside the house!

but as Metallica says, "Careful what you wish, you may regret it. Careful what you wish, you just might get it." Perhaps John the colorist was right: I shouldn't have jumped so eagerly into the deep end of the proverbial brunette swimming pool.

This move over to the dark side took place a few days before New Year's Eve. On that first brunette day in late December 1999, I decided to take my new brown hair for a spin and met up with Suzanne for drinks that evening. She had been at the hairdresser that same day and was experimenting with a funky, new haircut that wasn't so much "funky" as it was a mullet. A freaky lady mullet.

But Suzanne and I had both wanted something totally new and different, and the novelty of my brown hair and her mullet still hadn't worn off. At the bar, we played pool, drank some bad domestic beer, and gingerly danced around the fact that we were both beginning to regret our drastic hair changes. "It's cool to try something new, ya know? Right?" I asked her, as though I had simply purchased an edgy new shirt for a night on the town—not dropped a ton of cash and hours on hair that was now, seemingly, stuck this way. "Yeah, I mean, if I don't like this I can always just cut if off and go pretty short, and you can dye your hair back . . . it's fun!" Suzanne halfheartedly agreed while attempting to toss her newly shorn hair. The mullet mantra of "business up front, party in the back" played out on Suzanne's head with the hair toss, as the "business" didn't move much but the "party" swayed gently. We were both up to our ears in denial, the first stage of Elisabeth Kübler-Ross's famous model of the five stages of grief. And we were both grieving hard: Suzanne for her non-mullet hair and me for my blonde hair. We were in the thick of denial, and we didn't even know it. As I like to joke, denial ain't just a river in Egypt: It's also a powerful defense mechanism in which you refuse to accept the reality of a given situation.

The guy I had been seeing at the time, Eric, was hosting a big New Year's Eve party at his place, which was a post-collegiate faux fraternity house. On the afternoon of New Year's Eve, I gave him a call to tell him my hair color news (because everyone cares!) and confirm plans for that night's festivities. He didn't seem very excited about the news that I was now a brunette, and I tried to play it off as a wacky, impulsive decision that could only come from a super-chill party girl who will try anything once (spicy!). Eric got off the phone quickly, saying that he and his housemates had to run out and buy beer for the party and that he would call me back. Then a few hours passed without a call, so I decided to call his house. This was back in the days of landlines and the potential for you to be away from your phone. The dark ages. Eric wasn't at the house, allegedly, so I spoke to one of his housemates and left a message. An hour later, I still hadn't heard from him, so I called again.* Another one of Eric's housemates answered. I could just sense that I was getting the runaround and his friend's insistence that Eric was "still at the packie"† had to be bullshit. How much time can you spend at a liquor store!? Finally, I laughed on the phone with one roommate and sarcastically said, "He's *still* at the liquor store, huh? Well, Happy New Year's to you all. Bye." It was nine p.m. on New Year's

---

* This sounds bonkers, I know, but just *days* prior, Eric had called my house and left messages three times in a row while I was out at the mall, so I felt like I could call him two times in a row. Yes, girls keep track of that shit.

† "Packie" is Massachusetts-speak for a package store, or an establishment that sells liquor or beer.

Eve, and now I had no plans. Things were looking bleak.

After making a few last-minute phone calls, I rang in the New Year at a friend-of-a-friend's house party, where I spent most of the night talking to a random high school girl about how much she hated high school. I feel an odd sense of obligation to listen to angsty teen girls because nobody ever listened to me during those high school years of misery. So I sat there and paid it forward, listening to this stranger's onslaught of gripes and complaints about the misery and boredom of high school. In the back of my mind, I kept thinking that there must have been a miscommunication with Eric. He must be trying to reach me and furiously calling my parents' house, right? Or was he just a complete jerk? Why had his feelings changed so completely and so suddenly? That night, as the clock struck midnight on December 31, 1999, the world didn't explode into some Y2K mushroom cloud of bad computer data as everyone had predicted. Something worse happened: I was stood up. And a brunette.

A few days later I moved to London to study abroad for a semester and unconsciously entered into the second stage of grief for my formerly blonde hair: anger. My assigned room-mate, Mary Beth, had the patience of a saint and listened to my blonde-vs.-brunette ranting without judgment. I blamed every misfortune that befell me on my dark-haired status. Poor Mary Beth, a natural brunette, had to endure hours of my hair color kvetching and blaming. Stubbed toes, missing the Tube, snippy Brits—all were blamed on my brown hair. I was convinced that anything and everything would have been infinitely better if I were still a blonde. As a brunette, guys didn't even notice me! Nobody was staring at me or chatting me up! I was angry and jealous of women with blonde hair—even subpar blonde hair. I felt like a lady in a coma who can still hear, think, and process what is going on, but cannot talk or register emotion. I wanted to scream, "Is everything so hard because of my brown hair? I'm blonde in here! Hello! Why is no one talking to me!? Get me out of this dark-haired hell!" I received a grand total of *one* compliment during my time in London, and it came from a muscle-bound bouncer at a cheesy bar. One night he told me that I had nice eyes. Yes, blue or green eyes pop beautifully when you have dark hair—we know this. After he complimented me, I wanted to say, "Of course I do . . . they're blue and with this dark hair, it's unexpected, as you normally see blue eyes with blonde hair." Sigh. *Tears.*

I felt like a reverse "Englishman in New York" that Sting so beautifully sang about. I was like an alien, a legal alien living in London as a brunette. Too many unfamiliar things were happening concurrently. It didn't help that Mary Beth and I managed to alienate ourselves from most of the other American students living in our building. Philip was the sole Brit among us, and he was the resident adviser for the five flats* in in our gorgeous home on a tree-lined street. The building contained a mess of guys in the dungeon-like basement apartment, three girls on the first floor, a gaggle of ladies jammed into the second-floor apartment like a can of somewhat bitchy and styleless sardines, Mary Beth and me with the run of a three-bedroom duplex apartment on the third floor, and Philip and a motley assortment of American students across the hall from us. In short, Mary Beth and I had lucked out, and for a sweet springtime semester, we shared an apartment that resembled a penthouse in one of the nicest neighborhoods in London.

---

* Brit-speak for apartments.

Two of the three girls on the first floor were nice, albeit a bit serious and prudish. Those two attended a women's college and seemed to find Mary Beth's and my energy and antics barbaric. We were interested in London nightlife, and we went on dates with British and Greek guys—we had fun and met new people, while the women's college ladies mostly hung out with other Americans who they knew in London. I wanted to tell them to chill out and have some fun, would ya? We're on a six-month vacation during which we have to crap out a few papers—eat some curry fries and loosen up!

Those two women's college girls were sweet, though, which is a whole lot more than I could say for their third roommate. She hailed from California and was crazy thin, super pretty, insanely snobby, and completely intimidating. Her holier-than-thou attitude covered many areas but seemed rooted in the fact that she hailed from the birthplace of Vince Neil and porn. She was so stiff and unfriendly that around her, I felt like an adolescent boy with a crush—I'd stumble on my words, get dry mouth, and freeze up. As I'd try to talk to her and flail around, I'd think to myself, *Selena! You are not a sixteen-year-old guy trying to get into a classmate's pants! You're just trying to coexist with the snob downstairs—calm down! Mouth, let's get some moistness back in here, OK?* She resembled Posh Spice with her inexplicable ability to pull off a (universally unflattering) pixie haircut and somehow make it work. I guess that a skeletal frame can pull off any haircut, no matter how ill-advised. Her color was fantastic, though; light-brown base with expertly painted golden-blonde highlights. The kind of color that is achieved either with a lot of luck or a lot of money. Her wiry body somehow supported a normal-size head, which gave her that lollipop look made famous by the (allegedly) anorexic cast of *Ally McBeal*, circa 2000. Because of this lollipop look, Mary Beth and I nicknamed her "Lollipop Guild," despite the fact that this is a name for friendly dwarves from *The Wizard of Oz*. Who doesn't love a good mixed pop culture reference?*

During my British brunette era, I had a relatively light schedule (because "study abroad" is mostly "abroad" and not so much "study"). Four days of the week I had classes, and one day midweek I enjoyed a totally free day during which Mary Beth was in classes all day. Time for me to receive college credit for hours spent tea-drinking, McVitie's-eating, and BBC1-watching, followed by some late-afternoon London exploration and pubhopping. I love education!

One such morning, Mary Beth and I were both hustling around the apartment. She headed out for a long day of engineering classes while I cleaned up the apartment and finished a quick load of laundry. I went down to the lobby to transfer my clothes from washer to dryer, letting the apartment door shut behind me. I was busy staring at the British currency and wondering if I had enough five-pence coins to ever get my clothes sufficiently dry and fluffy. (I would later learn that British dryers simply don't do "dry and fluffy," and you're lucky to achieve "kinda damp but semitolerable.") I stuck coins into the dryer, thinking about how this foreign currency felt like Monopoly money, as I still wasn't totally familiar with the exchange rate just yet. Once the dryer was shaking, I trudged back up three flights of stairs and thought about my day of relaxation at home, only to find the door to my flat closed and locked. I jiggled the handle, but it was sealed tight shut. The door and door frame were in an embrace tight enough to seem vacuum-sealed. This

---

* The copyright holders of said pop culture item, that's who.

is a door, not a can of nuts that you want to keep fresh—why such a snug seal!? This door wasn't budging, that was for sure.

The apartment building, while beautiful and in a gorgeous London neighborhood called Kensington, was also ancient and required large keys at every door. Even worse, construction over there is actually made to last, so I knew there was no way that I could pick the lock with a credit card. *Why can't this be crappy American construction?* I thought, staring at my closed apartment door. *If I were in a slipshod McMansion in the States, this door would be made of faux wood boarding, it would be completely hollow, and it would pop open if I so much as thought about it. But noooo—construction in England has to be sturdy and well done. Ugh. How come the Brits can't transfer that level of craftsmanship from carpentry to dentistry?* My dreams of flimsy construction and a credit card break-in were useless. Not that I had anything on my person—no credit card, no cell phone, not even a way to escape. That antiquated building required yet another giant old-timey key to get in *and* to get out. Yes, we lived in a complete firetrap.

And so began a long and painfully boring day during which I was trapped alone in a stairwell and small lobby area for six hours. It was even more of a mind-numbing time suck than R. Kelly's song "Trapped in the Closet" (though with a bit more leg room, I suppose). It was just me, the pudgy and brown-haired fish out of water; a washer and dryer tucked beneath the stairwell like a robot Harry Potter; and hours of solitude staring me in the face. To make matters worse, the lobby area where I was confined was absolutely freezing because Britain doesn't believe in heating buildings, so my hours of boredom were punctuated by the chattering of my (straight white American) teeth. I wasn't prepared for a full day exposed to the elements—I was dressed in ratty sweatpants, socks, and a crummy T-shirt from my college improv comedy troupe, Yoda-pez.* Every year my troupe would receive a generous grant from the college and what money we didn't spend on strange comedy props like tricycles, kiddie pools filled with ketchup, and matching unitards for all members, we'd spend on troupe T-shirts—the weirder, the better. That year, we had designed T-shirts with photos of frightening-looking criminals that we'd pulled off the Internet, from FacesOfMeth.us. Each T-shirt was emblazoned with pictures of these weirdos positioned in *Brady Bunch*–like tiled format, with one team member's name below each photo. From above "Selena" stared out an emaciated vagrant woman with no teeth and a cigarette dangling out of her mouth. The best part? The T-shirts were the color of urine. Well, urine if you are a mildly dehydrated human.

My full day of forced isolation made me feel like Tom Hanks in *Cast Away*, only without the tropical temperatures, tan, and volleyball companion. All I had for "entertainment" were the local real estate catalogs that cluttered the mail area. That day, I read every single one cover to cover and gained a better appreciation of the insane prices of real estate in the Kensington neighborhood of London. I guess the royalties from such hits as "Rock DJ" and "Millennium" were treating Brit pop god Robbie Williams pretty well, as he lived in the neighborhood. Unfortunately, an appreciation of overpriced flats doesn't keep you warm when you're locked out of your apartment and stuck in an unheated stairwell for a full day.

I had so much time to myself that I unknowingly entered into

---

* Our group's name came from a Pez dispenser with a Yoda head on top. *Comedy!*

stage three of the Kübler-Ross grief model: bargaining. You're probably not supposed to pray for a different hair color, but I needed to put this problem in the capable hands of a higher power. *Please, God, make me wake up a blonde. Just take me back to where I was before I became hell-bent on being a brunette. Please—let me just wake up blonde tomorrow. I'll never complain about missing the Tube ever again. I'll stop making fun of the odd characters who live in this building. I'll even stop visiting that pub down the street most nights of the week—I'll get it together. Just please, PLEASE, God, let me wake up and open my eyes a centimeter and see a head of yellow, brassy hair.*

After hours of solitary confinement, I finally heard the sweet sounds of help—a key in the front door. *Yes! Freedom! Whoever is there will help me,* I thought. *At least I can go sit in an apartment and warm up a bit, maybe have some food, and wait for Mary Beth to come home and unlock our flat.*

The door opened a crack and a normal-size head peeked through, followed by an emaciated skeleton body. Fucking Lollipop Guild. *Of all the building residents who could come home right now, it has to be her. Dammit!* I thought. I huddled in the chilly stairwell as she entered, and I was painfully aware of how disgusting I looked in my urine-colored T-shirt and ratty sweatpants. Plus, I had brown hair, which made me look exhausted and brunette at all times.

"Hey," Lollipop Guild said flatly as she walked by me to go open her front door.

"Oh my goodness, I'm so glad you're home!" I said as I thought to myself, *Why the hell am I acting like she's friendly or we're friends at all? She's a jerk, and you're punchy from having no human contact for too many hours. Stop being so needy, Coppock!*

"Get this—I locked myself out of my apartment this morning!

About six hours ago! I've been trapped in this friggin' freezing stairwell all day!" I rambled on, while thinking, *Selena—please stop saying "friggin'" in front of people, OK? We aren't at a Celtics game with Sully and Quinny.*

Lollipop Guild swiveled her giant dome until she was looking directly at me, her highlights glittering in the hallway lamplight. The blonde streaks taunted me, as if to say, *Selena, you should have followed the advice of your mom's colorist, John, and eased into brunette life. You could have gone for light-brown hair with blonde highlights, and you probably wouldn't be in this lockout mess in the first place. Bad things come to those who go too dark brown, as the old saying goes.* She looked at me blankly.

"Huh. Where's Mary Beth?" The monotone of her voice revealed her indifference to my plight. Her affect was so flat and unsympathetic that Lollipop Guild seemed like a bad actor just phoning it in on a sitcom that she's ashamed to have been cast in but she needs the paycheck. I'm painfully aware of my proclivity for spazz-like behavior and more than one ex-boyfriend has said that I am "too much," but Lollipop Guild was a bad actor *in her own life.* As if the stakes were never high because there were never any stakes. As if every interaction in her life was as unimportant as, say, choosing vanilla or chocolate ice cream if you enjoy both equally. Lollipop Guild was simply a skeletal body with *zero* emotion.

Lollipop Guild looked me up and down and her eyes lingered on the photo of "Selena" (the filthy, smoking, vagrant version on my pale-yellow T-shirt) while I silently cursed myself for wearing such goofy shirts to bed. Desperate for a warm place to sit, I barreled forward in my pleas for help.

"Mary Beth is in class all day. I had a whole day

planned—walking around, getting some coffee, exploring . . ." I yammered on, while thinking, *Again, Selena, all of this is too much information—Lollipop Guild doesn't give a rat's ass about the adventures you had planned for the day! Her idea of a great free day would be spent sucking on ice cubes, working out in a raincoat, and staring at a map of her beloved Golden State.*

"But I got locked out of my apartment . . . and locked into this stairwell, so I've been stuck in here all day. . . . It's like I'm in a weird carpeted jail . . . that's just small jail areas on multiple floors . . . and the clothes are better than orange prison jump-suits, I suppose . . . and we have nice windows . . . and I'm not stuck with anybody else here . . . no other prisoners . . . except for my own thoughts and boredom." *Good God, Selena!*

Lollipop Guild stared at me blankly, whispered "Whoa . . . sucks," then walked into her apartment and shut the door. As her door slammed, stage four washed over me: depression. *Why does nothing go my way?* I thought. *I'll be stuck with unflattering hair and trapped in this stairwell for the rest of my life. There's no way out. I'll never leave the entryway of this Brit building. My college pals will graduate from Hamilton College without me, get married, have kids, and I'll still be here reading real estate catalogs. The London police department will find my corpse here when I'm ninety. I'll still be in this weird college improv troupe T-shirt. I'll have a head of horrible roots. I won't even be able to play it off like I'm doing an ombré look, those roots will be so bad.*

I had come on too strong with Lollipop Guild, and apparently great highlights do not a kind soul make. I felt like a tween boy who had just asked a girl way out of his league to be his date for the big school dance, only to be given the Heisman hard and fast. Like a good boxer or a bad glutton for punishment, I wasn't down for long, though. Within minutes, I saw another figure approaching the door and was elated. I'd take what I had learned in that Lollipop Guild interaction and apply it here. *Be cool, Coppock,* I thought.

This time it was Angela from the overcrowded bunkhouse that was the second-floor apartment. Five girls crammed into a tiny apartment (bunk beds and all), and they seemed to resent Mary Beth and me because our apartment was so spacious. I wanted to explain to them, "We didn't set up the room assignments, ya cunts. Just give me a chance—I'm fucking *nice!*"

As I anxiously watched Angela pull her key from the front-door lock and begin walking into the lobby, I thought back to my sole interaction with her. It was during our first few weeks in London, and all of the students living in the building were gathered in the first-floor apartment (home to Lollipop Guild and the Prudish Twosome[*]) for a party. Mary Beth and I had brought along a few cans of Strongbow because (1) our parents raised us well, teaching us that you don't ever visit the home of a friend and arrive empty-handed[†] and (2) we imagined that their idea of "enough alcohol for a party" was definitely not enough alcohol for a party, so we had to bring provisions.

After the standard initial pleasantries and greetings, Mary Beth and I found ourselves chatting with a few of the second-floor ladies, who already seemed to hate us for our dumb luck on the apartment front. Like a standup comedian doing "road material" (so called because it can be done anywhere for any audience, usually on the road), I initiated conversation about the astronomical cost of living in London. We can all agree that

---

* Hell of a good band name right there.
† More on bringing gifts as good manners in Chapter 11.

airplane food is bad, men and women are different, and living in London is pricey. Perfect! Let's commiserate, second-floor ladies who resent me for my sick apartment.

"Oh my goodness, it's ridiculous," Mary Beth agreed. "My college back in the U.S. is in the middle of nowhere, Pennsylvania, so I guess I just got used to the prices and rent around there, ya know?"

"Yeah! Cigarettes in upstate New York are about five dollars right now, but here in London I have to spend five pounds on my Marlboro Lights, and that's about seven fifty!" I chimed in.

"And the price of going out at night! You don't have to pay a cover to get into a pub, but the more lively bars and dance clubs all have cover charges, then once you're in there, the drinks are so pricey, too!" Mary Beth contributed.

"Yeah, well, that's why we really don't go out very much," said Angela from the second-floor apartment. "I mean, I'd rather wear my money than drink my money," she snapped and gave us a smug smile.

Mary Beth and I looked at her strangely while the wheels were spinning in my head and I thought, *Yeah, well, I'd rather experience London and explore neighborhoods and enjoy the nightlife than spend money on flimsy, poorly made clothes from Topshop that I'll inevitably outgrow and get sick of. Also, what was with that icy one-liner? Had we unknowingly offended her by enjoying London nightlife and dating guys who wore leather pants? We were just going with the flow of la vida London!*

Back in the freezing stairwell, I was desperate and ready to say whatever I had to say to get into a warm apartment. So what if Angela had sad hair and self-righteous logic, and was letting her London experience pass her by—I was locked out of my apartment and freezing. Time to turn on the charm.

"Hey, Angela," I said as she looked over the assortment of catalogs and envelopes cluttered on the mail table.

"Hi, Selena—how are you?" she asked.

OK, this is good, I thought. *We're engaging in conversation. She doesn't think I'm a total asshole, it seems. Maybe just a bit of a party girl but not an asshole. Let's just stay calm and not compare this lobby to a carpeted jail or say the word "friggin'," OK?*

"Oh man, not so great. I got locked out of my apartment this morning—"

"This morning! It's five p.m. now!" she exclaimed.

"I know! Brutal, huh?" I said, elated that Angela possessed emotions and a willingness to empathize with others, unlike Lollipop Guild. "I'm such a moron—I came down here to put money in the dryer, and I managed to totally lock myself out of my apartment! Mary Beth's in class all day, and I've been stuck here freezing in these scrubby clothes," I said, hoping that my acknowledgment of how gross I looked would prevent her from hating me for wearing a T-shirt whose premise was "ugly people = comedy gold."

Just then, the magic words rolled off her Topshop-shopping tongue: "Do you want to come sit in my apartment until Mary Beth gets back?"

"Oh my goodness, would you mind!? That would be fantastic!" I tried to stop myself from appearing too excited.

We went up to her apartment, where I warmed up and ate some McVitie's cookies. The second-floor bunkhouse looked just like Mary Beth's and my apartment upstairs, just with more bodies per square foot. Their apartment was carpeted with the same indestructible dark-gray carpet as ours was. Their walls were almost blindingly plain white, and the living room had only a few pieces of dorm furniture that were so dinky and insubstantial that they felt like children's furniture.

Angela took her personal mantra of "I'd rather wear my money than drink my money" quite seriously, as her tiny bedroom was filled with clothes from Topshop, Selfridges, and H&M. Everything was bland and made of synthetic material, not surprisingly. She was perfectly nice, and I began to feel a sense of guilt that perhaps I had prejudged this random girl from the floor below. Her system was to shop instead of party—that's fine. She made an offhand, smarmy remark once, but she probably meant nothing by it and she just saved me from going insane in the lobby. Who knows how long I would have been stuck there if she hadn't appeared? Lollipop Guild hadn't been willing to help, but Angela had been and her kindness was touching and inspiring. The gratitude I felt toward Angela led me to stage five: acceptance. An odd calm came over me and I reveled in the fact that I was a brunette for a little while. What a kick! What a different, interesting experience.

About an hour later, Mary Beth arrived home, and after I told her the tale of my lockout, I went into my bedroom to look at some photos of me with dark hair. I didn't look half bad, I thought. It looked very unfamiliar to me, but that didn't make it bad. I just wasn't used to seeing myself with brown hair—it was a shock to the system. But I needed to accept it. I hadn't missed the Tube because of my brown hair. I had brown hair and I lived in London—people do it all the time! To quote Dr. Phil,[*] I needed to get real with myself: I missed being blonde, and I was being a whiny brat about it. To quote another one of Dr. Phil's myriad mantras: I had to name it to claim it. I just wanted to

---

[*] Mixing Elisabeth Kübler-Ross and Dr. Phil McGraw is blasphemy in the psychiatry community, I'm sure. Sorry, guys!

be blonde. Having dark-brown hair was a fun experience, but perhaps I should have just experimented with a wig. I knew what I needed to do: I needed to quit brunette life. We'd had a good run, but blonde hair is in my veins (not literally, but you know what I mean). I needed to get back to feeling like me. The lessons of my time on the dark side weren't lost on me, though.

In my time spent walking down the boulevard of brunette dreams, I developed a great respect for bombshells such as Jane Russell, Cindy Crawford, Elizabeth Taylor, Penelope Cruz, and Ava Gardner. These women ooze(d) sex appeal without utilizing a drop of peroxide, and for that I was (and still am) in awe of them. Unfortunately, despite Cameron Diaz's inspiration, I just couldn't find a comfortable spot to lay my head in the brunette community. I rued the day that I bullied John the family colorist into making me almost raven-haired. But what was I to do? Hit up the British pharmacy Boots the Chemist and see if they had hair dye? Could I handle this dye job at home? What if I tried to go back to blonde but ended up orangey, like Brenda Walsh in that episode of *90210** where she dyes at home, then is forced to wear a *Blossom*-style hat to West Beverly High!? I'll take Dylan McKay as a boyfriend, but orange hair would be even worse than brown, I feared. What if I thought I was buying hair dye but it turned out to be something else, like the time when Mary Beth and I went shopping for pants (as in, clothing covering your crotch, ass, and legs that Lady Gaga rarely wears) and specifically asked a clerk for "tight pants," only to learn that in Britain, "pants" is what you call underwear. Tight pants! We'd unknowingly been seeking snug undies!

Mary Beth had endured enough of my brunette bitching and

---

* The original on Fox, not the CW reboot. I'm not a tween tool.

finally marched me to Boots, where we bought two highlighting kits. Yes, Mary Beth decided to jump on the blonde-highlight bandwagon, too! We could only find kits that were the draconian pull-through cap system for at-home highlighting, but it would have to do. Thankfully, MB and I worked as a team, with her jabbing a metal hook into my scalp and pulling hair out through the plastic cap for me, and vice versa. Within the hour, I was a brunette with lots of blonde streaks, which, in some blonde-starved countries, passes for blonde.

My time as a brown-haired lady was brief—just six months. Yes, I managed to pass through the Kübler-Ross five stages of grief in only six months. Like an embedded reporter who experiences life in the trenches, I have fought the battle of brunette life and lived to tell the tale. I have war stories, London photos in which I'm barely recognizable, and a closet full of jewel-tone tops to show for it. I encourage you to experience life on the dark side firsthand, as a personal challenge to test out a new look, a tool to engender sympathy and understanding for your fellow woman, and a gutsy endeavor to prove your own strength to yourself (like people who do triathlons). Sure, adopting a head of dark hair is a tough task for the true blonde, but one must endure winter to experience the spring. Peering at the world through brunette-colored glasses will make you appreciate the attention, levity, and energy of life as a blonde. And if nothing else, brown hair is a good foundation on which to layer gorgeous caramel highlights.

PART THREE

Blonde Behavior

CHAPTER 11

RULE: *Keep It Classy*

Earlier we discussed the brassy-vs.-ashy phenomenon. If you aspire to be an ashy blonde, Grace Kelly, ice queen type, then you'd better review your Emily Post etiquette book because women like that wouldn't be caught dead using the wrong fork. Grace Kelly and other cool, withholding blondes all have one thing in common (other than their use of purple shampoo): class. Your class is revealed to the world through your clothing, behavior, activities, and disposition. In Europe, where the classes are extremely stratified, manners and etiquette are hugely consequential. In the United States, the American dream is built on the concept of class ascension. As Americans, we believe that anyone can move classes and quite easily marry up or marry down. It's not just for socialites anymore! As a by-product of that, manners and etiquette are given less weight in the United States. This difference between Europe and the United States means that Americans traveling in Europe can easily offend or horrify Europeans by lacking manners and being ignorant of etiquette. And as my mother says about etiquette gaffes, "There's really no recovery from that. You are expected to know how to behave—especially in Europe."

My parents frequently lament the loss of manners and social graces in American society, and I learned everything I know about manners from them. When I was a kid, my parents, sisters, and I ate dinner together every night, and we'd all talk about our days and catch up. My sisters and I weren't permitted to leave the dinner table until we asked to be excused, and we were expected to help with clearing plates, loading the dishwasher, and the like. When my parents had friends over to the house, the three of us daughters were put to work greeting guests, putting away coats, passing hors d'oeuvres, and generally learning how to be polite. I didn't realize it at the time, but these family rituals taught me how to be a well-behaved kid and I grew into a classy blonde. When we reached our teen years, my father bought tome-like etiquette books for my sisters and me, and these books have served as useful reference manuals. Both of my parents are very gracious and know a lot about the appropriate things to do and ways to carry yourself based on the circumstances, and they passed that down to my sisters and me. My mother spouts off un-PC and hilarious advice and tidbits about manners. Some of her greatest hits include: "When a person snaps her gum, it's as though she is telling the world, 'I'm dumb, I'm dumb, I'm dumb.'" "Cruises are horrible." "Red Lobster is seafood for landlocked idiots."

I sat down with my ashy blonde mother and grilled her about assorted tidbits for keeping it classy that you might not find in your standard etiquette book. My mother was educated at a Swiss boarding school (just like that mean, icy blonde stepmother threatens in *The Parent Trap*) and at an all-girls school on the Upper East Side of Manhattan (just like *Gossip Girl*). If anybody knows about hostess gifts or the proper way to RSVP to a wedding, it's Susan Coppock.

When I sat down with my mother to receive her data dump of etiquette rules accrued over her sixty-plus years as a classy blonde, the first thing on her mind was finger bowls. Yes, finger bowls. An antiquated part of a black-tie place setting, a finger bowl is a bowl of tepid water with a circle of lemon floating in it perched atop a small plate with a doily on it. You are meant to submerge your fingers into the water between the main course and dessert. A finger bowl is tantamount to a tiny, lemony sink that is delivered to each place setting—the old-timey equivalent of antibacterial hand gel. Outside of a manicurist's salon, I have never encountered a finger bowl. I suspect that they were pulled out of rotation around 1968, but it was my mother's first thought. Keep in mind that at her Deb ball at the Plaza Hotel in New York City, she had to perform a dramatic public curtsy and was escorted by not one but two males. Her father was a Victorian—born in the late 1800s—no joke. She's from a different era, when propriety was paramount.

"Finger bowls—first thing you should have in this chapter. It's about how to be classy? OK. At a fancy dinner, when a finger bowl is placed at your setting after the entrée, it will be placed on a paper doily and a plate. When you are done using the finger bowl, pick up the bowl and the doily and move them away from you and to the left of the plate that remains in front of you. Put it where your bread plate had been before," she instructed me. So, should you travel back in time to a black-tie dinner circa 1940, you'll be all set. But let's go occasion by occasion and review some etiquette advice that my mother shared with me over the years. These are tips that you might use in the present day told through the precious lens that is me.

Dinner Parties

- Never arrive at a friend's home for a party or gathering empty-handed. Always bring something—it makes you seem rich and in the know. A small gift for the house or a bottle of nice wine is an appropriate item to take along to a dinner party or cocktail party in a friend's home. Never bring something that the hosts must tend to immediately (cut flowers, a small rodent) as they'll already have their hands full. Just hand them whatever brilliant gift you have brought and make a beeline to the bar or, better yet, the unmanned booze table.

- If the party is a cocktail party or has a cocktail hour, you will probably find yourself attempting to hold a glass and a small plate while feeding yourself hors d'oeuvres. Humans simply do not have enough digits or hands for this! If only you were a spider at a cocktail party, am I right? This juggling of wine and plate while consuming said treats simply can't be done, and you'll probably end up spilling wine on the host's carpet or, even worse, on your own clothing. So think strategically: What do you need more right now, a drink or food? If you're hungry and need to fill up a bit, focus on food only. If the food is really good, get down on it[*] because it ain't going to last long as the party fills up with people. Shovel those miniquiches and cheese ball

---

[*] That Kool and the Gang song was about dinner parties. Nuts, huh?

things in your mouth with reckless abandon so that you can switch to drinks pronto. I usually eat a snack at home before cocktail parties, which leaves me free to just hold on to a cocktail and not worry about getting seeds in my teeth. Plus, that way nobody has to be traumatized by how I look when I start chowing down on a miniquiche. It's not pretty. I can polish off an entire tray of those babies in no time flat.* That type of chowing down is best done, as my mother would say, *en famille*.

- If the passed hors d'oeuvres includes something hard to eat like shrimp on skewers or drumsticks (yes, I've seen both served as friggity hors d'oeuvres—I know, are you friggin' shitting me?), just don't do it. Do you want a wrasslin' match to go down? You vs. shrimp skewer? The skewer will take that title belt every time. I was once at a party where a young woman was absolutely mowing on a drumstick as she tried to talk to me. I was horrified. I was probably talking about something completely uncouth and ridiculous (as I am wont to do), but her caveman-like chow-down was stunningly inappropriate. You're under no obligation to help the hostess polish off her (horribly chosen) hors d'oeuvres. Nancy Reagan's antidrug refrain from the 1980s is what your oversize hors d'oeuvre refrain from the new millennium should be: "Just say no."

- Always offer to help the host. If it's a party without a catering staff, then offer to pass hors d'oeuvres or refill wineglasses. It's always greatly appreciated when someone pitches in. Plus, that way you get first dibs on the good stuff.

---

* I grew up and traded in a bronzer addiction for a quiche addiction. I have an addictive personality, so what? At least it's not heroin.

- Once seated at a dinner party, know what belongs to you using the childlike "lowercase *b*–lowercase *d*" trick that you can do with your thumb and pointer finger. This trick reminds you that your bread plate is the one to the left, and your drinks are to the right. You might have a few different glasses at your setting. You'll probably have water (a regular-looking tumbler), a white wine glass (a traditional wineglass, but skinnier than a red wine glass), a red wine glass (pretty fat—picture a mouse drinking his way to the bottom, then passing out*), and possibly a champagne flute (tall and thin for maximum jazzy bubbling). Be sure to put the napkin on your lap as soon as you sit down in your seat.

- If you are seated at a dinner party and being served by a cater waiter, don't start eating the food placed in front of you until everyone has been served and the host (or hostess) has begun eating. If you are at a benefit sort of event, where your table doesn't have a "host," then you wait for the oldest woman at the table to begin eating and you may begin after her. If you're at a work event or it's at all unclear, just wait for everyone to be served and for somebody else to start eating. Then lean into that dinner plate like a pig at a trough, or pour the entrée into a small bag and strap it around your ears, feedbag style.†

- If the dinner party is out at a restaurant and you are being taken out to dinner, don't order the lobster if your host is getting the pasta. Follow his or her lead with regard to price of entrée. If the host orders a salad to start and a

---

* Just trust me on this visualization exercise.
† Just kidding. Do *not* do that.

medium-priced entrée, you can order a salad to start and a similarly priced entrée.

- When eating at a restaurant, the person who orders the bottle of wine becomes the "decider" on wine.* The waiter will bring the bottle to that person and ask him or her to taste it, look at the cork (potentially), and give the green light on that bottle. Once that person approves the bottle of wine, the waiter should pour it for the women first, then the men. Yes, formal wine service at a restaurant was the original impetus for Queen Latifah's 1989 jam "Ladies First."

- During the dinner party, attempt to include everyone in conversation. Be a good guest—ask questions of the people around you; talk about safe, noncontroversial topics; and engage in conversation with people on either side of you. If you act interested and ask people about their interests, you will be a dream guest (which will get you invited to more dinner parties and mean more free dinners—eyes on the prize, kid!). Don't dominate conversation, but certainly contribute and share funny anecdotes. After you share a story, it's nice to sort of lob the focus to another person. Like a tennis match, minus the tiny white skirts and un-ending cardio. If you feel like you have nothing in common with the person sitting next to you, ask them about their pets, their home, or their children. They probably have at least one of those things and people love yammering on about all of them.

- When you are done eating, place your knife and fork to-gether in the center of your plate. This indicates to the

---

* The George W. Bush of wine, if you will.

waiter that you are done eating, but it should be done whether or not there is a waiter clearing plates. If you are at a dinner party in a home, offer to help clear plates once all diners' forks and knives are positioned this way. If the host takes you up on your offer to help clear, simply pick up a plate (and fork and knife laid across) in each hand. Don't scrape food or stack plates too high—carrying one in each hand is plenty to make you the VIP of the dinner party.

- Don't overstay your welcome. If you attend a dinner party in a friend's home, don't linger much longer after dessert and coffee have been served. I have been on the hosting end of this situation when a friend just kept on chatting and drinking until four a.m., despite my comments that I was tired and really needed to hit the hay. Don't be that guy.
- If the dinner party was particularly well done, labor-intensive, or part of a visit to a friend's home (and you spent a night or two), send a thank-you note to the host. Send a real one via snail mail. People love snail mail. Even more than they love actual snails.

Weddings

- When you receive an invitation to a wedding, check your calendar as soon as possible and reply in a timely manner. As harsh as this might sound, many brides and grooms have second- and third-string invite lists (I know! It's like high school football!), so you should RSVP to a wedding immediately so that the couple can get a head count quickly and invite additional friends if there's room. Respond to the invitation in whatever manner is specified by that couple. Some couples include response cards, and all you need to do is check a box (chicken or fish?) and write your name. Others include the more classic blank response card, and you must write out a full response on that card. The response should be written in third person (completely weird, I know) and reiterate all necessary information. The template for this is "Selena E. Coppock accepts with pleasure the kind invitation of [insert names of people throwing the wedding] to the wedding of Alison and Brian on Saturday, September 28, 2013, at 5 o'clock in the evening."

- If you must travel for the wedding and/or stay in a hotel, book that travel and room as quickly as you can. Don't you dare be that guy who calls the bride a week before her wedding and is like, "That hotel is all booked up—where else can I stay?" You're an adult—book a room in the hotel block early on, or figure it out on your own. This includes transportation to and from the rehearsal dinner, the wedding, or brunch the next day. Most weddings have shuttle buses or at least small maps or directions available at the hotel, but if this wedding doesn't, you've simply got to figure it out on your own. Do not bother the bride or groom in the days leading up to the wedding. They are busy fighting with their parents while posing for photos.

- Dress appropriately for the event—dress, nice shoes, shawl, clutch. I always have a shawl with me at weddings because

I prefer to be a bit covered up while inside the church, and then I can simply put the shawl on my chair at the reception if necessary. Later in the night, once you have busted out some sweet moves on the dance floor and worked up a sweat, the shawl can even be used as a makeshift towel for a personal sweat wipe-down.

- You have twelve months after the wedding to get the couple a gift. If you have a bunch of weddings coming up, it might be easiest to simply order the gift online via the couple's registry (wedding websites have made all of that so simple) and check that off your to-do list so that you don't forget. If you attend the wedding alone, a gift worth fifty to a hundred dollars is pretty standard. If you brought a date, you'll probably want to hit the high end of that rate and send a gift that's at least a hundred. If you're hard up for money, don't be shy about coordinating with friends to buy a joint gift that might be easier on everybody. That's completely fine—no one should melt their American Express card trying to keep up with their friends' weddings. Unfortunately for me, that's a lesson that I learned a bit too late. About twenty weddings too late.

Miscellaneous

- People really appreciate traditional snail mail. A condolence card should always be sent via traditional mail. Condolence cards can be hard to write, oftentimes. Everything feels clichéd and impersonal. You can certainly lead with the standard "I'm so sorry for loss," but then you should incorporate a few sentences about the deceased—share a positive anecdote or memory about that person. Not a memory of "that one time when we drank a bunch of Zima, then went skinny-dipping," but a family-appropriate memory. You can keep that Zima/skinny-dipping memory to yourself.

- If you are staying at a friend's home, always bring something along when you arrive. This hostess gift can be of any sort, really, since the hostess isn't busy with a dinner party in that case. Nice ideas include something for the home (a candle, potpourri, a seasonal tabletop decoration) or food (a nice bread or jam for the next day's breakfast, or a bottle of wine).

- Try to remember personal anecdotes or things that friends or acquaintances tell you. This makes you seem really sweet (even if you're faking it) and thoughtful. Develop memorization techniques to aid memory. I'm a very visual person, so I do visualization exercises where I think about the person and picture whatever it is that they told me. For instance, if my friend Ali says that her laptop was stolen, I'll picture that scene in my head. Then, the next time I'm in the card section of CVS buying a card for my lovely grandmother (we're pen pals*), the image of Ali losing her laptop might spring to mind and I'll buy her a card just to say hello and wish her well. Visualization: If it's a good enough strategy to help sports stars win big games, it's a good enough strategy to help me remember random bullshit.

---

* Yes, I'm the best granddaughter ever. Duuuuudes.

My classy blonde mother and brown-haired father taught me many useful lessons in childhood, but manners and appropriate behavior are the ones that pay off every day. You can't fake that stuff—you must know how to function in polite society. That way, even if your color has gotten a bit faded and might be considered brassy, you're still considered a classy blonde.

CHAPTER 12

RULE: *Channel Blonde Wisdom*

Dear reader, you're savvy enough to laugh at blonde jokes but deep down know that blonde gals are smarter than they look. Public opinion is certainly shifting, but it's up to us blonde ladies to complete the dismantling of blonde stereotypes by showcasing our smarts whenever we can. Let's push forward with intelligence, hope, and change (but not be afraid to embrace the stereotype when it's handy).

This chapter is a useful gathering of million-dollar words that you can drop in conversation when necessary. If you should find yourself trapped in conversation at a cocktail party or dinner gathering with a smarmy jerk who is being patronizing and you can tell that he thinks that you're just another ditzy blonde, drop one of these bad boys and watch what happens. I can guarantee that the know-it-all's entire world will be turned upside down by the mere suggestion that you might be even remotely intelligent. Revel in this moment, as you stand by and watch this jerk bag have a *Death of a Salesman*–like existential crisis. This type of person seems to almost resent when a spunky gal with good hair dares to understand complicated issues, possess sophisticated vocabulary, or hold her own in conversation. Know-it-alls tend to think that there is a finite quantity of intelligence in the world, and if you have any, that means that there is less for him. So toss out "zaftig" in reference to a portly congresswoman and watch what happens. It won't be pretty, but it will be awesome.

You were smart enough to pick up this book, so obviously you're whip-smart, but your smarts may be somewhat specialized. Perhaps you're like me, and a lifelong addiction to hair metal bands has resulted in your near-encyclopedic knowledge of metal band minutiae. Or maybe you're a hypochondriac, and as a result, you know a ton about diseases and disorders. Or perhaps you spent many happy hours during childhood watching your local major league baseball team, so now you know everything about America's favorite pastime. That's great. Don't be shy about revealing that stuff during conversations with strangers. You're a smart cookie—show it off.

Some wise women take the opposite tack and embrace the assumption that they are idiots. They play it up, deliberately acting naïve and unknowing. These blonde ladies know full well that they are smart and savvy, but they don't need to answer to anyone or seek outside validation of their intelligence. They'd rather fly under the radar and play the role of a dumb blonde, then come out on top because of incorrect expectations. It's a brilliant negotiation tactic. Dolly Parton and Pamela Anderson are two perfect examples of this phenomenon. Both ladies are assumed to be moronic nitwits who are all boobs and big blonde hair. In reality, both Dolly and Pam are savvy, self-sufficient businesswomen. Dolly Parton was one of twelve children raised in a one-room shack in the mountains of Tennessee and grew up to be a wildly successful singer, songwriter, actress, musician, and philanthropist. She laughs off the naysayers and jokes about her plastic surgery and style, saying, "It takes a lot of money to look this cheap." Pamela Anderson is a Canadian-born actress, model, and activist who has used her celebrity platform to share her struggles (hepatitis C) and support the issues that are important to her (veganism and animal rights). With her roles in the hit series *Baywatch* and *V.I.P.* and the film *Blonde and Blonder*, Anderson's self-awareness and ability to laugh at herself are refreshing. But not everyone wants to play up the dumb-blonde stereotype, and that's understandable. I find it more enjoyable to decimate expectations and assumptions immediately when faced with judgmental pricks.

The modern blonde is inquisitive and alert, eager to learn more and unafraid to get intellectual when the situation calls for it. If you aspire to be this self-assured but aren't quite there yet, arm yourself with these five-star vocab words to boost your confidence in any conversation. And don't stop building your lexicon at the end of my list—collect new words like Carrie Bradshaw collected heels!

- **myopic**: short sighted, narrow-minded. Smart people *love* dropping this one. To describe something as myopic (and it's an adjective, so it's used as a descriptor) is saying that it's self-centered and simplistic. For example, you know John Cougar Mellencamp's song "Small Town"? Great song. The anthem of small-town pride across the nation. But Mellencamp showcases a pretty myopic worldview through the lyrics of this song. Born in a small town, parents still live in a small town, you admit that you'll probably die in a small town? That's a great example of a myopic life.

- **debacle**: a complete collapse, a train wreck, a chaotic mess. I'm convinced that the only reason I was accepted to my wonderful alma mater is because in the interview I referred to my high school's delayed building renovations as a "chaotic debacle." I'm often tempted to refer to something as a "shit show" or "train wreck," but when judgmental, uptight people are listening, I'll sub in the word "debacle" instead.

- **Faustian**. Get ready to blow judgmental people's minds when you drop this gem. Faust is a character from a classic German legend who makes a deal with the devil, trading his soul for unlimited knowledge and worldly pleasures. Sound familiar? It should since this premise has been used time and time again in film, plays, songs, and more. Two of my favorite uses of a Faustian deal with the devil are Tenacious D's "Tribute" and "The Devil Went Down to Georgia" by the Charlie Daniels Band. An example of a Faustian bargain would be if I sold my soul in exchange for perfectly blonde hair for the rest of my life (I suspect that some people think that I have made this agreement, but I assure you I have not. I have good genes and a great colorist.)

- **Dickensian**: like the conditions in a book by Charles Dickens, which is to say bleak, squalid, poverty-stricken. As you probably know, Dickens was all about depressing stories of poverty, orphans, and debtors. In the way that Michael Jackson was known for his one bedazzled glove during the 1980s, if Charles Dickens were known for any type of glove, it would be the fingerless glove.* There's just

---

* And I'm not talking about a glove without fingers to make cigarette smoking easier. I'm talking about fingerless gloves like you see in those

something so broke and dirty about fingerless gloves. So if something is described as Dickensian, it's probably pretty dark and broke. If you find yourself at a super-swank cocktail party, you might hear a comment like "Did you see the cloak room? It was freezing and horribly lit—positively Dickensian!"

- **Machiavellian**: characterized by sleezy, cunning moves; dishonest. I love words like this. It's derived from the name of Italian renaissance diplomat and author Niccolo Machiavelli, who wrote *The Prince*, but you might recognize it as (almost) the pseudonym of rapper Tupac Shakur: Makaveli. (More on Tupac in a minute.) Psychologists can assess and measure a person's Machiavellianism, which indicates that the person is sociopathic, has no regard for others, and is only focused on his or her own self-interest.* So, in cocktail party conversation, you might refer to a coldy pragmatic, ruthless politician as "Machiavellian." Tupac Shakur was inspired by Machiavelli's book *The Prince* and its assertion that a leader could eliminate his enemies by all means necessary. Machiavelli: code for a tricky, selfish, dishonest person and the pseudonym of a great West Coast rapper whose talent was snuffed out during the East Coast vs. West Coast rap battles in the 1990s.†

- **Shakespearean**. Another gem of a million-dollar word. This can be used to describe many things, as poet-playwright William Shakespeare invented many literary phenomena that we now take for granted. For example, many films and

---

period dramas on the BBC.
* Sounds like a few of my ex-boyfriends—HEYO!
† Seriously, guys—who killed Biggie and Tupac?

TV shows will use stormy weather to portend doom or to build tension—that was totally Shakespeare's idea first! It's known as "Shakespeare's storms," and now everybody's doing it! He was an innovator and you can still feel the effects of his ideas on theater, poetry, and literature. A lot of his comedic plays are about hilarious and elaborate misunderstandings, so keep the descriptor "Shakespearean" in mind when you're at a cocktail party and someone is rambling on about a misunderstanding with his wife's car and the babysitter and what time to pick up the kids. That sounds like a Shakespearean scene! (A very boring Shakespearean scene.)

- **pedantic**: excessively academic, showy in one's smarts. I get a nerd high from using the word "pedantic" around people who I find pedantic. Double word score! (Or something.) A lot of ugly, straight, white dudes whose mothers doted on them too much during childhood eventually grow up to be pedantic adults. They've got to name-drop their academic achievements because they are clueless about social interaction. A pedantic person might go out of his way to detail his résumé and academic achievements while you are making small talk at a cocktail party. Shut it, guy. Let's just focus on chugging these free gin-and-tonics, OK?

- **puerile**: childish, immature, trivial. You can remember this one using the handy trick that Purell (hand sanitizer) is good to use after you have been around immature children (because they are usually filthy and their fingers are covered in germs). Use Purell around puerile kids. In cocktail party banter, you might say something like, "My friends and I recently enjoyed a day of paintball—a totally puerile activity but lots of fun!" People will be thinking, "Whoa—she's smart, active, *and* has great hair."

- **bourgeois**. You don't grow up with a mom who teaches French and not learn a few French words (and eat a lot of madeleine cookies). Originally, the term "bourgeois" signified a member of the upper class (within Marxism). Over time, though, it has come to mean a person who is flashy or ostentatious with his or her wealth. Now, "bourgeois" and "nouveau riche" (French for "new money") mean the same thing essentially: newly wealthy people who show off their wealth. In James Cameron's 1997 film *Titanic*, Kathy Bates played the role of Margaret "Molly" Brown (an actual person, not just a character in the film), who was nouveau riche/bourgeois. The other first-class passengers on the *Titanic* looked down on her because she was categorized as "new money," which they deemed vulgar and loud. Margaret Brown was indeed new money—her husband, James Joseph Brown, was a wildly successful engineer, and she went from growing up as a poor kid from Hannibal, Missouri, to being a wealthy socialite and philanthropist. If there's one thing that old money hates, it's new money. So, despite its original definition, today the word "bourgeois" has a negative connotation and means a person who has new money and is ostentatious with it.

- **nostalgie de la boue**. Let's stay on this French kick with "nostalgie de la boue," which translates to "a yearning for the mud" and means an attraction to what is crude or degrading—a romanticized notion of the class below you. If a person at a cocktail party is telling a story about when he was twenty-one and lived with five friends in a tiny apartment and they subsisted on ramen noodles, and he's marveling at how simple and fun those times were, that's definitely nostalgie de la boue (and you should identify it as such, so the guy knows you're smart and thinks you're multilingual). Be careful with this phrase, though, because correct pronunciation is imperative here. So if you're shaky on your high school French, don't use this one.

- **louche**. This one is pronounced "loosh," and it's an adjective that means dubious, shady, or disreputable. You see it often in modern literary reviews, but you almost never hear it in conversation, which will win you points from the judges.* I would say that my favorite dive bar, with its oddball characters, unmarked entrance, and honky-tonk jukebox, has a certain louche appeal. Or you might say that you don't usually go to a certain neighborhood because it's quite dangerous and filled with louche characters.

- **zaftig**. This adjective is a poetic way to call a woman fat. Well, not straight-up fat but proportionately and pleasantly plump. One might say that Rubenesque models are beautiful and quite zaftig. A similarly impressive word with the same meaning is "embonpoint." "Embonpoint" can be a noun or an adjective.

- **zeitgeist**. That last Z word reminded me of another killer Z word: "zeitgeist." "Zeitgeist" means the spirit of the times, the current cultural movement or pulse. One might say that AMC's hit show *Mad Men* accurately represents the cultural zeitgeist of the 1950s and '60s. Trashy as this sounds,

---

* Only kidding. Life isn't like an episode of *Family Feud* with judges looming overhead, no matter how many times I say "Judges, will we accept that?" in conversation while looking skyward.

one could even describe the month (or so) in 2009 when Snuggies (those body-covering blankets) were popular as a time when Snuggies were part of the cultural zeitgeist. They were the hip thing, even if for a moment.

- **twee**: something that is sweet to the point of being sickeningly sweet. I'm a cynic, so I find many things overwhelmingly sweet or sentimental. For example, if you saw a grown woman on the street carrying a lace parasol and wearing all pink, you might say, "That's a twee display." I find it horribly twee when a new parent writes a thank-you note from the perspective of the baby, writing something like "Thank you for the nice book. My mommy and daddy love reading it to me!" So twee it hurts.

- **Sisyphean**. A personal favorite, and I really mean it this time. Like "Machiavellian" earlier, the word "Sisyphean" has a great origin story. Sisyphus was a character in classical mythology. Sisyphus pissed off a god, and his punishment was to roll a huge boulder up a hill, but as soon as he had completed his task, the boulder would simply roll back down the hill again. Sisyphus would have to start over again and again and again ad nauseum. So if something is Sisyphean, it's an unending labor that is never truly completed—a life sentence, of sorts. In small talk at a dinner party, you might refer to a horrific project at work that feels never-ending as a "Sisyphean task."

- **nebulous**: hazy, vague, or confused. Fantastic word because it has to do with astronomy and I love reading my horoscope. (Are these different things? Huh?). "Nebulous" is a great million-dollar word to drop instead of using "confused." If you are asked to retell a funny story during a dinner party, you might kick it off by saying, "Gosh, I have a somewhat nebulous recollection of what happened, but here goes nothing," then launch in on a story of the time that you and your best friend almost vomited at the hotel pool during your last party weekend in Vegas. That Vegas story makes you sound like an irresponsible, party machine, but your use of the word "nebulous" will balance things out.

- **reify**: to convert into or make into a concrete thing. You might say, "If you've ever walked out of the colorist's salon crying, that trauma serves to reify the importance of communication between client and colorist." Drop that one and watch their heads spin.

- **ablutions**: washing of hands, body. A weird word to drop in conversation, but it's a personal favorite thanks to one of the many wonderful high school English teachers I had the pleasure of learning from. He used to speak frequently about the importance of "morning ablutions," which struck me as funny and quirky at the time, but in retrospect perhaps he was encouraging me to shower more. Either way, it's a hell of a word. Drop "ablutions" in conversation and people will probably think you're pretty weird . . . and wicked smart.

So remember our strategy: Talk about topics that you know about (when possible), and if that isn't an option, drop some million-dollar vocabulary words. If you still feel overwhelmed by a conversation, then it's time to heed the advice oft-repeated maxim "Better to remain quiet and seem a fool than to open your mouth and erase all doubt."

CHAPTER 13

RULE: *Be Mindful of the Attention that Blonde Attracts*

Blonde hair is undeniably eye-catching. As Anita Loos wrote in *Gentlemen Prefer Blondes* back in 1925, "Gentlemen always seem to remember blondes." There's a reason that Madonna and Lady Gaga—the two most in-your-face, attention-craving, envelope-pushing performers of the past few decades—are natural brunettes who switched to blonde: Blonde is what gets attention. Pale hair reflects light and catches the eye. But make no mistake—that attention is of both the positive and negative variety.

The adjective "blonde" is a loaded descriptor. You rarely hear someone described as "great with children, really generous, blonde, thoughtful," and so on. The adjective "blonde" is usually paired with "dumb" or "leggy" or "bombshell." Take the quick (but telling) mention of a blonde character in the song "Amen" by the country trio Edens Edge. This song is about the singer's elation that her crush has finally escaped from a bad relationship. The lyrics go: "I heard Mary Jane down at the Powder

Puff Beauty Shop / Sayin' that blonde in her tube top / She left our Jimmy for a boy in Illinois / Someone give me an amen." The song goes on to say how both her crush's mother and the entire town are relieved that he finally woke up to the evil of the blonde in the tube top. Of course the Beelzebub character is a blonde in a tube top! What else would she be? We'd never hear a description of this evil heartbreaker as a "brunette in a tube top"—it just doesn't pack the same punch as an evil blonde in a tube top. This widespread disdain for the sexy blonde is fueled by the perception that blondes have it easy: They're (somehow universally considered to be) clueless (so others take care of things for them, which makes them . . .), spoiled, and entitled, plus they get all the attention.

But this blonde quandary is a chicken-or-egg question: Are blondes universally prejudged and hated because they get so much attention, or do blondes get so much attention because of these universal prejudgments and assumptions?

To explore this question within the world of Internet surfing, I reached out to professional web-click maximizer (and brilliant storyteller) Jeff Simmermon. He shared with me some interesting information about how blondes catch the eye and get positive attention online. Jeff used to work in AOL's Communities section, which was essentially a precursor to today's social media. On this site, people would have forum discussions and read articles. It was Jeff's job to manage those forums and maximize clicks on AOL's web content. AOL's research-and-development department studied how to maximize these clicks and gathered a ton of data about the online behavior of visitors to websites. This data was aggregated across the United States, the world, and millions of different web pages. It revealed what items, pages, or pictures people tend to click on or interact with more than others. Based on these findings, Jeff organized AOL's home pages a certain way as far as imagery, articles, text placement, and so on. The findings were this: If you have an article that you want people to read, you must post some sort of a photo along with the headline. That is, links to articles that included a photograph "viewed better" (got more clicks) than links to articles that were simply text (just the title of the article). So photos seem to draw web surfers to an article—OK. But AOL's findings dug much deeper. Just one step further, the data shows that photos of people get more clicks than photos of other items (still lifes, landscapes). To go another step, photos of women get more clicks than photos of men. (Let's take for granted that the models in these photos are all extremely good-looking.) And further still, photos of blonde women get the most click traffic—more than photos of beautiful women with any other hair color. Beyond all of that, photos of celebrities get even more click traffic than anything. So web designers' formula for maximizing click traffic is to find a reason, any reason, to post a photo of a blonde female celebrity.

So, for example, if AOL had an article called "What to Know Before Saying 'I Do,'" they might want to put a photo of a blonde Jessica Simpson with text to draw a thin connection between the article and the photo, perhaps something like "Jessica and her man should read this one!" This photo of a blonde female celebrity would maximize clicks on an article that isn't actually related to Jessica Simpson at all. So you see, blonde hair catches eyes on the computer screen. But it isn't limited solely to the digital world—it also happens in the real world. And, as we touched on before—this eye-catching can be of the positive or the negative variety. As Voltaire (and Stan Lee and FDR and Churchill) supposedly said, with great power comes great responsibility. And nowhere is that adage more applicable than in the world of blondeness. Blonde power should be wielded wisely, for it can have catastrophically bad or stunningly good results. I have experienced both bad and good things as a result of my blondeness.

I certainly have gotten some useful attention or perks as a result of my light hair. I've had many nights out with pals when a guy would come over and chat me up, specifically, when I'm out with a mix of ladies. Some guys have even admitted that my hair caught their eye so they thought they'd buy me a drink or introduce themselves. On a summer Saturday night back in high school, Suzanne and I were cruising around the suburbs, looking for something to do, and we stopped into a local convenience store for soda and candy. As luck would have it, a crew of cute guys was in the convenience store, and they invited us to their party, saying, "We looked over and two blondes had just pulled up, so we had to come over and invite you." We went to the party and were *not* murdered, despite what *Dateline NBC* would have predicted, and we had a wonderful time! Score one for blondes getting positive attention!

But the eye-catching nature of blondeness can also be a negative, "nowhere to run, nowhere to hide" situation that makes you stand out when perhaps you'd rather blend in. Because their yellow hair stands out in a crowd, blondes must be thoughtful about the types of establishments that they frequent. It's all too easy for an evening of live music to turn into the legendary night when your best friend (and fellow blonde) gets punched in the face.

In late summer 2004, I was living back at home with my parents after my year of living in Chicago. Yes, I was a "boomerang kid" (graduated from college and ended up living back in my parents' house) before it was big. I got in on the ground floor of that sad phenomenon, my friend! One evening a few weeks after my return from Chicago, I was reclining on my childhood bed, staring up at the ceiling, which I had covered, twelve years prior, with glow-in-the-dark stars. I thought to myself, *So I guess this is rock bottom? Being twenty-four years old, broke, and sleeping back in your childhood twin bed with glow-in-the-dark stars overhead.*

The phone rang (yes, a landline—I'm a Luddite), and it was my lifelong best friend, Suzanne, mercifully inviting me out of the suburbs and into the city. Suzanne and I fell right back into our usual routine of hanging out and having fun, and thank God we did. Suzanne helped me resocialize back to Boston life. That night, Suzanne asked if I wanted to drive to her apartment in Brighton because a Guns N' Roses cover band called Mr. Brownstone was scheduled to play at the live music hall Harpers Ferry that very night. Her then-boyfriend, Paul, had seen them before and reported that they didn't just play Guns N' Roses music; these guys dressed up as Guns N' Roses and put on a hell of a show. Wait—a lineup of five hard-rocking, bewigged dudes belting the sweet melodies originally created by Axl, Slash, Izzy, Duff, and Steven? Before you can say, "I might be a little young, but honey, I ain't naïve,"* I was driving into Boston for the night's festivities.

I parked my parents' car (because I was going hog with the whole "reverting to high school life" thing) on the street and climbed the stairs to Suzanne's third-floor walk-up apartment. It was a dingy three-bedroom apartment, but it boasted a big

---

* The lyrics to "Rocket Queen," Guns N' Roses two-songs-in-one big finish to the album *Appetite for Destruction.*

front porch with a beautiful view of L.A. (Lower Allston)—
specifically Brighton Avenue, the street on which Harpers Ferry
was located. So we were stumbling-distance from the concert
venue—clutch. Suzanne; her new beau, Paul; and his handsome buddy Ben (well hello there!) were all drinking beers on
the porch when I arrived. I was glad to meet Paul as he and
Suz had recently started dating and I wanted to suss out if this
guy was good enough for my best friend. By transitive prop-
erty, it earned Paul some points that his best friend, Ben, was
not only hot but his love of all things Guns N' Roses almost
rivaled my own. After Bud Lights on the porch,* we walked
the few blocks to Harpers Ferry, paid the ten-dollar admission
fee, bought some cheap beers, and got ready for our minds to
be blown thanks to Mr. Brownstone. I was prepared for the
universe to explode when the GnR cover band Mr. Brownstone
played the song "Mr. Brownstone" as it would be a critical mass
of Brownstone-themed rock.†

The band's blond-wigged drummer (the would-be Steven
Adler) caught my eye first as his platinum locks caught the multicolored lights. He wasn't as heroin-chic emaciated as the real Steven Adler, but that was probably a good thing for the stability of
the cover band. Three guitarists then came out and I looked them
over, assuming the other blond-wigged guy was Duff, the short

---

* What I often refer to as "cocktails on the veranda."
† In a similar scene, I was once at a tiny upstate New York bar whose
exterior sign bragged that it was "nothing but a good time." Their staff
was very earnest about this theme, and it cracked me up because this bar
was a lame watering hole in a tiny town. But it was a good time, I'll admit.
Alas, just when we were having a good time at this bar (the self-anointed
epicenter of good times), my friends and I put money in the jukebox
and played Poison's "Nothing But a Good Time" and then the universe
exploded.

brown-wigged guy was Izzy, and of course the curly-wig-and-top-hat combo was the unmistakable Slash. It's common knowledge that a good Axl can make or break a GnR cover band, and while theirs was a pudgy Axl, he rocked the serpentine dance with such skill that it didn't matter.

The band Mr. Brownstone rocked hard and put on a hell of a show, just as Paul had predicted. They blazed through songs off of *Appetite for Destruction*, *Lies*, and both *Use Your Illusion*s as the crowd ate up their hard-rocking antics. Pudgy faux Axl's thick white legs poked out from beneath his kilt as he enthusiastically shrieked that he was loaded like a freight train and yet simultaneously flying like an aeroplane. Who doesn't love songs about modes of transportation? *Come on!*

After a few ditties, Suzanne, Paul, Ben, and I made our way toward the front of the standing-room-only audience. We were all singing along with GnR's hit song "Paradise City," which was advancing toward the second half of the song, when the drums switch to double-time and it gets pretty nutso.* Slash shreds on the guitar, and the song sounds like it's spiraling out of control as Axl shrieks, "Take me down! Ohhh yeah, spin me round . . ." The power of this chaotic double-time section washed over the crowd, prompting a spontaneous mosh pit to form around the four of us, and we couldn't fight that wave of madness. We found ourselves at the center of the pit, with assorted limbs flying around us in white-kid rage soup. I just tried to stay with Suzanne, Ben, and Paul as bodies were moving and swirling around us. It was difficult to stay with the group and see where the guys were, though. To that end, Suzanne's platinum hair

---

* I know a *lot* about music, as you can see from my refined musical vocabulary.

was extremely helpful—I kept my eyes out for Suzanne and hoped that Ben and Paul would do the same. She could be our lighthouse so we wouldn't lose one another in the madness of "Paradise City."

Just then, a random fist appeared out of nowhere and connected with Suzanne's cheekbone. "Holy shit, what the shit!?" I shouted, stunned at what had just happened.

"Oh my God!" Suzanne exclaimed putting her hand to her cheek. She'd just been punched square in the face. Suzanne immediately bent down to register the fact that she had been punched in the cheekbone by a random guy. I looked at her boyfriend, Paul, who was horrified, frozen, and unwilling to do anything about this. Thank God Paul's friend Ben turned out to be less of a pussy as he had seen the stranger punch Suzanne and he was ready to brawl.

"Who the fuck did that? What the fuck!?" nonpussy Ben shouted as he scanned the crowd and tried to find the offending fist. But we were about to see *Random Fist Punch: Part II* as the perpetrator's balled fist was heading straight for us yet again, this time clutching a makeshift weapon. The drunk jerk thrust a beer bottle in the air and was about to bring it down on our heads. On our *heads*! On our platinum-perfection domes! He was aiming it toward us, like an upside-down parabola of unprompted drunk rage.[*] I have no idea why this random stranger was in attack mode and can only guess that he got too caught up in the mosh pit experience. Perhaps he had been rejected by hot

---

[*] Please note: I literally got an F in Algebra II when we studied this stuff. So if this is wrong, I wouldn't be surprised. Nor would my teacher whose educational theories on algebra incorrectly assume that every student gives a rat's ass about math.

blondes back in high school and was eager to unleash some payback on arbitrarily selected members of the blonde community. Perhaps Suzanne's white-blonde hair just happened to catch his eye and she was in the wrong place at the wrong time. But the wrong time was about to happen again. The stranger had an upturned longneck bottle of Bud Light in his hand, and it was heading straight for Suz and me. I watched it descend upon us as if in slow motion.

"What the shiiiiiiiit?" I slow-mo choked out just as Ben saved the day and intercepted the bottle's trajectory with his hand. The bottle then broke all over Ben's hand, which ran counter to everything I knew about Physics and Anatomy and Physiology. *How did that Bud Light bottle just break on Ben's hand? Is that even possible? The glass that beer bottles are made of is so thick, most likely so that it won't easily shatter in a bar fight. Yet one just smashed all over Ben's fleshy paw. Are his fists made of friggin' cement!? How did a fun night out in Brighton turn into a scene from the cinematic masterpiece* Road House?* I thought.

Within seconds, blood was pouring from Ben's hand and shards of glass were everywhere, including jammed into his hand and wrist. That was when this Guns N' Roses concert got a little bit more Guns N' Roses, as Ben balled up his hand into a bloody fist and wailed the bad guy in the face. I'm almost ashamed to admit that watching a bloody fist connect with a dude's face to the double-time second half of "Paradise City" is the closest that I have ever come to spontaneous orgasm.

We missed the song's final refrain of "Oh, won't you please take me home?" because our entire party was shoved out a side

---

* Minus the chicken wire stage cage and Jeff Healey's brilliance.

door by a posse of beefcake bouncers. The four of us found ourselves in a dark alley next to Harpers Ferry as Ben's hand continued to bleed.* Using Boy Scout–style survival skills, Ben removed his shirt, wrapped it around his hand, and applied pressure to stop the bleeding. I already thought that Ben was great for pounding his bloody fist into a dude's face, but now he was also shirtless in a dark alley. This night had gone from great to awesome. The moonlight illuminated his muscular body as I noticed that Ben had tattoos on his chest and arms. The night had ticked even further up the continuum of radness from great to awesome to amazing. The dim starlight and nearby streetlights bounced off Suzanne's ashy blonde bob, and I thought about how her head caught the eye and ire of a drunken stranger, thus making this night out into an eventful one.

We four walked down the alley and onto crowded Brighton Avenue. Ben and Paul hailed a cab and headed to Mass General Hospital so that Ben's hand could be looked at and stitched up. The guys knew that they'd be in for a few hours of sitting around the waiting room, so they told Suzanne and me to just go home and crash. Suzanne needed to get some ice on that cheek anyway.

"I'll call you in the morning," Paul told Suzanne as I stared at Ben and thought, *I'd like for you to call me in the morning . . . but I hardly know you. Nonetheless, I feel like we could build a relationship based on our mutual love of Guns N' Roses, tattoos, and unbridled aggression. In the words of Axl Rose, "When you're in need of someone, my heart won't deny you," so when you're all*

---

* GnR fanatics might say that we took Axl's lyric "I'm going to watch you bleed" a bit too literally.

stitched up and your fist is ready to bash in faces of other dudes at concerts, please call me.

Paul and Ben sped away in a cab while Suzanne and I re-traced our steps and walked back to her apartment, our blonde heads bobbing along Brighton Ave.

"What the shit?" I said.

"Yeah—wow—what a night," Suzanne agreed.

"Crazy the kind of rage that can be incited by two hot blondes at a concert, huh?" We laughed.

It's that type of mayhem that can confront blondes, apropos of nothing. We have a tendency to stand out in a crowd, and sometimes that protrusion is enough to make us the target of a punch or errant beer bottle. Color blindness is a sex-linked condition carried on the X-chromosome, so males express the condition at a much higher rate than females. Many color-blind males report that the color of blonde hair stands out dramati-cally to their eyes. Get some of these color-blind guys drunk and stick them in a mosh pit, and they just might swing their fists and beer bottles at the first head that attracts their eyes. So in a real-world context, the bold quality of blonde hair can be dangerous, but in the computer world, its eye-catching proper-ties mean a maximum number of clicks. As the old saying goes, damned if you do (have amazing light hair), damned if you don't (have amazing light hair).

CHAPTER 14

RULE: *Be Capable*

I can tolerate a lot of things: smelly subway cars (you get used to them after about ten minutes and you don't notice the stench anymore), materialistic loudmouths (sometimes I feel like these people have got me surrounded), disorganized junk drawers (it's a junk drawer—it's just where you toss random crap). But one thing I cannot abide is helplessness. Nothing makes my blood boil more than seeing a coworker who needs to send some documents via FedEx but can't be bothered to figure out how the shipping website works. Or a person who refuses to learn how to drive, so she's stuck hitching rides from friends and family and being at the mercy of others. Or a person who claims to hate a book or movie or sport, but only because he doesn't understand it. This type of person—the willfully obtuse—drives me semibananas.* As people of

---

* Question: Does the term "semibananas" make you picture a semitruck filled with bananas, half of a single banana, or a bunch of half bananas?

earth, and especially as women of earth, it's so important to be capable. An incorrect stereotype about blondes is that we are vain, defenseless, and clueless. Well, we may be vain, but we're certainly not defenseless or clueless.

Every blonde should know a few things and have a few key skills up her sleeve: know the basics of football, America's most popular sport; know how to read a subway and street map; and know how to pump her own gas. You might already have those skills and, if so, good on ya. For you, we have a few advanced skills: know a few phrases in major languages and know how to throw a drink or a punch when in danger. Let's learn these important items.

- **Know Football Basics**

    It's imperative that blonde gals understand the basic tenets of football in order to debunk the stereotype that women don't understand complex sports. Any sport can be fun to watch once you understand the basic concepts. Also, football metaphors are often used in the workplace and politics, so it's good to know what somebody means when they make a comment like "Time is running out for this project—we're in the fourth down."

    Football is a long game that resembles a recurring pig pile for three hours. To me, the only bright spot in football is the tight pants worn by the players (and adopted by trainer-to-the-stars Tracy Anderson). These pants are fantastic: They're made from shiny, stretchy fabric; the capri cut is fun and playful; and most football

---

I use that question with people like a conversational Rorschach test for whether or not they're psychopaths.

players have beautiful, round bums that are showcased wonderfully in these uniforms. But football is more than matching outfits and shiny, metallic hats—it's about moving the ball down the field, ten yards at a time.

In football, two teams of eleven play against each other, and the game is played in four fifteen-minute quarters. The clock is stopped a lot during the game, though, so the entire game takes a lot longer than an hour. Plus, sometimes you have a jazzy halftime show adding to how long you'll be watching a game. To start things off, the referee (zebra-looking dude) conducts a coin toss and the winning team decides if they'd prefer to kick the ball or receive it in the initial kickoff—that is, the decision of whether to play defense or offense first. With football, you might hear a lot of talk about Xs and Os, and that stands for defense and offense. (When coaches are mapping out plays, they draw the different players using Xs and Os. Xs are defense, and Os are offense.)

The kickoff is what starts the game, and another kickoff commences the second half (after the halftime show). Within the game, each team has four "downs" to advance the ball at least ten yards. Many teams need only three of these downs to move the ball ten yards or more, so often they won't even use the fourth down. Think of the fourth down as a spare tire in the trunk of your car: It's there when you need it, but you can probably get where you're going without it. To advance those ten yards (or more), a team uses coordinated maneuvers called plays—running plays, passing plays, trick plays. On TV, you might see a team and the announcer says that it's "first and ten" and all the dudes are lining up on the line of scrimmage.* "First and ten" means that this is the first down (just starting off) and the team needs to advance ten yards. The line of scrimmage is the line on the field where both teams get into position against each other. On TV, it's usually a yellow line that is digitally inserted into the shot. As we discussed, during their four downs, the team who is on offense (trying to score) must advance ten yards down the field from the line of scrimmage. If it's a close call, you might see referees come on the field with two tall poles connected by a chain. This isn't an elaborate torture device: This is a ten-yard-long chain that measures if the team moved the ball far enough. For example, you could have a situation in which a team uses all four downs but is only able to advance the ball nine and a half yards. The refs with the tall poles will come out to check it out. If the team doesn't advance ten yards in their given four downs, then the ball goes to the other team and the line of scrimmage remains where it was. So then the teams switch up and the team that before was on offense (trying to score) is now on defense (trying to block the goal), and the team that was on defense before is now on offense. This switch-up starts things over again, so the other team is on first and ten now (first down, trying to move ten yards). See, it's not so confusing!

Points are scored either when a player runs into the end zone (the end of the grid-like field, where the player

---

* Before I made an effort to learn about football, I hadn't heard the word "scrimmage" since I played high school field hockey and a scrimmage was a preseason game that wasn't on the record. This isn't what it means here.

who just scored usually breaks out some dance moves) or when a ball is kicked into the uprights (the goalposts, which are usually yellow or white and look like a box with three sides but no top side). A touchdown is worth six points, and after a touchdown, the team can kick the ball through the uprights for one point or they can opt to do a two-point conversion for two points (obviously). The two-point conversion is a bit trickier because it's not a kick or a guarantee—it's a play on the field that could potentially go wrong if the other team blocks it. It makes sense that the one-point option is 99 percent guaranteed (unless you have a "LACES OUT" situation like in the film *Ace Ventura: Pet Detective*) and the two-point option is a bit harder but with a bigger payoff. That's life for ya. A field goal (which is another time when a team kicks the ball through the uprights—just in a different situation during the game) is worth three points.

As with many sports, the plays in football require special "teams" or specific groups of players. The quarterback is usually the guy on the team who gets the most credit and fame—Tom Brady, Eli and Peyton Manning, Brett Favre, Joe Montana. He calls the plays, and then, when the action starts, he has to find a person to pass to or he has to run the ball himself—the quarterback is pretty clutch.

The defensive guys are the truck-like fatties who are mostly hunched over and tackling people, and they are the Xs that I mentioned earlier. The positions on the line are defensive tackle, defensive end, nose tackle (also called nose guard), linebacker (outside and middle), corner (also called cornerback), and safety.

When the offensive line comes out, they aren't screaming profanities,* but rather they are the aforementioned Os who will be on offense, trying to score. Their specific positions have names like offensive tackle, guard, center (who snaps the ball to the QB between his legs), quarterback, tight end, wide receiver (one type of wide reciever is called the split end, natch), and running backs (fullback, tailback).

If a play starts and the QB, looking for who is open and where he can throw the ball, gets tackled by a member of the opposite team before he has a chance to throw it, that's called a "sack." It's usually outside linebackers or middle linebackers who pull off a sack, and it's pretty sweet to watch. I also love that it's called a "sack." Let's end this orientation to football on that double entendre, shall we?

- **Know How to Read a Map (Subway or Street)**

I have a pretty good sense of direction (until you get a few cocktails in me—then I'm useless and gunning for a fight), but nonetheless, navigating a foreign city or

---

* Get it! Offensive line? Offense jokes! (This is why I was never good at sports—I don't care about the sport. I care about jokes and wordplay.)

unfamiliar neighborhood can be confusing. Above all, try to act casual and not lost. Walk with confidence, even if you're secretly thinking, *Where the F am I? This neighborhood is terrible and I'm scared!* Never let 'em see you sweat. If you must refer to a map, I recommend using a hardcopy map, not your smart phone or, heaven forbid, an iPad. Sure, a hard-copy map might make it obvious that you're lost, but at least it's not an expensive miniature computer that could be snatched from your hand. Walking around an unfamiliar area while staring at a map on your phone or iPad just looks like an advertisement for thieves that says, "Hey, thief! Here's an expensive gadget for all to see! Take a look and come over and punch me if you want it!" So go with the old-school paper map like Chris Columbus used to use (but please have a better knowledge of geography than he did). And don't be shy about how you hold it. I find it easier to get my bearings if I am holding the map to match up with exactly what is in front of me. So if I am pointed south and looking to walk south, I hold the map upside down. There are no rules in map handling! Cartography may be filled with standards and rules, but holding maps is not. So hold it however you like.

Most major cities have subway systems, and they're pretty logical, despite the color-coded, crisscrossing maps. I have rocked public transportation in Boston, New York, Chicago, Paris, London, Venice, Rome, Prague, Edinburgh, Glasgow, and possibly Athens (my three days there are a blur of ruins and disappointing food). I don't speak the language in many of those places, but a subway's a subway's a subway and if you can match up letters, you can find your way. Your best bet is to look at the last stop on the line of the direction you want to go. So, for example, if you want to visit a neighborhood in Brooklyn called Windsor Terrace (where I currently live and where Mindy Kaling lived when she was broke and unfamous—what what!), you'd take the orange-line F train—specifically the one that ends at Coney Island (a mystical place filled with fried food, tattooed vagrants, and a surprisingly awesome beach). So if you were in Manhattan, you'd hop on the Brooklyn-bound F train that says "Coney Island" on it. You're not going all the way out to Coney Island,* but the train is telling you that Coney Island is the last stop on that train line. Also worth noting is that sometimes you may need to take a train "inbound" to get to an "outbound" train.† This is the way it sometimes works with the T in Boston. You might be thinking that you need an outbound train because you're trying to get out from the city (and go to an outer area like Brighton or Brookline). But if you're transferring trains (perhaps from Red Line to Green Line), you may need to take the Red Line inbound (to Park Street) to get the Green Line outbound. It's like the old saying goes, "You gotta get up to get down," right? Wrong? Huh?

- **Know How to Pump Your Own Gas**

   This section doesn't apply if you live in New Jersey or Oregon, two states where self-sufficiency at the pump is, strangely enough, illegal. But if you live in any of the

---

* Unless you're in a modern-day remake of *The Warriors* and you and your leather-vest-wearing friends have just "gotta get back to Coney!"
† At times like those, Bruce Springsteen was right: Sometimes it feels like you're a rider on a downbound train.

other forty-eight states of the union, you have no excuse. Everyone should know how to pump his or her own gas— it's simple and important. How many horror movies have scenes set at a desolate gas station with a creepy attendant and a car full of frightened coeds? Don't be that helpless girl—pump it your damn self.

Know which side of the car your gas tank is on so you don't pull into the gas station wrong and have to do a sixty-four-point turn flipping around to the other side. Turn off the car when you pump. This isn't required and, in theory, you can leave your car idling while you pump, but I think it's a bad idea. Whenever I have done that, I have forgotten that I've left the car idling and unthinkingly turned the key in the ignition once I got back in the car, prompting a horrific screeching sound and disdainful looks from other patrons. To avoid doing this, I make it a rule to turn off my car whenever I gas up. More and more gas stations demand that you pay (whether with cash or credit) before you pump to ensure that you don't pump and run. So if you pull your car into a spot next to a pump, the first thing you might need to do is swipe your credit card into the machine above the gas choices or hand over your cash to the dude in the bulletproof box.

Gas choices! Let's talk gas choices. You can use regular or diesel in most cars, but know this: Diesel cars take diesel gas, and everything else takes regular. Unless you drive a German-made sports car, you probably don't have a diesel engine. Read the signs at the gas station carefully, though. You do *not* want to put diesel gas into a nondiesel engine. That would be like regularly using deep conditioner if you already have limp, fine hair—it is *not* a good idea. It will ruin your day and possibly your week. So, if you're 99 percent of America, just use regular gas and don't worry about buying the more expensive gas for your car. Unless you drive a Lamborghini, your car doesn't need high-grade gasoline.

So you've positioned your car next to the pump on the correct side, turned off your car, opened your little gas trapdoor, unscrewed the cap, and swiped your credit card. Time for the real pump n' grind of pumping that gas into your tank. Isn't this fun? Like a 1994 song by R. Kelly! OK—there probably will be three pumps in a row on the gas stand. After you have swiped your card, select your gas choice by pressing the giant (sometimes illuminated) button. Once you have selected that, you should grab the nozzle, which probably resembles a penis made of accordion. While you're doing all of this, you should not be smoking or talking on your cell phone. I'm not a scientist, but both of these activities, when combined with gas pumping, cause explosions. It looks cool in the movies, but in life it's a total bummer. Don't ask how this cell phone/cigarette/gas cocktail works—just follow my advice blindly, OK? So take the nozzle, put it into the hole in your car that leads to the gas tank, then turn back to the pump stand. Once the nozzle is resting firmly in the hole, you may need to turn back and flip the lever thing, where the nozzle was resting before, back at the pump. This will enable gas flow, but it won't start until you pull the trigger. So flip that thing, then get both hands back on the accordion penis, and pull the trigger. You should feel gas flowing, and at this point, you may wish to cry out, "I RULE! You think I'm stupid, but I'm not—YOU ARE!" at whoever is near you. Congratulations—you're pumping gas like a pro!

Now let's talk dismount. Once your gas tank has filled to capacity, the gas will automatically stop. Magical robots, huh?* If you are trying to hit a certain amount of gas (perhaps just ten dollars' worth), you can simply stop the accordion penis when you get to that quantity. You do that by pulling the trigger again. Either way, once you have all the gas that you want, make sure that gas is no longer passing through the accordion penis, pull it out of your car, and place it back on its original holster (you may need to flip this down, also). Put the lid back on the gas tank, close the elfin trapdoor on your car, and you're good to go! Drive out of that gas station giving the two-finger salute (flippin' the bird, my friends) to the haters. Or just safely drive out, with both hands on the wheel. It's your life, you decide!

You got all those down? Then let's jump into some more sophisticated assignments: I'm talking linguistics and pugilism.

• **Know a Few Phrases in Major Languages**
Here are some key phrases that you should know how to say in a few languages in case you find yourself abroad and in dire need of help. These crucial phrases are listed below, with their translations after that.

"Where is there a hair salon I can visit?"

---

* We may be living in an Orwellian *Nineteen Eighty-Four*–esque land, but occasionally it makes life easier. And the automatic cutoff at the gas pump is one of those times. I love you, Big Brother!

"I am blonde and proud!"

"Where is the bathroom?"

"I don't speak your language, but my amazing hair makes up for it, no?"

SPANISH

"¿Dónde está la peluquería puedo visitar?"

"¡Soy rubia y orgullosa!"

"¿Dónde está el baño?"

"No hablo su idioma, pero mi cabello increíble lo compensa, ¿no?"

ITALIAN

"Dov'è il parrucchiere piu vicino?"

"Sono bionda e fiera!"

"Dov'è il bagno?"

"Non parlo la tua lingua, ma con i miei capelli bellissimi, non mi sembra che c'e proprio bisogno di parlare!"

GERMAN

"Wo gibt es einen Damenfriseur?"

"Ich bin blond und stolz darauf!"

"Wo ist die Toilette?"

"Ich kann deine Sprache nicht, aber mein tolles Haar macht das doch wett, oder?"

FRENCH

"Où puis-je trouver un bon coiffeur?"

"Je suis blonde et fière de l'être!"

"Où se trouvent les toilettes?"

"Je ne parle pas votre langue mais pour compenser j'ai les cheveux superbes, n'est-ce pas?"

- **Know How to Throw a Drink or a Punch**

I'm not encouraging you to become a surly brawler who is always itching for a fight, but I do think it's important that you know how to take care of yourself. Blondes are often perceived as weak and defenseless, so knowing a few tricks for how to throw a drink or a punch can help us overcome this (only if you absolutely must, of course).

Throwing a drink is a good go-to if you're in trouble and you don't want to get too close to the target or you don't want to potentially injure yourself. Perhaps you're a hand model who simply can't be doling out uppercuts and haymakers, so drink tossing seems like a better option for you—go for it. Throwing a drink is a good move if you are at a bar and a creepy random is trying to rub up on you or has forced you up against a wall or into a corner. Much like the opening credits to the moronic display of humanity that is *The Real World*, situations like the bar creeper are times when you must stop being polite and start getting real. Throw that drink with attitude and impunity. Usually a drink toss will be an underhand maneuver, in which you simply unload the liquid into the perpetrator's face. Aiming for the face or head is your best bet—it will be most effective and give you time to scramble away. It's also hilarious and cartoonlike to watch, so revel in the situation for a moment, then jet out of there in case the drenched person tries to chase you down.

Throwing a punch is a bit more intense and can lead

to hand injury, but sometimes it's simply necessary. To get comfortable with landing different types of punches, you might wish to take some boxing classes at your local gym. I belong to a very mainstream gym, and they have a really basic cardio-boxing class that introduced me to the uppercut, jab, and cross. This class also enabled me to become acquainted with a hot, jacked instructor who loves the music of Marky Mark and the Funky Bunch almost as much as this Masshole writer. Nothing gets me ready to whip my fists at a hot guy's padded mitts quite like a teenage Mark Wahlberg, fresh out of the juvenile detention center in Boston Harbor (now closed), telling me to, "C-c-come on, swing it." Yes, the hot teacher is calling the punches that you should throw and you're punching a padded mitt that he's holding up. Contact sports, yes, please! But seriously—if you find yourself in a situation where you need to defend your own life, throwing elbows is a good strategy, but nothing feels quite like landing a punch. Form a fist with your dominant hand and remember to keep your thumb outside of that fist. Do not fold your thumb into the center of the fist (even though it feels so natural to do that thumb tuck), as this will cause you to break your own thumb when you land the punch. I know that it feels weird to keep your thumb out, but trust me, you want to keep your thumb out. As you are swinging, aim to land your knuckles first, as the primary impact. Knuckles aren't just for cracking to annoy others—they are big-ass chunks of bone that can do damage and should be used to your advantage. Another smart strategy is to wear rings that can help your cause, too. I wear big silver jewelry (and I joke that the only person who likes chunky silver rings more than I do is Axl Rose), and I often think that if I needed to throw a punch, my giant silver-and-turquoise rings would be helpful. Don't be afraid to rock the boat, my friend. Sometimes you have no choice and you must defend yourself—be ready for that.

Now you know about (or have received a refresher on) how football is played, how to read a subway or street map, how to pump your own gas, how to express a few crucial ideas in an assortment of languages, and how to throw a drink or a punch. You've tackled the basics and the advanced assignments—nice work! If I were an accredited university, I'd give you a diploma for being a jazzy cat. The modern blonde should strive to be informed, self-sufficient, and, above all, not helpless, and this information will help you achieve that. These skills, and a head of gorgeous blonde locks, are all you need in life! You're welcome.

CHAPTER 15

RULE: *Beware of Blond Bullies and Date Outside Your Color Group*

I only date dark-haired men, and my reasoning is a combination of eugenics, self-hatred, and a burning distrust for blond men. Yes, when it comes to light-hued locks, what's good for the goose is not, in fact, good for the gander.* I blame my fear of blond-haired men on the glut of blond bullies who populated television and film in the 1980s and early 1990s, the days of my towheaded youth. The blond bully was a ubiquitous character in the media of my childhood, and a handful of those characters are forever seared into my memory bank. This group includes the platinum Cobra Kai leader from *Karate Kid* (William Zabka), Dolph Lundgren in *Universal Soldier* (the guy who wears a necklace made of *human ears*, then delivers the line "I'm all ears"), super-snob James Spader of *Pretty in Pink*, and Dolph Lundgren (repeat offender!) in *Rocky IV*. That's just the tip of the proverbial blond-boy, bad-boy, bully iceberg, but those are

---

* And who uses a word like "gander" anyway?

those ones who most traumatized me. The 1980s taught us that blond men are capable of, at the very least, making you feel poor (Steff of *Pretty in Pink*) and, at the very worst, brutally cutting off your ears to fashion a necklace (Sergeant Scott of *Universal Soldier*). The archetype of blond men as creepy bad guys was implanted in my brain long before I ever began dyeing my own hair to be blonder . . . and blonder . . . and blonder. And that characterization persists in entertainment even today. The brilliant Harry Potter book series features pale-haired evil wizard Draco Malfoy (played by Tom Felton in the movies) in contrast to brown-haired and bespectacled Harry and his dark-haired and red-haired best friends. J. K. Rowling created this bully character who possessed a pointed face, an elitist (to the point of racist) attitude, and, of course, white-blond hair. Another current-day blond bad boy is found in HBO's wildly popular series *Game of Thrones*. Prince Joffrey Baratheon (Jack Gleeson) is a blond sociopathic brat.

For a person who loves all things blonde as much as I do (I even prefer blondies over brownies when it comes to dessert), you'd think I would have more respect for blond guys. Sorry, Hitler Youth—I don't. I love me an olive-complexioned, exotic, dark-haired (and often quite hairy) man. Not one guy, specifically. One of that type. Someone in that wheelhouse, whatever a "wheelhouse" is. So keep it in mind when you're peeping out potential dates for me, would ya? Bonus points if he's a bit hefty. Heavier guys really do offer "more to love," make you feel stick-thin, and appreciate your attention, ladies. Some might say that they are America's greatest undertapped natural resource . . . after solar power. We should tap that resource . . . and tap that ass. (OK, that was cheap, but why else would you pick up this book, dear reader, if not for forced references to Guns N' Roses and thinly veiled sexual metaphors aplenty?)

My affinity for Italian, Greek, Albanian, Jewish, Mexican, or just any old dark-haired guy can be traced back to one hugely influential leading man of the '80s: Erik Estrada. As a child, I was a pretty big *CHiPs* fan—as much as an eight-year-old can be a "fan" of anything other than her security blanket and juice boxes. *CHiPs* was on TV in reruns when I was a kid, and I would use my hour allotment of television time per day to watch the bizarre stories of the California Highway Patrol play out. (Live wires on the freeway! Women delivering babies in the darnedest places!) My sisters and I used to ride bikes and carefully coordinate simultaneous turns while shouting, "CHiPs Patrol!" Like the majority of the American public, I always liked the gregarious and kooky Ponch (Erik Estrada) better than straitlaced Jon (Larry Wilcox). Jon was a vanilla, white-bread California surfer boy; Ponch was a swarthy, exotic charmer whose smile could stop California highway traffic. Ponch and I would be the perfect couple: His Mediterranean looks would contrast with my alabaster skin and blonde hair in a yin-yang marriage for the ages. Sure, he'd keep crazy hours with his job as a California highway patrolman, but I'd keep myself busy in our beach bungalow, where I'd have closets jammed with vintage '70s-style housedresses.

I had inspiration from the relationships of Loni Anderson and Burt Reynolds, Christie Brinkley and Billy Joel, and Jerry Hall and Mick Jagger.* All were blonde ladies matched up with darker-haired beaus, and that dynamic persists in plenty of high-profile couples today. Take current couples Gwen Stefani

---

* Sadly, none of these couples are still together.

and Gavin Rossdale, Kelly Ripa and Mark Consuelos, and Blake Lively and Ryan Reynolds. These women are obeying one of the cardinal rules of blondeness: Date outside your hair color group. At the risk of sounding too much like infamous Nazi doctor Josef Mengele on opposite day, blonde-on-blond procreation often results in children who are practically allergic to the sun and must live under cover of darkness. But blonde-on-brunet/black-haired reproduction will build balanced children who can be exposed to direct sunlight without issue. So it's imperative that natural blondes and fake blondes alike date partners with darker hair (for matters of potential procreation and aesthetically pleasing contrast, respectively).

But where can you meet such swarthy (or at least light-brunet) suitors? Where do dark-haired dudes hang out? It's a question that has boggled the minds of scientists for millennia. Let's break it down.

Who are dark-haired men in terms of heredity? Many have bloodlines that connect back to the Mediterranean, India, Africa, and the Caribbean. So a smart blonde (not an oxymoron!) would find herself at cultural gatherings for these groups—Italian street festivals, Caribbean parades, Indian restaurants, Greek Orthodox churches, Catholic masses, or your city's own "Little Italy." It's a law of averages: There are simply more dark-haired potential partners at these types of events—they're more concentrated—so you can chat up and be noticed by more of them than you would if you walked into a random pub. I'm nothing if not efficient in my dating rules.

If you don't have the guts to storm a Greek Orthodox church service for the purpose of scouting "talent" (and I wouldn't necessarily blame you—my strategies are pretty shameless), what are some other locations where you might meet dark-haired men? Dance clubs on the Jersey shore, the Sunglass Hut in your local mall, your local tanning salon, and nail salons that offer waxing services. Or really anywhere out in the world—they walk among us.

Dating any nonblond hair color is acceptable, though. Give redheads a spin! Test-drive a gray-haired dude who used to have brown hair. Go out with a bald but swarthy beauty! The options are limitless! Just do not engage in blonde-on-blond romance, or you and your mate will end up resembling the painful blond spectacle that was Hulk Hogan and his ex-wife. Or, worse, the brassiest blonds to never blow on a brass instrument, Dog the Bounty Hunter and his equally brassy wife and partner. As evidenced by these two couples, blonde-on-blond dating is not synonymous with class and taste.

My dreams of ending up with Ponch never came to fruition, in part because Ponch is a TV character and therefore not real, and in part because I was eight when I had a crush on him and even Appalachia won't permit that type of generational mixing. But he did set the template for my ideal guy: tan, dark, and hardworking. To this day, I'll take an overweight, hairy, brunet guy over a conventionally handsome blond guy every time. And you should, too, unless you want your family's holiday cards to resemble promotional photos for *Dog the Bounty Hunter*.

PART FOUR

Blonde Friendship

CHAPTER 16

RULE: *Have a Blondetourage*

The world can be a harsh place for golden-haired goddesses, which is why blonde-on-blonde friendship is so important. Every light-haired lass should have an entourage of fellow blondes—a blondetourage—to help her make her way in the world today (after all, it takes everything you got*). You need a crew of friends because blonde backlash is a real phenomenon and it can be harsh. In pop culture, when a posse of blondes appears on screen (in film or television), it's cinematic shorthand that sends the message: These are the characters you're supposed to hate. The only way to explain this is to fall back on the thing I love best, second only to my hair, pop culture trivia.

---

* *CHEERS!* Hell yeah, Boston! Go Red Sox!

To wit, we have the popular girls from the 1986 John Hughes film *Pretty in Pink*, all light-haired and all snobby, mean girls (before "mean girls" was even a thing). The movie's protagonist, auburn-haired, working-class Andie (Molly Ringwald), is taunted by caramel-blonde rich girl Benny (Kate Vernon) and her wealthy bitch crew. Going back further in pop culture history, in 1978, John Landis directed *National Lampoon's Animal House*, which gave us frigid blonde sorority girls Mandy (Mary Louise Weller) and Barbara Sue (Martha Smith). We first meet these beautiful blondes at the uptight Omega Theta Pi house, because of course these opportunistic, gold-digging blondes only date the rich, popular guys.* The blondes don't care if the big-man-on-campus guys are nice or share their interests, as blondes will date whoever happens to be popular at the moment, or so we learned from the *Revenge of the Nerds* film franchise. Beautiful, blonde cheerleader Betty (Julia Montgomery) is a collegiate triple threat: a cheerleader, a sorority sister, and the quarterback's girlfriend. A hat trick of blonde stereotypes! During the course of the film, Betty works at a kissing booth but refuses to kiss a nerd (talk about bad customer service!), has sex with a nerd who she mistakes for her boyfriend (that's effectively rape!), and is just as stunned as the audience when she ultimately falls in love with a nerd. Another surprising blonde-on-nerd love connection from 1980s cinema is found in an earlier John Hughes's hit, *Sixteen Candles* (1984). While redheaded protagonist Sam (Molly Ringwald again) is pining after dark-haired leading man Jake

---

* But at the close of the film, we learn that Mandy eventually married Bluto. Some blondes can outgrow their shallow, judgmental ways, it seems.

Ryan (Michael Schoeffling), his stuck-up blonde prom queen girlfriend Caroline (Haviland Morris) is busy hosting a house party, getting her hair caught in a door, then letting an unlicensed driver take her parents' Rolls-Royce for a spin. That unlicensed driver is geeky freshman Ted (Anthony Michael Hall), who Carolyn takes a liking to, proving that everyone can outgrow shallow high school cliques somewhat. The message seems to be that we're all trapped in our respective high school roles and characterizations. Interestingly, Haviland Morris, who played the prom queen girlfriend Caroline, is actually a natural redhead and was asked to wear a blonde wig for the role. The filmmakers had a specific look in mind for the role of the irresponsible, snobby prom queen and it was blonde.

In pop culture, "blonde" is quite often synonymous with either "bitchy" or "bubbly"—mean girls or cute idiots (with cute idiots being played by the likes of Meg Ryan and Reese Witherspoon). Hell, there's a band whose entire existence is based on their pride in having any hair color that isn't blonde (4 Non Blondes). That's some serious backlash.

Thankfully, some of that anti-blonde sentiment can be mitigated through good old-fashioned friendship. We find presentations of blonde friendship and loyalty in cinema, television, literature, and even in the real world.

In 1990s television, we saw a strong blonde-on-blonde friendship between Donna Martin (Tori Spelling) and Kelly Taylor (Jennie Garth) in *Beverly Hills, 90210*. Donna and Kelly remained best friends forever, and both actresses were part of the *Beverly Hills, 90210* franchise for all ten years of the show's existence. These platinum pals are lucky that their characters were never written out of the show with a story line about a move to London for drama school (cough—Shannen

Doherty—cough). Donna and Kelly endured a lot together: Kelly's mom's alcoholism, Donna's lame-o boyfriend David Silver, Donna's abusive boyfriend Ray Pruit (who uttered the legendary line "Pruit with one *T* because that's all my momma could afford"), the whole "Donna Martin Graduates" revolution (oh, suburban kids and their "causes"), Kelly's nose job, Dylan and Kelly's love affair during which he ditched Brenda ("Policy of Truth," baby!), and the ladies' shared Hermosa Beach bungalow. Not to mention enduring Steve's awful hair, Brandon's gambling problems, and Andrea's bus rides over to the wrong side of the tracks.

If we consider the Sweet Valley High book series as "literature," then blonde friendship is the centerpiece of a whole lot of literature. Starting in 1983, the (low-level) reading public got to follow blonde twin sisters Jessica and Elizabeth Wakefield as they navigated every conceivable teenage and young adult situation known to man. Jessica and Elizabeth loved each other dearly, despite their vastly different personality types and the ups and downs of their relationship. These experiences occurred over the course of 181 books, if you can believe it. This barrage of books include 143 in the "core series" (the only core more intense than that is Eric Nies's core circa *The Grind*), twelve Super Editions, nine Super Thrillers, five Super Stars, twelve Magna Editions, a few spin-offs, a series of prequels, and a TV show. In the TV show, Jessica and Elizabeth were played by twin sisters Brittany and Cynthia Daniel, who were Doublemint Twin models before they became TV stars.

A model of healthy, supportive, loyal, blonde-on-blonde female friendship comes to us from the most unexpected of places: season three of Bret Michaels's reality TV dating show *Rock of Love* (VH1). Yes, this show lasted a full three seasons and yet somehow, Bret Michaels still never found love on *Rock of Love*.* Season three was quite literally a "departure" from the previous seasons as it mostly took place on tour buses as the show rolled through the highways and byways of America, mimicking Bret's real life on the road.† Seasons one and two had taken place in the same filth-laden mansion, but season three took the show on the road and was officially called *Rock of Love Bus*.

Season three was by far the best season, and it's in large part thanks to blonde participants Farrah and Ashley. These two became fast friends on the show because of their myriad commonalities: Both women have breast implants, are tattooed, are (former or current) strippers, and are unapologetically pro-blonde. Of course, they aren't just pro-blonde politically—they are both towheaded in real life, as well. Farrah and Ashley formed the crew that they named "the Blondetourage," proving that, if nothing else, blondes can smush words together to make even better words. Another *Rock of Love Bus* contestant, Gia, was a short-lived member of the Blondetourage, and she wasn't disqualified because of her two-tone hair (which would technically make her half a blonde and thus half a member of the Blondetourage—so at its roots,‡ the Blondetourage was a crew of 2.5 blondes). Gia stood out from the hard-partying pack (which is a mighty feat) with her wild antics and excessive drinking, and Bret had to let her go. Or as Bret told Gia when he revoked her backstage pass during the elimination ceremony, "Your tour ends here."

Thank goodness Ashley and Farrah made it through most of the season, or the American public would have missed out

---

* It almost feels like he wasn't *really* looking for love during those three seasons in front of the cameras. Hard to imagine, I know.
† Traveling from tiny venue to bar room venue to nostalgia showcase.
‡ Yes, that's a hair pun.

on some amazing blonde debauchery, pro-platinum propaganda, and classic quotes. Ashley, the more surly and deadpan of the duo, gave us some gems during the course of that show and in post-show interviews. She's a proud blonde who always speaks her mind, and it often gets her in trouble. In that way, she reminds me of myself (though we differ in a few respects, namely that I am required to wear clothes at my job, and Ashley is required not to). In one episode, the girls played football in the mud and whichever girl was declared the game's MVP would be rewarded with a one-on-one date with Bret. Boisterous blonde Ashley was especially eager to win that face time with Bret, saying, "I am going to do whatever it takes to win this MVP. Even if it means that I have to get muddy, so I look brunette." Later, in a post-show interview on VH1's blog, Ashley spoke about when she picked a fight with brunette *Rock of Love* contestant Marcia. When asked if she hated Marcia because of Marcia's brown hair, Ashley responded, "It wasn't really that. Marcia was obnoxious and a really drunk, annoying person. She just happened to have brown hair, but even if she had blonde hair, I still would have made fun of her." So the Blondetourage from *Rock of Love Bus* isn't founded on a complete hatred of all nonblondes. If you're an annoying drunk, even a head of blonde hair can't save you from their wrath.

On a more serious note, though (as serious as you can get about a competition in which strippers vie for the affections of an aging rock star), watching Farrah and Ashley's friendship grow and blossom during the course of the season was heartwarming and hilarious. In the world of reality TV, where the drunk and dysfunctional willingly lock themselves in L.A. McMansions for weeks at a time and insist that they "didn't come here to make friends," it was surprising and sweet to watch such a genuine, loyal friendship blossom between Farrah and Ashley, like a dandelion growing through a tiny crack in the asphalt, against all odds. The Blondetourage knows what we all should know: that blondes need to back each other up. Today's blondes should cast off the outdated model of mean girl blondes and instead be kind to others, support blondes and nonblondes alike, and, above all, never be bullies.

Within the realm of female friendship, blonde-on-blonde friendship is important because no one understands blonde issues quite like a fellow blonde. A sister in blondeness understands why you occasionally use purple shampoo (to keep your color from getting brassy), why you never dunk your head in a chlorinated pool (it could ruin your color and you'd end up with a green tint), why you wear a scarf on your head at the beach (again, to protect your color), and why you rarely wear shirts that are yellow (clashes with hair color).

I have been the lucky participant in a lifelong blonde-on-blonde friendship with a pal who is like a sister/soul mate to me: my best friend, Suzanne.* We've been besties since our mothers put us in a playgroup together, through nursery school, grades K through 12, and still to this day. We lived together during our wild twenties in South Boston, and I was a bridesmaid in her wedding a few years back. She married a wonderful guy who I went to college with, and whenever I'm home in Boston, the first order of business is to catch up with my family and Suz. She has fantastic platinum hair, and we regularly text about roots, our colorists, and being blonde (among other family updates, thoughts, and general shit-talking). She has had my back since

---

* You certainly know Suzanne by now, what with the tales of all our adventures and accidents already covered in this book.

playgroup, and we have seen each other at our best and at our worst. This story, dear readers, is an example of when I was at my worst.

During our respective freshman years of college, Suzanne and I both acquired ID cards to get into twenty-one-and-older bars. Mine was from a batch that was made by an acquaintance at my college, Hamilton. He cranked out about twenty fake IDs for the majority of my sorority pledge class and dozens more for other underage students. He had quite a setup: backdrop and camera, laminating machine, the whole shebang. All of the IDs were Maine state ID cards, each with a real photo of the person, a fake birth date, and a fake hometown of Limestone, Maine. Yes, everyone who got a fake ID from this guy was supposedly from Limestone, Maine. All of us. It was terrible when ladies from my sorority pledge class went out to bars together and tried to use these ID cards at the two bars downtown. What were the chances that a posse of twenty gals from Limestone, Maine, had driven eight hours to Clinton, New York, for a night on the town?* But when I was home in Boston for the summer (without nineteen of my closest Limestone pals), the ol' Limestone, Maine, ID card worked wonders. I had memorized everything—my fake birthday, my astrological sign based on that birthday, and, just in case the bouncer was a real stickler, I'd even memorized a few tidbits about growing up in Maine.† An unfortunate fact that I learned pretty quickly is that Limestone, Maine, is a tiny town of about two thousand people and it's almost exclusively a location for Phish shows. Claiming to live in Limestone, Maine, is like a rural version of saying that you

---

* Limestone, Maine, *rolls deep*!
† Lobster everywhere! Coastline all over the place!

live in Madison Square Garden. Fortunately, most Boston bar bouncers aren't well versed in their Maine geography and history, so the Limestone, Maine, fake ID was a ticket to partying for a few summers. Suzanne had hit underage fake ID mecca: She scored a real ID card from an older girl in her sorority. It resembled her enough, in that the ID's real owner was also pretty and blonde.

When we'd go out to use our fake IDs in downtown Boston, Suzanne and I would be vigilant about "acting over twenty-one." We had a very specific way that we thought people over the age of twenty-one acted, and we thought that playing the twenty-one-and-over role masterfully was the key to public drinking. Being twenty-one meant ordering drinks as though you have ordered a million drinks in your life—just super blasé. You're a twenty-one-year-old gal on the town! Who cares? No biggie. Cop a little attitude. Recite a drink order in a way that shows just how over twenty-one you are. Another part of our twenty-one-and-over exercise in overanalysis was that Suzanne and I would dress in professional-looking clothing. Based on our work attire, the waiter would be able to tell that we'd just come from our nine-to-five, postcollege, real-world jobs because we were over twenty-one. We were doing it just like Huey Lewis and the News used to croon, "workin' for a living." This was our scheme.

That summer we both *were* working for a living, just as Huey Lewis had said. Suzanne was a lifeguard at a pool near our hometown, and I spent my days working as a temp for a hotel chain that is featured in countless rap songs: the Holiday Inn. I was the "gal Friday" in the catering and corporate sales department of the Holiday Inn right next to the last stop (Riverside) on a branch of Boston's public transportation, the T. It was a pretty clutch location—walking distance to the T, so easy access to

Boston. Late one summer afternoon, I cut out of work a few hours early and Suzanne and I headed into Boston in search of cocktails. Suzanne drove to the T station in Newton (next to my place of employment), parked her mom's beautiful Saab (which had become Suzanne's recently), and met up with me on the train platform, and soon we were Boston-bound. Our big plan was to walk around Newbury Street and shop, then get some drinks with dinner. Suz and I had our fake IDs, were dressed up, and had already carefully planned how we'd order our cocktails. At the appointed time, we'd casually say to the waiter, "Margarita on the rocks with salt," and this blasé recitation would show that we were obviously over twenty-one. We knew the lingo! We knew exactly how we liked our margaritas—the waiter would know that this wasn't our first time at the rodeo. We were over-twenty-one gals just having dinner after a day's work.

As the late afternoon sun bounced off the expensive cars parked along Newbury Street, Suzanne and I walked down the brick sidewalks and thought about how we could use adult lingo to get cocktails into our eighteen-year-old mouths.

"Where should we eat? I mean, which restaurant do you think will have a cool enough waiter to either—one—not card us—two—card us and not know that our IDs are fake, or—three—card us, know our IDs are fake, but serve us anyway because we're cute blondes?" Suzanne asked.* I wasn't totally sure. We needed a restaurant where the food would be good even if, worst-case scenario, we were forced to simply eat dinner

---

* Suzanne and I have always loved debating possible plans using elaborate, numbered tallies or pro/con lists. It's the best way to explore all possible options, especially when you're grappling with important issues such as restaurant selection.

and drink water or soda. We settled on Charley's, a standard American-fare restaurant with enough background noise that even if our IDs got us in trouble, it wouldn't be that much of a spectacle. We were seated quickly, and soon a handsome young waiter was introducing himself and reciting the specials. As he talked, I fidgeted and picked at my cuticles, nervous about the impending launch of Operation: Drink Alcohol in Public.

"Can I start you ladies off with some drinks?" the hottie waiter inquired.

"Yeah, I'll have a margarita on the rocks with salt," Suzanne ordered casually, just as we had discussed.

"Me, too, I guess . . . yeah . . . I always like that whenever I go out . . . which is a lot . . . so yeah, same thing for me—margarita on the rocks with salt." I overdosed on blasé attitude.

"Great—I'll be right back with those drinks and to take your food order." He walked away. Suzanne and I stared across the table at each other, stunned at the miracle that had just unfolded before our very (blue) eyes. We were about to be throwing back some drinks right there in Charley's, right in public, like real twenty-one-year-olds. I repressed my desire to grin from ear to ear and tried to blankly stare out the window while waiting for a margarita, like a real twenty-one-year-old would.

The margaritas arrived, and Suzanne and I quietly squealed and grinned at each other, like twenty-one-year-olds never would. The food selection was where we ran into trouble. Not trouble with the restaurant or the waiter. Trouble like when indigestion becomes panic and you need to find the nearest bathroom. What was that recipe for disaster? Margaritas on the rocks with salt followed by chicken Caesar salads. We were so focused on ordering our drinks in a relaxed, nonchalant way that we gave no thought as to what food might go well with margaritas. It certainly wasn't chicken Caesar salad, yet that's what we both ordered.* If something was going to expose us for what we were—eighteen-year-olds who could barely contain our glee at drinking tasty cocktails in a public restaurant instead of our usual skunked beer in the woods or the backseat of a hatchback—our ill-conceived food-drink combo should have. The waiter humored us, though, and delivered our matching chicken Caesar salads as we casually sipped on our matching margaritas on the rocks with salt.

"How friggin' cool is this?" I whispered to Suzanne as we chomped on our salads.

"I know! We're adults! Here we go! Just having some drinks, having some food. No big deal," she agreed.

"Just spaghetti and beer," I marveled. "Spaghetti and Beer" was a theory that my brunette pal (with gorgeous caramel highlights) Alexa and I had developed early on in high school. Back in those days of desperate partying (in the form of drinking Zima or Bud Ice in a deserted Christmas tree farm during the dead of winter), we'd fantasize about what it must be like to be an adult. To have beer or wine or liquor in your home and drink it whenever you want. It struck us as such a magical and exciting idea, having alcohol with your dinner—specifically spaghetti and beer. Yes, when we were sixteen years old, the pairing of spaghetti and beer seemed like the pinnacle of adulthood and delicacy. And here were Suzanne and I, enjoying proverbial spaghetti and beer.

---

* Over the years, we have done a lot of identical ordering and shopping. The one that I find the most cringe-worthy is a shopping excursion we once took to Newbury Comics on Route 9, where we proceeded to buy identical sunglasses and the same album (311's *Greatest Hits*). Told ya it was cringe-worthy.

After we finished our oddly late to be lunch/early to be dinner meal, Suz and I hopped on the T back out to Newton, where Suzanne's car was in the parking lot next to the Holiday Inn. It didn't occur to us to keep drinking in Boston—we were both so excited we'd been served once that we didn't want to jinx it, so we headed back to the suburbs. The T ride back out to Newton is a long one (about an hour), so Suzanne and I had plenty of time sitting on the train to chat and marvel at our good fortune. It was then that I began to feel sharp pains in my stomach. My stomach was rumbling, and it wasn't a rumble of hunger—it was a toxic rumble that portends a wicked case of diarrhea.

"Woodland is next, then last stop is Riverside," the announcements blared overhead as my stomach turned.

"Whoa, Suz . . . my stomach feels weird. Does yours feel weird?"

"Nope—I feel fine. Are you OK?" Suzanne asked.

"I think that something didn't quite agree with me. Oww . . . my stomach hurts," I explained as I tried to avoid doubling over. I managed to keep it together until the train pulled into the station at Riverside. Now we had to walk out of the station and across the giant parking lot to Suzanne's car. But with every moment, the pain increased and the pressure on my excretory organs doubled.

"Whoa, Suz . . . whoa . . . I'm not sure if I can walk," I explained as I carefully stepped out of the T train and onto the platform. "Hold on . . . I may need to go slow." My churning stomach had turned into an urge to move the bowels (to put it politely), but from the feel of it, this wouldn't be a solid passing.

"Fucking roughage and alcohol . . . oh my God," I muttered as Suzanne and I slowly walked toward her car. The pressure was escalating, and a liquid shit was knock, knock, knocking on my asshole, just like the song that Guns N' Roses covered better than anybody else.

"Suz! I'm afraid I'm going to shit my pants!" I exclaimed. This was bad. Sweet Suzanne couldn't help but laugh, but her laughter would make me laugh, which could spell disaster, I feared. We were making progress, though—almost at her car.

"Don't laugh! Please! I'm sorry! I'm just afraid . . . I can't control—" I was sweating profusely now. I was wearing a favorite bebe skirt and a miniscule thong as I climbed into Suzanne's mother's Saab. The seats were leather, but not "leather" like my father's station wagon. Real leather. There was a tag and everything to prove it. And only a tiny piece of fabric separated a powerful spray of liquid feces from this leather seat.

"Drive to the Holiday Inn!" I commanded.

"It's that bad?" Suzanne marveled.

"Back entrance!" I bellowed. I sat in the passenger's seat, crossed my legs, and then wrapped one calf and foot around the other, like that move that is normally done in a yoga class, not when you're trying to lock up your digestive track. Suzanne couldn't help but laugh as I tensed my body, closed my eyes, and encouraged her to "step on it." Because of my job at the Holiday Inn, I knew exactly where the restrooms were located, and the back door would be our best bet. I wanted to avoid the front entryway, where I'd potentially run into a crowd of guests or, worse, coworkers. If I hightailed it in the back door, I could bolt into the bathroom in time to avoid releasing diarrhea in my pants (err, skirt). Things were dire.

Suzanne efficiently steered the small car past the Holiday Inn's front entrance, down the side driveway, and beneath the parking area, coming to a stop at the back entrance. I opened the car before she had even come to a complete stop and started walking forward. The Holiday Inn's back entrance opened based on a motion sensor mounted above the door, so I stuck my hand up like a brainwashed constituent showing undying dedication to a psychotic leader and the doors opened immediately. I didn't even break my stride. I kept on moving down the long corridor of patterned carpet. I was holding my sphincter shut by sheer force of will, and I was so close. But you know when you're this close and everything falls apart because you're so close? I pushed open the public restroom door. In just a few more steps, I'd be inside the dinky walls of the bathroom stall and this margarita-on-the-rocks-with-salt-and-chicken-Caesar-salad nightmare would be over.

"Holy shiiiiit!" I whispered as I hiked up my bebe skirt and the diarrhea flood commenced. My thong was an innocent bystander in the melee, but I managed to get my rump on the toilet and release the liquid deuce. I was breathing hard—deep breaths and heaving sighs of relief—when I heard the bathroom door open a crack. I peeked through the gap between the bathroom stall door and the walls, and my watery eyes made out a sliver of Suzanne's platinum dome.

"Remind me *never* to order a margarita with a Caesar salad ever again." I laughed.

"Haha, oh my goodness, Lenny,* are you OK?" Suzanne asked, adding, "Don't worry—nothing got on the seat in the car, everything's fine, and we don't have to tell anybody about this."

"Oh, I'm not keeping this one a secret. That was insanity!" I said. Timidly, I emerged from the bathroom stall. "Suz—I'm so sorry I barked at you. I just didn't want to get diarrhea on your mom's leather seats."

---

* My nickname. How much does it rule?

"Don't worry about it! I'm just glad that we made it the Holiday Inn bathroom in time!" Suzanne smiled. We hugged and laughed. Almost every time we get together, Suzanne and I get ourselves into a ridiculous situation much like that unforgettable blondetourage of Romy and Michele.

I hope that you never find yourself on the verge of a diarrhea disaster resulting from an ill-conceived dinner-and-drinks pairing, but if you do, I pray that you are in the company of a steadfast, trusted blonde bestie like my BFF, Suzanne. A blonde best friend who will explore the world of fake IDs with you, then calmly drive your diarrhea-filled carcass to the nearest toilet as you sweat, yell, and hyperventilate? Now that's a blondetourage.

CHAPTER 17

RULE: *Expect Blonde-vs.-Brunette Tension*

In the 1980s, Pantene peddled shampoo by introducing the now legendary tagline "Don't hate me because I'm beautiful." In that first commercial, a brunette beauty (Kelly LeBrock) uttered that famous mantra, but it's the blonde community who should adopt this phrase as its siren call. You might be the sweetest, warmest gal on the block, but if you have a head of gorgeous, platinum locks, you might someday experience brunette-vs.-blonde tension. Let's set off, dear reader, on an exploration of this dynamic throughout pop culture and develop a few strategies for how to dissolve this tension. This rivalry isn't limited to brunettes, though, so perhaps I'll broaden this warning and say that you should brace yourself for tension with other ladies. Being in possession of great hair and self-confidence has a way of drawing the hatred of others. Don't believe me? As that legendary Pantene commercial used to close with, "You'll see."

One early instance of blonde-on-brunette drama within pop

culture is found in the immortal *Archie* comic strip (founded in 1946). Redheaded male protagonist Archie spent eons vacillating between the affections of Betty, the impoverished, sweet blonde, and Veronica, the calculating, savvy brunette whose family was filthy rich. (They re-created a mall in her home, fer crissake!) This blonde-brunette tug-of-war over a guy is certainly believable, and it provided fodder for *Archie* comic book story lines for years. What is not believable is that two hot ladies would waste so much time brawling over such an indecisive fire crotch.

Competition between blondes and brunettes isn't limited to cartoons or works of fiction—it can and does happen in the real world. Another example of blonde-vs.-brunette tension comes from a "reality" that is harsher than most: Hollywood. If you think it's hard to get over a breakup in the real world of the average American, try doing it when your ex's face is plastered all over gossip magazines. Recovering from heartbreak in Tinseltown sounds positively nightmarish and practically impossible. In 1955, pale, blonde, Texas-born Debbie Reynolds, America's sweetheart, married handsome (and swarthy) singer and actor Eddie Fisher.* The couple had two children (Carrie and Todd) and were close friends with actress Elizabeth Taylor and her then-husband, producer Mike Todd. In 1958, Mike Todd died tragically in a plane crash, and soon Eddie Fisher and raven-haired beauty Elizabeth Taylor began having an affair, unbeknownst to Debbie Reynolds. This now legendary Hollywood scandal unfolded beneath the glare of the cameras, as Debbie Reynolds and Eddie Fisher eventually divorced and he married

---

* She followed my directions about dating outside your hair color group, as we discussed in Chapter 15.

Elizabeth Taylor. In the aftermath of that messy break-up, Debbie Reynolds emerged looking like a bit of a dolt and Elizabeth Taylor was a dark-haired, violet-eyed, savvy sexpot who got whatever she wanted. Score one for the tally of blondes as clueless simpletons.

A somewhat similar scenario played out in Hollywood about fifty years later between Jennifer Aniston, Brad Pitt, and Angelina Jolie. Jennifer Aniston is one of America's sweethearts, and while I wouldn't necessarily classify her as a true blonde, she certainly has enough sun-kissed highlights to be a tertiary member of the club. Aniston was married to actor Brad Pitt for almost five years, until he filmed *Mr. & Mrs. Smith* with brunette sexpot Angelina Jolie. Soon after filming wrapped, Aniston filed for divorce from Pitt, and promptly thereafter, Pitt and Jolie formed a family unit. The couple later adopted children and Jolie gave birth to a few of their own. The Jolie-Aniston drama consumed gossip magazine headlines and inaccurately painted Jennifer Aniston as a boring girl-next-door, while Angelina was an exotic temptress with long dark locks, impossibly pouty lips, and a whole lot of badass tattoos. America loves a good reality-based "catfight," and some classless retail stores were even selling "Team Aniston" and "Team Jolie" T-shirts as this human drama played out.

Another time when blonde-on-brunette tension played out in the public eye occurred during the 1994 Winter Olympics in Lillehammer. Tonya Harding was a muscular, brassy blonde figure skater with an impressive résumé and unprecedented triple axel skills. Nancy Kerrigan was a lithe, graceful brunette figure skater who already had an Olympic bronze in her pocket as she approached the 1994 pre-Olympic events. While she was at the 1994 U.S. Figure Skating Championships in Detroit, Nancy

Kerrigan was attacked by a man who was hired by Tonya Harding's ex-husband and her bodyguard. The injuries that Kerrigan sustained during that attack were bad enough that she was unable to compete in the national championship, which Tonya Harding subsequently won. Both women were selected for the 1994 Olympic team, and their every movement was watched with great curiosity and anticipation throughout their stay in Lillehammer. The contrast was striking: Dark-haired Kerrigan's costumes were minimalist, classic, and mostly white or gold, while Harding's blonde hair and makeup were severe, and her costumes were bold, sequined, and gaudy. The press loved capturing Kerrigan and Harding in photographs (on the rare occasion when they shared the ice for practice sessions), showcasing the tacky blonde next to the classy brunette.

In the cinema, the blonde-vs.-brunette dynamic is given pitch-perfect portrayal in the contrast between the two leading women of *Grease*: golden-haired perpetual naïf Sandy and brash, ballsy brunette Rizzo. Rizzo insults Sandy in song and dialogue, singing, "Look at me, I'm Sandra Dee / Lousy with virginity / Won't go to bed 'til I'm legally wed," then mocking Sandy's unwillingness to smoke, drink, or rat her hair.* Childlike Sandy doesn't quite get it, asking Rizzo at the end of the song, "Are you making fun of me, Riz?" At the end of *Grease*, Sandy finally gets the guy by letting her hair be wild and voluminous (guys can't resist that volume), smoking, and wearing tight black clothes. Heck of a lesson for young girls—you want a guy to like you? Just stop being yourself, smoke cigarettes, and

---

* "Ratting" your hair was what teasing your hair was called in that era. Gross, huh?

dress like a member of a motorcycle gang whose clothes were accidentally put in the dryer.*

In the 2001 film *Legally Blonde*, the platinum protagonist Elle Woods (Reese Witherspoon) is portrayed as a materialistic sorority party girl. Within the first ten minutes of the film, she gets dumped by her boyfriend, Warner Huntington III (Matthew Davis), because he is law school bound and his days of frivolous college antics are over. Warner says that he needs to get serious and grow up, and he doesn't picture blonde, fun Elle in that adult phase of his life. Elle is a lot smarter than she seems, though, and she manages to win admission to Harvard Law School along with Warner and, once there, attempts to win him back. Warner begins dating a Harvard peer of the more typical law school variety (serious, dry, and academic): a frumpy brunette named Vivian Kensington (Selma Blair). Elle may be naïve and clueless, but she's charming, has a heart of gold, and wins friends everywhere she goes. Before Elle finally realizes that Warner isn't worth her time, she and limp-haired brunette Vivian are rivals for his affection, setting up a classic blonde-vs.-brunette tension. Elle is bubbly, energetic, and willing to wear a Playboy Bunny costume to a Halloween party (that is a setup to make her look stupid), while Vivian is condescending, patronizing, and, worst of all, brunette.†

Television has given us a multitude of classic blonde-vs.-brunette pairings. In NBC's show *30 Rock*, unlucky-in-love,

---

* It's because of this terrible lesson in the end of *Grease* that my high school theater director always refused to put up the show at our high school. I completely understand and respect his decision, but come on, Mr. Minigan, my blond hair could have *rocked* the role of Sandy!
† Blonde-vs.-brunette tension need not be lifelong, though, as we saw when Elle and Vivian eventually became best buddies.

awkward brunette Liz Lemon (hilarious everywoman Tina Fey) is the centerpiece of the show because viewers can identify with her. The story lines of each episode usually focus on steady Liz and the crazy cast of characters who orbit around her at the comedy-variety show *The Girlie Show* (*TGS*). Jenna Maroney (gorgeous, amazingly coiffed Jane Krakowski) is the vain, vapid actress who possesses a head of beautiful blonde curls and not a clue. Their relationship toggles between blonde-against-brunette and blonde-in-collaboration-with-brunette, with Liz serving as Jenna's sounding board and Jenna acting as a fun, crazy pal to Liz. One episode of *30 Rock* explored their unlikely friendship as a story line, with Liz seeking out more like-minded brunette friends and Jenna making friends with equally vapid, self-obsessed ladies. At the close of the episode, Liz and Jenna came together, secure in the knowledge that opposites attract and their rivalry-based friendship is exactly what each woman needs.

Going back into the television archives, *Three's Company* explored the blonde-brunette dynamic with a blonde and a brunette as two of the three roommates in a San Diego beach bungalow. Suzanne Somers has built a career on playing ditzy blondes (and peddling Thighmasters). Chrissy Snow, her character on *Three's Company*, was an executive assistant from Fresno, California, whose idiocy was the linchpin of many jokes and setups. Whip-smart brunette Janet Wood (Joyce DeWitt) was a florist and a good straight man for the antics of Jack Tripper (the late, great John Ritter) and the stupidity of blonde Chrissy. The archetype of "dumb blonde" was nonnegotiable on *Three's Company*, as we saw when Somers quit the show (due to a salary dispute) and was promptly replaced by another blonde actress (Jenilee Harrison) who played Cindy Snow, Chrissy's country cousin. Cindy moved into the San Diego apartment with Janet and Jack, and not only was she a dumb blonde, she was also clumsy! What a multifaceted character! Cindy fulfilled the role of the token, clueless blonde for two seasons and to such great effect that the show received criticism from viewers for its one-note, disparaging characterization of blondes. During the final three seasons of *Three's Company*, Cindy was replaced by a new blonde roommate, Terri Alden (Priscilla Barnes), who the writers deliberately crafted as a smart nurse. Through all of these stereotypes-as-characters, the balance of the zany blonde and the steady brunette was a constant presence in *Three's Company*. During season six, brunette Janet even tested out life as a blonde, wearing a blonde wig to boost her confidence. It's obvious which hair color the writers associated with sexuality and confidence.

In the same era as *Three's Company*, the American public was introduced to *Charlie's Angels* with its original cast of Farrah Fawcett, Jaclyn Smith, and Kate Jackson. It's worth noting that Farrah Fawcett was only a full-time cast member of *Charlie's Angels* for one season,* but she's the most legendary of the Angels (even including the *Charlie's Angels* franchise reboot during the '90s). Her soft, layered blonde hair inspired a million hairdos, and her hard nipples poking out from a red bathing suit in that legendary poster inspired even more hard-ons.† The two brunette angels were certainly famous and celebrated, but blonde Farrah garnered the most attention in that trio.

Another classic television portrayal of blonde-on-brunette tension was found in ABC's hit prime-time soap opera *Dynasty*.

---

* Fawcett returned as a guest star in a few episodes of seasons three and four due to contractual obligations.

† This poster hangs on the walls of fraternity houses to this day. Now that is staying power!

Alexis Carrington vs. Krystle Carrington was a blonde-brunette rivalry for the ages. Alexis (Joan Collins) was the brunette first wife of oil tycoon and silver fox Blake Carrington (John Forsythe). Krystle (Linda Evans) was the ashy blonde second wife, and a love of shoulder pads and gaudy jewelry was the two wives' only common ground. The Nielsen ratings for *Dynasty* were flat during its first season (1981), but in season two, when brunette first wife Alexis arrived and initiated the blonde-vs.-brunette tension between wives, the ratings skyrocketed. The American TV-watching public is, sadly, always interested in a good brawl. And brawl they did—Alexis and Krystle engaged in some unforgettable hair-pulling fights, oftentimes in pools. They just don't make television like that anymore. (Well, they do, but it's not character acting anymore—now it's depressing reality.)

Around the time that my older sisters were watching *Dynasty*, I was inhaling episodes of *Punky Brewster* like they were fluffernutter sandwiches (something completely verboten in our house so I'd shamelessly chow them at friends' houses*). On this show, Margaux Kramer was the uppity blonde "friend" (but more of a prototypical frenemy) who wore a lot of pale pink clothing and was completely out of touch with dark-haired Cherie and Punky. Margaux was the focus of an entire episode when the Kramer family—*gasp*—lost their money and had to move out of their palatial home. Life is so hard! Brunette Punky was charming and somehow relatable, despite the fact that she was a runaway orphan whose bed was a wheelbarrow. The important takeaways from *Punky Brewster* are that blondes are icy, brunettes are scrappy, and you should never hide in an abandoned

---

* A very belated thank-you to Katie Ryan's family for enabling my childhood fluffernutter addiction.

refrigerator during a game of hide-and-seek. (I'm looking at you, Cherie!)

In somewhat more recent television, we saw some great blonde characterizations in two Aaron Spelling–produced shows, *90210* and *Melrose Place*, both on Fox. Perhaps Aaron Spelling was inspired by the blondes who were present in his personal life: wife, Candy (consistently blonde); daughter, Tori (on-again, off-again blonde); and even son, Randy (occasional frosted tips—we all made mistakes in the '90s!). In the original *Beverly Hills, 90210*, blondes Kelly Taylor (Jennie Garth) and Donna Martin (Tori Spelling) were Beverly Hills kids and already best friends when the brown-haired Walsh twins transferred to West Beverly High School. Of course brown-haired Brenda was the down-to-earth girl from a stable family comprised entirely of sensible brunettes. Kelly came from a semi-unstable home (of blonde alcoholics!) and had a nose job during high school, fulfilling the ol' "blondes are vain" stereotype. At least the character of Kelly Taylor wasn't completely detrimental to the reputation of blondes, unlike Donna "Donna Martin Graduates!" Martin. Donna Martin was the queen of bad implants and brown lipstick, and she certainly didn't do much for the blonde cause.

Immediately after every episode of *90210*, FOX served up the primetime soap opera that was the early 1990s in a nutshell: *Melrose Place*. The target demographic for *Melrose Place* was a bit older than that of *Beverly Hills, 90210*, but the standard tropes remained. All residents of the Melrose Place apartment complex (the corrupt doctor, the cool motorcycle guy, the lame couple) had their own story lines, but it was champagne-blonde man-eater Amanda Woodward who was pitted against the world, it seemed. Amanda Woodward (Heather Locklear) may have been brunette at the roots (inspiring a huge trend in the 1990s), but she was icy blonde on top. Ms. Woodward (if you're nasty) took no bullshit from anyone (not even hottie Billy, played by Andrew Shue!), and told the world to "F itself." And we loved her blonde guts for it.

In today's popular primetime soap opera on the CW network, *Gossip Girl*, we see another blonde-vs.-brunette matchup. The alternating friendship and rivalry between blonde Serena and brunette Blair provides interesting story lines and plot twists. Serena van der Woodsen (Blake Lively) is California blonde in color but Upper East Side blonde in heritage and location—the ol' blonde switcheroo—and a stark contrast to brunette Blair Waldorf (Leighton Meester).

Hair color tension isn't limited to women, though. Blond men and brown-haired males can have tense friendships, partnerships, and relationships, too. Take, for example, the tension among the assortment of hair colors found in '80s heavy metal supergroup Mötley Crüe. The Crüe is comprised of Vince Neil, Tommy Lee, Nikki Sixx, and Mick Mars. Mötley Crüe was a triumvirate of brunets before blond Vince Neil joined the band to sing lead vocals. When Vince Neil's drunk-driving accident killed Hanoi Rocks drummer (and friend of the band) Razzle Dingley in December 1984, the brunet trio turned their back on Vince during his darkest time.[*] It wasn't a dark enough time to force platinum Vince to darken his hair, though. The band worked through the tragedy and later emerged, ready to take America by storm again and kick-start more hearts.

All those rivalries between blondes and brunettes might

---

[*] There are two sides to every story, though. Read *The Dirt*, the story of Mötley Crüe, an American classic, for further information.

make for good TV and sell celebrity tabloids, but the modern blonde is in touch with her feminist roots and knows it's always better to show solidarity with her brunette sisters. Blondes today are too wise to get caught in this retrograde model of blonde-vs.-brunette tension. There might be a long tradition of this in pop culture, but it's time to cast this one off and shake things up. And so, sweet pussycat, I bring you the next rule: Befriend brunettes.

CHAPTER 18

RULE: *Befriend Brunettes (and Others)*

You can learn a lot from people who are unlike you and have different experiences, beliefs, hobbies, and, yes, even follicle colors. So I implore you, dear reader, to cultivate friendships and partnerships with all hair types: straight, curly, relaxed, natural, none, brown, black, white, red, badly dyed, well dyed, and generally anyone who doesn't look just like you. Their different and gorgeous hair might startle and intimidate you at first, but shared hair care tips can be the first step to lifelong friendship.

As I have mentioned earlier in the book, in addition to my platinum-haired mother, I grew up with two older brunette sisters and a brown-haired father. We lived in what I like to call a "mixed home." The five members of the Coppock clan get along despite our varied hair colors. We're family—we have no choice but to get along. My sisters, Laurel and Emily, have fantastic hair, I must admit. Their tresses might not be quite as stunning as mine, but their hair is better than the average human's. But, as sisters do, of course we got into sibling tussles every now and then. There were even times during childhood when I felt like the weird daughter because I was given a blonde bowl cut[*] while Laurel and Emily had dark, flowing locks. I'll even admit that I have felt threatened by their shiny dark hair at times. I know! What kind of a pro-blonde author am I? Like anyone, I have passed through some dark valleys during my journey to blonde perfection and self-confidence.

When I first moved to New York City in 2006 to find a new job in publishing and perform as much standup as possible, I was horribly intimidated at every turn. It felt as though around every corner and down every block was a wise New Yorker with more impressive work experience or funnier jokes or better hair. I worried that my professional résumé didn't stack up, I knew that my standup needed work, and I had left a fantastic Boston colorist behind, so I was all by myself colorwise. Within a few months of landing in Gotham, I found a job as a children's book editor and discovered some worthwhile open mics and shows where I could perform. My material was still a bit too provincial and Boston-specific, though. New York audiences just weren't taking to my hilarious jokes about bizarre characters seen at my beloved Dunkin' Donuts and sandwich shop D'Angelo's (probably because Double Deeze and D'Angelo's just aren't the cultural touchstones in New York City that they are in Boston—also probably because those jokes were straight-up awful). A comedian never realizes how insular his jokes are until he takes those jokes on the road and the punch lines that used to elicit uproarious laughter from audiences back home instead leave

---

[*] From ages three to seven, I was a dead ringer for Cousin Oliver from *The Brady Bunch*.

the room silent. I had a night like that about six months into my New York odyssey.

I was performing on a bringer show at the Laugh Lounge* on the Lower East Side of Manhattan. "Bringer" is standup parlance for a show in which any schmo can perform, provided he has five to ten friends who are nice enough to pay an exorbitant cover charge and drink at least two nine-dollar Bud Lights. Bringer shows happen at legitimate clubs, but usually earlier in the night (before the experienced comedians do their shows) or on off nights like Sundays or Tuesdays. The producer of a bringer show will also book a few veteran comedians so that the show isn't a complete train wreck composed entirely of nervous newbies whose friends are obligated to laugh at them. Bringers are somewhat unavoidable, though they are a scourge on the comedy industry. But young comedians will do these bringer shows just to get stage time and a tape out of it. Most of these clubs are willing to videotape your set (for a fee, of course), and once you have a good tape, you can use that to submit to comedy festivals or agents and managers.

So there I was, a New York City naïf sitting in a chilly basement comedy club on the Lower East Side, anxiously hoping that my friends who had said they would come to the show would actually come to the show. Oh yeah—that's the kicker: If your friends don't show up, you don't get any stage time. So if the bringer's producer has required the young comedian to have five audience members in attendance but only four of his pals make it, then he's shit out of luck. Yes, it's a terrible system that exploits aspiring comedians and crushes dreams like Gallagher crushes watermelon. That night, I was in the

---

* Like so many other comedy venues, this one is now closed, too.

middle of it and quaking like a California cul-de-sac.

"Hey—you're on the show, right? I'm Leah," a short brunette introduced herself to me. She was muscular, no-nonsense, and, I would soon discover, hilarious. She had been at the standup game a few years longer than I had, and it showed. Her stage persona was established, her writing was fantastic, and she was comfortable out there. Leah went onto that Laugh Lounge stage, destroyed (standup talk for doing fantastically well), then plopped down at a table among the keyed-up would-be comedians as though nothing had happened. I watched the stage lights reflect off her dark hair and winning smile as I thought, *Now that is how it's done.*

I nervously chewed at the fingernails on my right hand while I stared at the set list that I was clutching in my left hand. My heart was pounding, my hands were shaking, and my breathing was shallow. Back in those days, I was still shaky and visibly nervous on stage.[*] I would write "Loosen up! Be playful!" on the top of my set lists as though those reminders would salvage my performance somehow. It was during that era that I had a pre-show meltdown when an ex-boyfriend happened to appear at a comedy show I was booked on. (Looking back, why the hell did I stick with a trade that caused me so much anxiety and stress? I guess it's because when you kill on a standup stage, there's no better feeling. The waves of laughter wash over you, and that makes up for every crummy, stressful show you had to do in order to hammer out those jitters and nerves. I'm guessing that it's a feeling almost like heavy drug use—the highs are so high that they make you forget about the awful hangovers and withdrawal symptoms. I don't know about that type of drug use, and I'm

---

[*] A real joy to watch.

not just saying that because my parents are going to read this book. I actually mean it. The last thing I need are drugs to make me even more of a wackadoo. I'm high on life!) I knew that my material was too narrow and Boston-focused for New York City crowds, but I didn't know what else to do. Bracing myself to go onstage was extra nerve-racking because I knew that my jokes weren't strong and accessible, but they were all I had.

"She plays clubs and colleges all over the country.* Ladies and gentlemen, put your hands together for Selena Coppock." The host brought me onto the stage. I launched into my seven minutes that started off with a joke comparing my looks to those of then-relevant celebrity Paris Hilton. Yes, I kicked off the set with a blonde joke, effectively. It's a common thread throughout my life. The set wasn't terrible, but it certainly wasn't very good. My Boston-centric jokes required so much explanation that I lost any momentum or energy that I had established with the audience already. Plus, the long exposition required to set up the joke properly then screwed up my rhythm. Although I had performed improv comedy throughout college and for years after college, those skills of quick thinking and flexibility abandoned me when I was alone onstage with just a microphone. So for seven minutes I talked too fast and too much, my hands shook while I held the microphone, and the audience stared at me. Finally it was time for the big finish, a joke that made reference to my hometown—a place where, if entitled teenagers need money, they just visit the backyard of their parents' McMansions and pluck it off the old money tree, I joked.† I even

---

* Every standup will tell you that this introduction is what a host says when he doesn't know your credits or when you have no credits.

† There's more to that joke. Yes, unfortunately, much more.

said the name of the town (which was really bright since an audience on the Lower East Side of Manhattan definitely knows and gives a rat's ass about the name of the specific suburb of Boston where you grew up, right?), and after the word "Weston" escaped my lips, a shout of "BOOOO!" come from the back of the room. The "boo" wasn't ghosty, but it had a friendly, teasing tone, so it didn't freak me out any more than the entire experience already had. I managed to finish my awful joke and flee the stage to a smattering of applause, then bolt upstairs to the bar where I stared at my set list on that slip of paper and replayed every terrible second in my head while I wondered how the hell anybody ever got good at standup. I was bracing myself for the inevitable post-show comments from my sweet friends who had just overpaid to drink crappy domestic beer while enduring a pretty unfunny comedy show. No doubt they would assure me that they had loved the show and they'd tell me that I had "great energy up there," which was a nice way of skirting the fact that I was awful. As I wallowed in self-pity, I heard a shout from over my shoulder: "Wildcats suck! Warriors rule!"

I hadn't heard that refrain since high school, when the rivalry between the Weston Wildcats (my town) and the Wayland Warriors (the neighboring suburb) created battle lines across the myriad towns surrounding Boston with names that start with the letter *W.* I turned around to discover that the supposed militant Wayland Warrior was Leah, the brunette comedian I had met earlier. Oh no. Was she seriously going to hate me because of my hometown? I needed some savvy comedy friends to help me keep my head above water in the New York scene, and I had hoped she might be one. Her comedy had knocked my socks off, and despite how hilarious she was, Leah had seemed really friendly and approachable downstairs. But was she one of those tools who still believed in high school rivalries? I decided to take the bait.

"You think that Warriors rule? No way! Maroon and gray for life!" I jokingly shouted and laughed.

"Haha! Black and orange for life!" she laughed. This was good—we were both joking around and mocking losers who still believe in hometown football rivalries. "That was me boo-ing in the back. I just couldn't resist. That's nuts that you're from Weston—I'm from Wayland, and my father taught at Wayland High."

"I used to party with a lot of Wayland kids," I said. I was a little bit worried about that fact. I had gone out with a few Way-land guys in high school, and that made me none too popular with some of the girls from Wayland. Most of the girls were fantastic, but a handful of Warrior ladies were not pleased when two blondes from Weston (me and Suzanne) started cropping up at Wayland parties. I didn't blame them, but that didn't make me stop. Thankfully, Leah was not only unfazed by my years of socializing in Wayland, she was also exceedingly generous.

"Good stuff out there," she said.

"Oh, you're nice to say that—that was pretty painful. I'm hav-ing a hard time adjusting my standup to New York crowds."

"You can easily rework some of your material to open it up. Plus, with that last joke, you need to put yourself in the struggle."

"How can I do that with that last joke?" I asked.

"Well, it seems like you want to make rich people the butt of the joke, yes? That's not quite coming through right now. It feels like you are on the inside of that group you're mocking, and you need to establish that you're on the outside. Put your-self in the struggle." She was exactly right. Leah had watched me do seven minutes of jokes and pinpointed exactly what was wrong with my standup in that era. I had never analyzed and dissected my jokes with anyone, and I was beginning to see why my jokes weren't hitting. Leah was gentle and gracious with her input, and I knew that I wanted to be pals with this lady. But I didn't want to scare her off, so I squelched my urge to scream "You're just the friend I need! Please be my pal!" and instead just thanked Leah for her input and said that I hoped to see her smiling face and brown hair around the scene.

After that inspired meeting, I did see Leah around at open mics, and in time a fantastic friendship blossomed between us. She organized a comedian book club and invited me to join, which introduced me to gobs of other comedians. The "book" part of the book club never really got off the ground (does it for *any* book club?), but we were experts at putting back bottles of wine while gossiping about other comedians. I began coproducing a show in the basement of a pizzeria/VHS rental shop in the East Village, and she was one of the first people who I booked. She booked me on the show that she coproduced in the West Village and took me on the road with her a few times. (Yes, the Leah in the Constantine stalker story is this Leah—she enabled my Constantine addiction that day but didn't judge me for it, bless her.) Through our years of performing together, Leah remained confident, hilarious, and witty, and I slowly got better at standup.

We coproduced and coheadlined a standup show in Boston called "Comedy Rivalry" where we played up the Wayland-Weston rivalry for laughs. The posters for that show were a fantastic contrast—me in an old maroon Weston jacket with my blonde hair reflecting the sun and Leah in a black-and-orange letterman jacket from Wayland, her brown hair just brushing her shoulders. We were an unlikely picture of friendship. We packed a comedy club in Boston's Faneuil Hall and brought down the house.

Leah's friendship has gotten me through some tough times, as well. I knew that this was a blonde-on-brunette friendship for the long haul when we both went through some dark eras simultaneously. The causes of our sadness were very different, but we were glad to have each other as we each needed a partner in wallowing. Sometimes you don't want a pal who will tell you to look on the bright side—you want a pal who will agree that everything sucks and just cry with you. During those times, Leah and I often ate dinner at a kitschy restaurant in the East Village because we knew that nobody would bat an eye if we started crying into our respective, but matching, stir-fry entrées.

Now Leah lives in Los Angeles, so our friendship has been split between two coasts. Initially, I worried that her move across the country might weaken our friendship, but it hasn't. On the short weekends when she comes back east, Leah jokes that she only has time to visit with the "varsity squad" of friends, and I'm proud to be part of that elite crew.

When I was fifteen, if you had told me that someday one of my best friends would be a sporty brunette Warrior from Wayland, I would have told you that you have quite an imagination. But Leah has taught me so much about standup and self-love that I hate to imagine what my life would be like if I had never met her. I'm so glad I jumped at the chance to befriend a brunette. A brunette from my rival hometown, no less!

FAQs with *Selena*

How should one answer the question "Do you color your hair?"

Ah, the inevitable, nagging existential query of blondeness. Here's the least helpful answer ever: Respond with whatever you are comfortable with. I know—I'm the worst! What am I, a jag friend whose relationship "advice" is the bullshit line that you should just "be yourself"? Fuck that! If I were myself when meeting guys, I'd fart and let my roots grow out—both are bad news. But back to the question at hand. The correct answer to this question depends on your personal preference as far as candor. There are two options when answering this type of question: You can use the playfully evasive line "Wouldn't you like to know?" paired with a mischievous hair toss maneuver. Or you can actually answer the question and wave your flag of fake blondeness (or "blondeness with assistance") proudly. I usually respond by saying, "I was born blonde, so technically it's natural . . . but now I give it a little help." Nobody needs to know that "a little help" is code for "I spend three hours and hundreds of dollars *one Saturday every two months to cover up the darker hair that somehow springs from my head. This is my happiness—don't judge." Use the response that works for you. If you're more comfortable avoiding the question, then by all means avoid the question. You don't owe this person anything, much less information about your sweet weave.*

What do you say to nonblondes who tell you that they wish to color their hair and become blondes?

Some days I am tempted to shout, "Welcome to the light side!" and embrace these people. Other times I'd prefer to say, "We're full up, thank you," because I've got enough competition in this group already. More often than not, though, I welcome these newbie blondes and take them under my platinum wing. I'll be honest with them, though—being blonde ain't cheap. Check your finances and make sure that you can handle the demands of blondeness: the trips to the colorist, the gentle shampoo for colored hair,* the purple shampoo to prevent brassiness (if you're into ashiness),† the conditioner to keep dyed hair from getting brittle,‡ and the ten-foot pole to fight off admirers.

How often do you wash your hair?

Truthfully, not much. Before you recoil and imagine the overpowering smell of body odor that must cloud around me like the Peanuts character Pig Pen, please note that I shower regularly. The bod gets washed—fear not. I just rock a shower cap to protect the delicate ecosystem that is my dope weave. The shower cap is key because you don't want hair exposed to the humidity of

---

* Or Johnson & Johnson baby shampoo.
† Aveda makes a great one.
‡ My current favorite is John Frieda's Sheer Blonde conditioner.

the shower—it's like a jungle in there (quite literally). *Just putting your hair in a bun or ponytail while you bathe upright isn't enough—you gotta get that hair sealed up in the plastic protective covering of a shower cap. I live by a pretty strict hair-washing schedule, and I take many variables into consideration: what activities I am doing on a given day, who I might see, what the weather has been like and will be like today, what season it is, if wearing a hat is feasible and not too Blossom-y, and if I need a workout.*

Depending on your hair type (thick vs. fine, curly vs. straight), you might require a daily shampoo and infrequent hair-washing might not be the right choice for you. Or you may be a good candidate for my every-couple-of-days hair-washing schedule. I have fine hair but a lot of it, and my hair doesn't get especially greasy until day three or so. If you have thicker hair or hair that's prone to become greasy more quickly, this schedule might not work for you. But if you have somewhat dry, fine hair, what I'm about to share might change your life forever. My personal day-by-day breakdown is this:

Day 1: Wash hair with a color-safe shampoo and a conditioner on the ends only. Apply product to damp hair (as mentioned in Chapter 7), then blow-dry with a paddle brush for most of your head and a smaller brush for trickier, face-framing sections. Wear hair straight and somewhat flat. Deal with flatness knowing that tomorrow, your weave will be big and bouncy.† Day 2 hair is worth the wait.

Day 2: Shower with a shower cap. Curl hair with curling iron.

---

* "Welcome to it!" —Axl Rose
† This is my version of "The sun will come out tomorrow"—big hair is my sunshine.

(I favor a 1.5-inch barrel iron for big, casual waves. Warning: 1.5-inch barrel curling irons are a bit harder to find than smaller curling irons.) After curling, brush out the curls a bit for shape, looseness. Spray a bit of hair spray over entire head to lock in style.

Day 3: Recurl if necessary. Wear tresses in a high bun or po-nytail, or clipped back half up and half down. Hairstyles like half up, half down require some volume and texture at the roots (for a '60s style that I favor), so days 2 and 3 are ideal for wearing that style.

Day 4: If you can handle it, rock a super-smooth ponytail on day 4.

Day 5: Shower and wash your hair, would ya?

What are your thoughts on color-enhancing products like Sun-In? Lemon juice? Beer? Cranberry juice? Coffee?

This question takes me back to eighth grade, when grunge mu-sic was big, flannel shirts were bigger, and all my friends were buzzing about DIY hair coloring courtesy of Sun-In, lemon juice, cranberry juice, coffee, and, yes, even beer. I think that I experi-mented with Sun-In during eighth and ninth grade, but I can't ex-actly remember because nothing traumatic happened. That's more than I can say for some brunette friends who ended up with freak-ish traffic-cone-colored hair thanks to Sun-In overdoses. Yikes. So my conclusion is that Sun-In can work if you are already blonde. For people with red or brown hair or darker, using Sun-In will be much like visiting Atlantic City: Be prepared to gamble and look like trash.

As for the "natural" hair color route of lemon juice (for blondes), cranberry juice (for redheads), and coffee (for bru-nettes), I think it's worth testing out if you're intrigued by it. These liquids aren't permanent dyes, so you can't do much damage, and experimentation is fun! And what about the beer in question? Supposedly, pouring beer on your hair will make it shiny. This idea was quite popular when my sister Laurel was in high school and she gave it a try. My parents were suspicious of the notion that shiny hair required their fifteen-year-old daughter to disappear upstairs with a can of beer and assumed that they were being had. Laurel insisted that she wasn't simply trying to score alcohol and that beer was indeed supposed to make your hair luscious and shiny, and eventually they believed her. Well, they believed her enough to pour half of a can into Tupperware, and she took that to the bathroom, where she dumped it over her head in the shower. Was her hair any shinier? Not really. But it was a worthwhile exercise that opened a dialogue about adolescent hair experimentation between a teenage daughter and her concerned parents, so it was an important rite of passage.

Who is your favorite blonde icon?

Without a doubt, Miss Piggy. Her hair is always phenomenal, she has tons of fantastic outfits, and she doesn't suffer fools gladly. Though I wish that she'd stop pining after the wimpy Kermit the Frog and move on. What about a date with Fozzie Bear? He's a comedian—wouldn't that be fun? Might get tiresome, though. What about Animal? I bet he has great connections to good parties and concerts.

Do you wear yellow?

Hell to the no! Because of my brassy, golden-blonde hair, a yellow outfit would make me resemble a banana. A fantastic banana who is spouting off witty quips and zinging them left, then zinging them right, but a banana nonetheless. Usually yellow clothing plus golden-blonde hair gives you a uniformity that is unflattering to all. I will admit to one blonde who looks fantastic in yellow, though: former Bachelorette Ali Fedotowsky. Initially, she was one of the many women on The Bachelor *who fought for the affections of Jake, the uber-corny pilot. That season was known as* The Bachelor: On the Wings of Love, *and I wish I were making that up. Ali appeared in multiple different yellow dresses and looked stunning every time. So I'll concede that some blondes can wear yellow, but not this blonde.*

What are your thoughts on highlights?

My feelings about highlights are "Do it and do it and do it and do it . . . and do it again," to quote that band of modern-day poets, the Black Eyed Peas. If you want some highlights, go for it! Highlights are a fun and easy way to play with color and dip your toe in another shade. In the fall and winter, red and brown lowlights are fun for a change of pace. Then, as soon as Punxsutawney Phil peeks his freaky groundhog head from his underground lair, start in on some champagne or goldenrod highlights.

How young is too young to start coloring hair?

Good question! I don't advocate for any hair coloring among the Toddlers & Tiaras *or* Honey Boo Boo *set. Kids should learn to appreciate their natural hair color, or at least make peace with it before they enter into a lifetime of changing it. The first fifteen years of life should be spent with whatever natural color you got. That undamaged, virgin hair will be beneficial in the long run. Then, once a kid is fifteen or sixteen, he or she can launch in on a lifetime of hair coloring.*

When you go swimming in a pool, do you worry about your hair turning green?

Yes, and that is why I haven't dunked my head underwater in a decade.

What's your favorite breed of dog?

Golden retriever.

What's your favorite type of brownie?

A blondie.

Conclusion

Sometimes, blonde life can seem like a Sisyphean task of constantly visiting the colorist for touch-ups and enduring unending blonde jokes. It might seem as hard as sacking the quarterback during the fourth down, or dating a man with great hair, or befriending an intimidating brunette from your rival hometown, or lasting through a Guns N' Roses cover band concert without being punched in the face. On bad days, being blonde even feels as difficult as doing your own highlights at home (something that isn't just difficult—it's damn near impossible to do well). But it's also a glorious life, when you're following in the well-worn path of legendary blondes such as Marilyn Monroe, Madonna, and Dolly Parton. Those blonde icons both fulfilled and flouted stereotypes, which is the best way to keep people on their toes. And you, dear reader, know how to keep people guessing because now you know thyself and you know how to work the weave and you aren't afraid to run in heels and you're smart as a whip because you're a classy gal.

A brunette pal once taught me a brilliant saying: "I am who I am without apologies." Without getting too touchy-feely or delving into "the last five minutes of a *Full House* episode" territory, the most important lesson here is self-love. The best way to go through life is to love yourself, take care of yourself, have your own back, and be your own first blonde bestie (you can work on forming a blondetourage later). Be proud of who you are and what you do, even if people assume that you're a helpless, vain moron because of your dope hair. Even if people say your hair is brassy or your roots are showing or your hair color makes you look like a trashy hooker (I've been there!)—if it makes *you* happy, that's all that matters. Whether you're ashy blonde or California platinum or, heck, even a nonblonde, learn to love you for you because you're fantastic and special and don't need to apologize to anyone for it—you shine, literally.

Acknowledgments

A huge thank you to Team Blonde: Stephanie Meyers, Elizabeth Evans, and Amanda Bergeron. Stephanie, you envisioned *The New Rules for Blondes* and you let me explore and execute—I am eternally grateful to you. Your vision and input on the early chapters were invaluable. My agent Elizabeth, your unending patience with me and confidence in this project kept me going. Thank you for making my dream come true. And my lovely editor, Amanda, your enthusiasm and positivity are an inspiration. Thank you for having faith in me and not vetoing even my most bizarre jokes.

Thank you to everyone at the Jean V. Naggar Literary Agency: Jessica Regel, Tara Hart, Jennifer Weltz, Ariana Philips, and Michelle Weiner at CAA. Everyone at It Books and Harper-Collins Publishers has been so helpful and making me feel so welcome. Thank you to Kevin Callahan, Joel Cáceres, Joseph Papa, Liz Esman, Elissa Cohen, Mary Elizabeth Constant, and Karen Dziekonski.

Acknowledgments

I owe a debt of gratitude to my wonderful friends who helped me with the book either by contributing expertise, sharing in these experiences, reading early chapters, or confessing to hair horror stories: Suzanne Thornfeldt, Jackie Hassell, Kendra Cunningham, Alison Sager, Glennis McCarthy, Alison James, Ginny Van Alyea, Sara Benicasa, Kambri Crews, Jillian Bell, Sarah Baker, Kristen Johnson, Nikki Glaser, Stephanie Shoemaker, Paul Case, Christian Polanco, Kevin Tracy, Tomas Delgado, Dmitry Komis, Danny Leary, Leah Dubie, Alexa Berk, Heidi Edsall, Mary Beth Betancourt, Michael Robinson, Jeff Simmermon, and Roman J. Watson. Big ups to my brilliant pal Scott Patterson of Point B Productions for creating the trailer and Thank you to its stars: Amy Clearwater, Kate Hendricks, Amy Bjork, Georgia Read, Mara Herron, Alison Leiby, Bobby Mort, and Greg Johnson. A special thank-you to Suzanne for being my best friend since nursery school and my partner in crime throughout many of the adventures detailed in this book. As we always say, sometimes you have to go through brownish lowlights to experience platinum-perfection highlights.

Thank you to the people who fostered and supported my comedic voice early on: John Minigan at Weston High School, Will Luera at ImprovBoston, Rick Jenkins at the Comedy Studio, plus Tim Paul, Sue Constantine, and Calvin Swaim.

Finally, my eternal gratitude to Laurel, Bobby, Emily, Jon, and Maren. You have all been so supportive and excited every step of the way and it has meant the world to me.

About the Author

Selena Coppock is a standup comedian, storyteller, and writer based in New York City. Her writing has also been featured on *TheFrisky*, *McSweeney's*, and *The Collared Sheep*. Her storytelling abilities have been showcased at shows around the country, including *RISK!* (live show and podcast), *Stripped Stories*, and, at *The Moth Story Slam* (where she tied for first place with her "After Hours" story in March 2011).

She has studied both improv and sketch comedy extensively, training at the Upright Citizens Brigade Theater (New York), ImprovOlympic (Chicago), and ImprovAslyum (Boston). Selena has earned spots in a multitude of comedy festivals, including the Boston Comedy Festival, New York Comedy Competition, Detroit Comedy Festival, North Carolina Comedy Arts Festival, the Out of Bounds Festival, the Ladies Are Funny Festival, and the Women in Comedy Festival.

On TV, Selena has been seen on *Big Morning Buzz Live*

(VH1), *The Revolution* (ABC), and *The Morning Show with Mike and Juliet* (Fox) and online on RooftopComedy.com, College-eHumor.com, ComedySmack.com, and PMSports.com. She has also been featured as *Time Out New York*'s Joke of the Week, and in the *Boston Globe*, *LA Weekly*, *Boston Metro*, and the *Boston Phoenix*.

The New Rules for Blondes is her first book.